A Sugarloaf Surprise

ROSEMARY WHITTAKER

A Sugarloaf Surprise

Rosemary Whittaker

Also by Rosemary Whittaker

The Cinnamon Snail

Sunshine State

The Wattle Birds

The Feijoa Tree

A Tale of Two Christmases

A Sugarloaf Valentine

A Sugarloaf Mix-Up

 Stopwatch Publications

First printing, 2023

ISBN-13: 978-1-922651-38-9

This book is a work of fiction. Names, characters, places, and incidents are the product of the author's imagination or are used fictitiously. Any resemblance to actual events, locales, or persons, living or dead, is coincidental.

Published by Rosemary Whittaker
www.rosemarywhittaker.com

Cover design by 100 Covers.

For Lynelle, who told me from the beginning I ought to be writing romantic comedy.

Chapter One

The car makes one final choking noise and sputters to a halt. I pull in to the side of the road before it gives up entirely. I look around, wondering where I am. Somewhere on the edge of the New-Forest, I believe. I noticed a sign a few miles back saying *Beware – wild ponies*. I'm not sure whether I'm supposed to beware of them, or they of me. The picture didn't make it clear.

The sign would have been correct to warn the ponies to beware of this car. I find it terrifying, and I'm sitting inside it. But not for long. I remember my driving instructor warning me never to stay in a broken-down car.

I climb out and scramble up the grassy bank to peer over the hedge. There are several fields of bright yellow flowers, but no people. There ought to be a farmer pacing his meadows and counting the flower heads, or whatever it is they do. Failing that, a shepherd. I look around for some sheep. But either they're hiding in the yellow flowers, or they've gone for a walk.

I sit on the bank and think hard. I have no clue where I am. I took a shortcut a while back because my phone suggested traffic was building up on the main road, and I thought it must know best. But it immediately followed up on its helpful suggestion by shutting down due to low battery. I switch it on again to check the map. The screen obligingly flashes into life, but there are no bars. I try to call the rental car company, but there's no connection.

It's a beautiful day. The sun is shining, and the birds are chirping. The yellow flowers are swaying gently in the breeze. I take a deep breath and try to enjoy the moment. Maybe this breakdown is a sign I should slow down and appreciate the simple things in life.

I heave a sigh and lean back against the hedge. This is just my luck – stuck in the wilds of the countryside with no phone signal and a broken-down car. What am I supposed to do now? I could try walking, but I have no idea in which direction. I could be wandering around for hours. What if I stumble upon the wild ponies? I don't feel prepared to face them on my own.

I switch off my phone again. I need to preserve whatever battery is left. Goodness knows when I'll reach civilisation again. This phone could be all that lies between me and complete disaster. I could sit here and wait for another car to come by, but I suspect I'd be here for a long time. I don't remember passing any other vehicles during the past ten minutes. Not even a tractor. Failing that, I'll have to start walking and hope I choose the right direction. If not, I may walk for miles before finding myself lost in a marsh or up to my neck in quicksand.

I remember I still have a half-eaten bar of chocolate in the dash pocket of the car. It's a cheering thought. With sensible rationing, it should help me survive for a couple more hours. And it's bound to rain soon. It always rains in the countryside. That's probably why they choose to grow crops there, rather than in cities. I won't have to worry about dying of thirst before I'm rescued.

It's the end of May, and the weather has been delightfully warm all week. On the other hand, the nights are still chilly. That decides it. I'm taking a chance and setting out in search of civilisation.

I scramble down the bank and extract my handbag from the car. I pull on my jacket and shove my phone into my pocket in case I can figure out a way to charge it from a nearby telegraph pole. I look up and down the narrow lane and decide the direction in which I was driving looks more promising than the one from which I came. I set off purposefully, but I haven't taken more than fifteen steps when I hear an engine, although I can't see any sign of a car. It may be on a parallel road to me, which would be frustrating. The sound grows louder, and a red sports car comes into view.

I'm so relieved that I almost forget to flag it down. Luckily, it's already slowing as it approaches. The driver must be wondering who's dumped a vehicle in the middle of nowhere and wandered off. Maybe he's planning to return with a truck and steal it. Horrified by the thought of having to explain myself to the rental company and possibly being charged a huge deposit, I turn and retrace my steps.

The driver has climbed out and is inspecting my car. He gives me a cheerful grin when he sees me. 'Hello, there! Having a bit of car trouble?'

'It's a rental,' I say. 'I have no idea what's wrong with it. It started making funny noises about an hour ago, and they got worse.'

'What sort of funny noises?' he says, looking amused.

'Just funny noises. Like sausages sizzling, or a popcorn machine, or a soda can after it's been shaken up.'

'And what did you do when you heard it?'

'I turned the radio up.'

I'm annoyed to hear him laugh. 'Of course, you did.'

'What else was I supposed to do? I'm not a mechanic.'

'Maybe find a mechanic?' he suggests. 'Or call the roadside services?'

'They aren't included in my rental package. The man told me this car was serviced only last week, and I didn't want to pay extra for something I wouldn't need. Besides, I was in a hurry. I wanted to get to my bed and breakfast before dark.'

'And now you won't get there at all.'

'Can't you fix it?' I say.

'I'm not a mechanic. I'm a photographer. There isn't a lot of overlap.'

I give a despairing sigh. 'Didn't they teach you how to maintain your camera at photography school? It's probably not much different.'

'I'm afraid not,' he says. 'It's a pity a chef didn't come along instead.'

'A chef?'

'As soon as you told them it sounded like sausages frying, they'd have it diagnosed in an instant. Sausages frying – transmission failure. Popcorn machine – overheating. Soda explosion – leaking brake fluid.'

Despite my annoyance, I find myself laughing. 'Thanks for trying to help, anyway. Could you possibly give me a lift into the next town? Even if there aren't any chefs on duty, I may be able to locate a mechanic.'

'I can do you one better than that,' he says. 'We're about five miles away from Honeywell. I'm staying in the village. You can call the rental company and ask what you should do.'

'I expect they'll say it's my fault,' I say gloomily. 'They weren't terribly helpful to begin with. And look what they've given me. They said it was a nice little runaround.'

He gives my car a disparaging glance. 'I wouldn't have thought it could do much more than stagger around.'

'Exactly! And now it's not even doing that.'

'Which is why they'll have to pay to fix it,' he says. 'If you're lucky, you may even get a night's accommodation out of them. Where were you trying to get to?'

'Dorchester.'

'That's about thirty-five miles from here,' he says. 'Where are you coming from?'

'Why?'

'I don't understand how you ended up here,' he says. 'We're nowhere near a main road.'

'I took a shortcut.'

'Who told you it was a shortcut?' he says, a glint of amusement in his eyes.

'It looked as though it *ought* to be a shortcut. The traffic was moving slowly, and my phone said it was getting worse. I thought I could bypass it and rejoin the main road later. But the road started winding away in a completely different direction. I tried to check the map, but my phone battery was almost dead. When I managed to switch it on again, I realised there was no connection.'

'It's a bit of a dead spot around here,' he agrees. 'It picks up again as you get closer to Honeywell. We have excellent connection there.'

'Congratulations! But that's not much help to me.'

'True, but I can give you a ride there. You can't sit here all day. You're lucky I came along when I did. You could have been here for hours.'

He opens his car door. 'That heap of junk will be fine here for an hour or two until they send someone out.'

I take a step towards his car, then stop. This may not be the best idea. I'm alone in a deserted area without a phone connection, and I have no idea who this man is.

He notices my hesitation. 'I'm Will Matthews. I'm a photographer, down from London for the summer. I have a few commissions in this area. One of them is to photograph places of interest for a book on local history, including Honeywell. That's where I'm currently staying. If I could get any connection, I'd show you my firm's website. It has my photograph on it somewhere. As it is, you'll have to take my word for it.'

I study his face carefully. He looks all right, but that doesn't mean anything.

'If you'd rather stay here and wait for a mechanic, that's fine,' he says. 'I don't know when they'll send one, but it may not be for a while. I have a bag of apples in my car I can leave for you. I also have three dozen eggs I bought from a farm shop a few miles back.'

'What do you expect me to do with eggs?' I say.

'That's up to you. If you happen to have any brandy in the car, you could make an eggnog.'

'If I had any brandy in the car, I'd have drunk it by now,' I say. 'It's been a rough week, and this breakdown has just about put the lid on it.'

'If I hadn't come along when I did, you'd have been forced to spend the night here,' he says. 'You'd have needed the brandy to stay warm. What would you have done if you'd drunk it all?'

'I have half a bar of chocolate,' I say. 'I was trying to work out how long that would last.'

'It's better than nothing,' he says. 'But not as good as my apples and eggs.'

'Raw eggs,' I remind him.

'True, but you may have seen them differently if you'd been stranded here all night. You'd be thinking longingly of steak tartare long before dawn.'

'I doubt it,' I say. 'Anyway, I wasn't planning on spending the night here. I was setting out to look for help when you arrived.'

'I saw that. There was a touch of the Captain Oates in the way you were striding along. "Now, there's a woman who may be gone some time!" I said to myself.'

'Was I at least going in the right direction?' I ask.

'It depends on what for. If you take a keen interest in automatic crop sprinklers or the latest fashions in scarecrows, you'd have had a wonderful afternoon. If you were dead set on finding a mechanic, not so much. We're only a few miles from Honeywell as the crow flies, but it's in that direction.' He points towards a clump of elms.

'Have you decided what you want to do?' he adds. 'Shall I go on ahead to warn the villagers that hostile townies are lurking nearby, or would you like a ride in so you can tell them yourself?'

I decide to take the risk. I don't want to sit here all afternoon.

'I'll come with you,' I say. 'Are you sure you know where we are?'

'I am. I can tell the rental agency exactly where to find your car.'

'If you insist on calling it that,' I say. 'I assume there's somewhere I can eat at this Honeywell place?'

'There's a very nice bakery. You won't need to bring your emergency chocolate ration with you. Leave it in the car for the next time you break down.'

'And your eggs are safe for now,' I say, settling myself into the front seat of his car. 'Why do you need so many? Are you making a giant omelette?'

'It's the school sports day tomorrow. I promised the head teacher I'd supply the eggs for the egg and spoon race.'

'It's lucky I didn't eat them,' I say. 'They'd have had to use something else for the race.'

'Like ping-pong balls?' he suggests, turning his car to face the opposite direction.

'Not ping-pong balls! They'd fall off the spoons if there was the slightest breeze. You'd need to use something much heavier. But not heavy enough to cause damage if it flew off and hit the other competitors.'

'You've obviously given this some thought,' he says. 'Are you an engineer or an assault course designer?'

'Not even close. I'm a veterinary nurse.'

'I take it from the fact you're lost that you aren't a local?' he says, turning onto a larger road, signposted Honeywell in one direction, and Ringwood in the other.

'I've never been in this part of the world before,' I say.

'Are you on holiday?'

I don't answer for a moment.

'It's none of my business,' he adds. 'I'm just naturally nosy.'

I don't know why I hesitated. I'll never see this man again. I should have agreed I was on holiday and left it at that.

'It's a sort of holiday,' I say. 'I wanted to be away from my flat for a few days, while ...'

'It's always good to take a break,' he says.

He turns the subject and points out various landmarks – a disused mill, and a pick your own strawberry farm. I'm grateful for his understanding.

He turns off the main road and weaves his way along several smaller lanes.

'There's Honeywell church,' he says, indicating a grey stone building on our right. 'The primary school is right next to it.'

We come to a crossroads, and he points to the sign. 'This is Honeywell high street. The Red Lion is over there, if you still want that brandy. Otherwise, you can get something to eat at The Sugarloaf Bakery. They'll do you an excellent cream tea. They also sell sandwiches and pies if you're after something more substantial.'

'What about the rental company?' I ask.

'Call them now,' he says, handing me his phone. 'My phone has plenty of charge.'

I dial the number and speak to a woman who tells me her boss has gone to lunch, but she'll get him to call me as soon as he gets back.

'Let's hope it isn't a three hour lunch,' I tell Will. 'I need them to sort something out for me as quickly as possible.'

'I'm sure it won't be,' he says. 'In the meantime, are you going to the pub or the bakery?'

'Which do you recommend?'

'The bakery,' he says without hesitation. 'I go there almost every day. They'll sort you out with a phone charger if you ask.'

'The bakery, it is.'

'Good call,' he says. 'You won't regret it.'

'It's awfully kind of you to go to all this trouble,' I say. 'You didn't have to.'

He grins. 'I couldn't leave you wandering around in the depths of the New Forest countryside, getting yourself more and more lost and falling into peat bogs.'

'But you were heading in the other direction. I've made you late for wherever you were going.'

'Not really,' he says. 'I was supposed to be photographing Wyndham Keep this afternoon. But I can do that anytime.'

He pulls up outside the bakery. 'Here we are. You must be ready for something to eat after all the excitement.'

'I could do something with a sausage roll or a sandwich,' I say. 'And those cream teas sound tempting.'

'You won't regret it,' he says. 'I may even join you there later. By the way, what's your name? I can't keep on calling you Jane Doe.'

'Olivia Sullivan,' I say.

I close the car door, and he rolls down the window. 'I've always liked that name. My aunt had a cat called Olivia.'

He gives me a friendly wave and drives away.

Chapter Two

I push open the bakery door and step inside. There's a counter in front of me, filled with brightly coloured cakes. I suddenly realise how hungry I am. It's been a long time since breakfast. I was planning to eat lunch in Dorchester, and it doesn't look as though I'll arrive there before dinner. But I could still be wandering around the countryside, getting progressively more lost. There are worse places to find yourself at lunchtime than a bakery.

A woman appears and greets me with a cheerful smile. 'Hi, I'm Isabella. How can I help you?'

'I'm not sure,' I say. 'There's so much to choose from.'

'That's our motto here at the Sugarloaf,' she says. '*Never knowingly underwhelmed.*'

'Is it really?'

She laughs. 'No, but it ought to be. Would you like some recommendations?'

'I was hoping to get some lunch.'

She looks at the clock hanging over the counter. 'It's half past three. Please tell me you mean second lunch?'

'I don't. My car broke down somewhere around here, and a helpful passer-by gave me a lift to Honeywell. He said this bakery would be a good place to eat.'

'He was almost right,' she says. 'It's the absolute best place to eat. There's the Red Lion too, but they don't have much in the way of lunchtime desserts, which I always think are the most important part of a meal.'

She shows me to a table and hands me a menu. 'We can offer you a variety of sandwiches and pies.'

'The man who gave me a ride mentioned something about cream teas,' I say, scanning the menu.

She looks pleased. 'We do the best cream teas for miles around.'

This woman doesn't seem overly troubled about modesty. She sees my expression and bursts out laughing. 'Someone has to say it, and it may as well be me. We make amazing cream teas. Our pastry chef has a secret recipe for scones that she refuses to share with me. It doesn't make any difference because I can't cook. Whatever she puts in them, they're delicious. We came second in the New Forest Mix-up last year, and I'm convinced it was partly because of our scones.'

'Do you have any chicken and leek pies left?' I ask.

'I had one earlier,' she says. 'But there were still a couple left. I don't think anyone has bought them.'

She disappears behind the counter and emerges with a pie. She puts it onto a plate and adds a few sprigs of salad.

I take a bite and sigh in contentment. 'This is delicious. Do you bake on the premises?'

'We do,' she says. 'We decided we wanted to make all our own pies and cakes when we bought the place.'

I remember my phone. 'The man I met said you might lend me a charger. My phone is flat, and I need to make some calls. I should have checked it before I set off this morning.'

She looks at the phone I hold out to her. 'No problem. That's the same one I have. I'll plug it in for you. You should be at least half full by the time you leave. I mean, your phone will. You'll be completely full.'

A woman comes out of the room behind the shop. 'Do we have any dried raspberries?'

Isabella nods. 'They're in the storeroom. I didn't get around to unpacking that last order. Were your ears burning just now? Our customer was saying how good your pies are.'

'This is Abby, our pastry chef,' she tells me.

'Hi,' I say to Abby. 'I'm Olivia.'

'I run the bakery with my partner, Lily,' says Isabella. 'She isn't here today because her baby has typhoid.'

'Typhoid?' I say, startled.

'A cold,' corrects Abby with a grin.

'Possibly,' concedes Isabella. 'I'm no baby expert. All I know is that I had to cover for Lily today because Daisy is seeing an infectious disease consultant from the rare tropical diseases department at the local hospital.'

'She means the health visitor,' says Abby. 'Nice to meet you, Olivia. I'd better get back to my cookies. Isabella eats most of them if she's left alone in the shop for too long, so we're always running out.'

'She and Lily are always making comments like that,' says Isabella. 'I can't think why. I taste the occasional product, but that's all. It's all part of being a conscientious bakery owner. Have you finished your pie? Would you like another?'

'I'm fine, thanks. It was the best pie I've eaten in a long time.'

She looks pleased. 'You must come in again and try one of our other flavours.'

'I won't have time,' I say regretfully. 'As soon as my car is fixed, I need to drive Dorchester. I've booked a room there tonight.'

'I'll fetch your cream tea,' she says. 'Do you have any preference for jams, or shall I bring you an assortment?'

'I'm not sure I can manage anything more after that pie,' I say.

'Of course you can! Our cream teas don't take up any room at all. I often eat one before I go home, and I'm still ravenous by dinner time.'

'You don't look as though you've ever eaten a cream tea in your life,' I say.

She laughs. 'Appearances are deceptive. I've eaten plenty of them. I tell you what. If you can't finish it, I won't charge you for it. You can't say fairer than that.'

She disappears into the kitchen and returns a minute later carrying a tray with a plate of scones, several small bowls of jam and cream, and a pot of tea.

'I've brought all the jams we have,' she says, setting down the tray and unloading it. 'My favourite is the gooseberry. Lily's mum makes it. She grows a lot of soft fruit, and she always makes too much jam, so we buy it from her and use it in the shop.'

I split open a scone and spread some of the jam on it. I sandwich it with a generous dollop of thick cream and take a bite. Isabella watches me anxiously.

'It's wonderful,' I say, swallowing my mouthful. 'I may finish it after all.'

'I knew you would!' she says. 'Everyone says they don't have room, but they never leave anything on their plates.'

She looks at her watch. 'It's only an hour before we close. I think I'll liberate a couple of scones. That gooseberry jam is making me hungry.'

'Why don't you join me?' I suggest. 'You don't seem busy in here, and I'd enjoy the company.'

She looks delighted. 'You're the best kind of customer. My two favourite hobbies are talking and eating. It's wonderful when I can combine the two.'

She disappears into the kitchen again, and I pour myself a cup of tea.

The shop door opens, and Will comes in. He looks pleased when he sees me. 'You're still here.'

I point to my plate. 'I may be here some time.'

'That's good. I was worried about you when we met. You looked so forlorn.'

'I was hungry,' I say. 'I hadn't had lunch, and I wasn't sure whether I dared eat that chocolate bar. I feel much better now. Thanks for rescuing me.'

'It was my pleasure,' he says. 'I came to tell you that the rental people called me. They must have thought you used your own phone to call them earlier. They've sent the local mechanic out to see your car. He's put the car on his truck and brought it back to Honeywell to have a look at it. What do you want to do next – wait for it to be fixed or ask the company for another one?'

I spoon raspberry jam onto my second scone. 'What I want is to sue the rental place for millions before pushing the car into the nearest river.'

'You can't do that,' he says. 'The council has extremely strict laws about fly-tipping.'

'I said push,' I remind him. 'I don't have to tip it in if the mayor will make a fuss.'

'Honeywell doesn't have a mayor,' he says. 'But the council would definitely object to finding a car in the river. We'll have to come up with another plan.'

'Another plan for what?' says Isabella, appearing with the scones. 'Hi, Will. Sorry I wasn't here when you arrived.'

He looks at her plate. 'You were probably otherwise occupied. Were you busy haranguing Abby about not making enough scones for your daily tea break?'

'I never harangue,' she says. 'I may have mentioned our stocks of eclairs are running low, but that's just business.'

She sits down at my table. 'Is this man bothering you, Olivia?'

I catch Will's eye and laugh. 'Yes. He's raising all sorts of objections about where I want to leave my car.'

'Olivia's a visitor,' she tells him through a huge mouthful of scone. 'She can park her car pretty much where she likes.'

'She wants to park it in the river,' says Will.

Isabella picks up another scone. 'I'm sure she has her reasons.'

'Will's the man who rescued me,' I tell her.

'Are you sure? I thought you said the man who brought you here was charming.'

I flush. 'I don't think I said charming. I expect I said helpful.'

'Probably,' she agrees. 'Will isn't charming. He's quite grumpy, really.'

He rolls his eyes. 'I told you I didn't have time to photograph all your cakes this week, that's all.'

'Are you putting the pictures on your website?' I ask Isabella. 'That's a good idea.'

'If that were the case, I might have made time,' says Will. 'But Isabella wanted the pictures for personal use.'

'What sort of personal use?' I say, puzzled.

His lips twitch. 'You know how people photograph their shoe collections or their antique bells? Isabella has decided she wants a photo shoot of all her favourite cakes. Something to look at during the long winter evenings.'

'It's an excellent idea,' says Isabella. 'Far more interesting than that stupid coffee table book you're working on.'

'That coffee table book will pay my bills,' he says. 'I suspect your collection of cakes won't.'

He turns to me. 'To make matters worse, Isabella wanted to pay me in kind.'

'You should consider it,' I say. 'Have you tasted her chicken and leek pies?'

'Well, no, but …'

Isabella gives him a triumphant smile. 'There you go. You're deciding without knowing all the facts. I told you he was judgemental, Olivia.'

'You said grumpy,' he reminds her.

'And pedantic,' she says.

The shop door opens again before he can answer. Isabella lays down her scone. 'I'll be right back.'

She walks over to the counter and starts talking to the customer.

'She's incorrigible,' says Will. 'But she's great fun. And when it comes to food, she leaves strong men collapsed in her wake.'

'She's really nice,' I say, wondering whether he and Isabella are seeing each other. It would explain their easy camaraderie.

He's a lucky man, if so. She's stunning. Add to that her sunny, friendly nature and infectious laugh, and I'd be surprised if half the male population of Honeywell weren't beating down the door of the bakery.

I shoot a surreptitious look at Will. I'm forced to admit Isabella wouldn't be doing too badly if she dated him. He's tall and strongly built, with dark, wavy hair and deep brown, amused eyes. Well, good luck to the pair of them. It's nice to know some relationships work out.

'Have you decided what you'd like to do tonight?' he asks, bringing me back to reality. 'Did you say you had a room booked in Dorchester?'

'That's right, but I don't know how I'm going to get there. Is there a bus or a train I could catch?'

'Possibly, but it's getting late. And you'd have to come all the way back here to collect your car, assuming you still want it. You might be better off cancelling your booking and staying here for a couple of nights.'

I look around me. 'Here?'

He laughs. 'I don't mean the bakery. That's Isabella's dream, not yours. But we could easily find you a place to stay for the night. There's plenty of accommodation in Honeywell. The holiday rush hasn't yet started.'

Isabella reappears. 'If I have to tell Mrs Glennister one more time that we don't sell soap powder! What are you two talking about?'

'Where Olivia is going to stay tonight,' says Will. 'I've suggested she finds somewhere around here until her car is ready.'

'That's a good idea,' she says. 'She can stay with me.'

'Great!' says Will.

'No, I can't!' I exclaim.

Isabella sits down and resumes her cream tea. 'Why not? We have a spare bedroom. You wouldn't be any trouble.'

When she says we, does she mean her and Will? I don't want to be a third wheel.

'My mum's away this week,' she says. 'So, the standard of cooking won't be up to much. I'm more of a baked goods girl myself. But we could order a takeaway.'

'That's ridiculous,' I say. 'I couldn't possibly land myself on you.'

'Why not? You have to sleep somewhere.'

'Don't bully the poor girl,' says Will. 'She probably doesn't want to spend any more time with you than she must, but she's too polite to say so.'

'That's not it at all!' I say.

'Of course, it isn't,' says Isabella. 'Why wouldn't she want to stay with me? Isn't that what you're doing here in the first place, Olivia? Having an adventure?'

'Not really. I was –' I break off, not sure how to describe to her what I'm doing. I'm not even sure how to describe it to myself.

'It's none of our business,' interrupts Will. 'Don't let Isabella bully you into doing anything you don't want to. We can find you somewhere else to stay.'

'I'm not bullying her!' she says indignantly. 'Am I, Olivia?'

Her expression is so much like an excited puppy that I laugh. 'Of course not. It's extremely kind of you. But I'm a complete stranger. I can't impose on you like that.'

'We won't be complete strangers after you've spent the night with my family and seen my sister's collection of gargoyle mugs,' she says. 'They may give you nightmares, but that can't be helped. Is that all?'

'Well, yes.'

She swallows her last mouthful of scone. 'Great! Your phone should be charged by now. You can call the place where you were supposed to be staying tonight and let them know you've had a better offer!'

Chapter Three

It feels strange to be setting off to a complete stranger's house for the night. But it's been a strange day, so I decide to go with it. To be honest, it's been a strange few weeks.

'My car's just over there,' says Isabella. 'I always try to park near the shop, but the customers usually beat me to it. I probably ought to get here before they do.'

'You must be running a popular business if the customers are queuing outside even before you open.'

She grins. 'It's the other way around. I mean, they're waiting for me to arrive and open the shop. I'm not the greatest timekeeper.'

'If that cream tea is a sample of your usual products, they probably don't mind.'

She looks pleased. 'Abby's a great baker, isn't she? She's been with us for just over a year. She came to cover Lily's maternity leave, but she stayed on. I can't imagine how we'd cope without her.'

'Lily is your partner?' I say.

'That's right. We bought the bakery together a few years ago. It's been in the village for ever, but business wasn't good. We wouldn't have been able to afford the bakery if it had been, even with both our families underwriting the loan. We expanded into the shop next door when they closed down, so now we have the cafe too. It was touch and go there for a while. We were drowning in debt, and there was no guarantee we'd be able to make a go of it. But we managed somehow. Business picked up, and now we're doing fine.'

'That's good,' I say. 'A lot of businesses seem to be struggling at the moment.'

'It helps that we're the only bakery for miles around,' she says. 'Honeywell isn't large, but most of the other villages near here are even smaller. So far, none of them has decided to open a bakery. I hope they never do. As it is, people who used to go into Christchurch or Ringwood are coming to us.

'I'm not familiar with the area,' I say. 'I grew up in Bath.'

'What do you do for a living?' she asks. 'Are you a mosaic tiler?'

'Why would you think I was a tiler?'

'My parents used to take me to Bath for the weekend when I was younger,' she says. 'I remember visiting the Roman baths and seeing lots of mosaics.'

'Made by the Romans,' I say.

'Originally,' she agrees. 'But they must have been redone plenty of times since then.'

I dart a look at her and see she's laughing.

'What else did you do in Bath?' I say.

'Oh, the usual. We visited the Abbey, took Jane Austen tours, and had tea at the Sally Lunn tea shop.'

She brightens. 'There's the most incredible fudge kitchen down one of the side streets. My parents always took me there if I didn't make a fuss about yet another tour of the Abbey. Do you know it?'

'I think I know the one you mean. They hand out free samples so you can choose a flavour.'

'That's the one!' she says. 'I used to go in wearing my hair in different styles to see how many samples I could get in one afternoon.'

'Did it work?'

'Amazingly, it didn't. My father had to buy several pounds of fudge to placate them. It was a win-win situation for me.'

'You appear to have a very sweet tooth,' I say, remembering the cream tea.

'I have several very sweet teeth,' she says placidly. 'And a fast metabolism.'

'Lucky you. I wish the fairies who attended my christening had been as thoughtful.'

'You have a great figure,' she says. 'And those fairies gave you that amazing red hair. I always wanted red hair. Proper red, the sort that looks as though your head has caught fire when you're watching a sunset.'

'And I always wanted blonde hair like yours,' I say. 'I spent most of my childhood being teased about my hair. However, short of spending an absolute fortune on hair dye, we're stuck with what nature gave us. We'll just have to make the best of it.'

'Until they perfect the art of head transplants,' she agrees. 'Here we are!'

She swings the car up a gravel driveway and pulls up outside an old stone house, hidden from the road by a row of poplars.

'The Lodge,' I read, peering at the sign over the front door.

'That's us.'

She jumps out of the car and picks up my bag. 'I live here with my parents and younger sister. My uncle and his family live up there in the main house.'

She gestures towards a massive building a quarter of a mile away up the hill.

'That looks like Downton Abbey!' I say, awed. 'Does your uncle have butlers and housemaids and chauffeurs and tweenies?'

'I've never noticed any while I've been visiting,' she says. 'But there's a large cellar and several attics, so who knows?'

'Your house looks lovely too,' I say. 'I wouldn't really want to live in a mansion. I like cosy houses.'

'They only live in one wing,' she says. 'They rent the rest of it out for conferences and as holiday lets.'

'Does it have a ghost?'

'Several,' she says, and I can't tell whether she's joking.

She opens the front door and ushers me inside. 'Welcome! I'll see whether anyone's home.'

She drops my bag in the hall and disappears. She returns a minute later. 'No one seems to be around.'

I feel a momentary qualm at the thought of being alone in the house with a complete stranger. For all I know, the house may not even belong to her. She may have broken in, disposed of the occupants, stolen their keys, and set up house here.

The front door opens, and I spin around, half expecting to see a police officer. But it's a young woman. She's several years younger than Isabella, but it doesn't take a genius to realise this must be her sister. They're incredibly similar, right down to the blonde curls and vivid blue eyes.

'Hi, Issy,' she says casually. 'Is dinner ready?'

'Not unless you've made it,' says Isabella. 'Georgia, this is my friend Olivia. Olivia, this is my sister, Georgia.'

Georgia lifts a hand in greeting. 'Hi, nice to meet you.'

She turns back to Isabella. 'I'm going out in half an hour. Is there anything to eat?'

'The kitchen's that way,' says Isabella, pointing.

Georgia sighs and disappears. We hear the crashing of pots and pans, followed by a muffled exclamation.

She reappears a few minutes later. 'I ate that pie in the fridge. I hope you weren't saving it for anything. I couldn't find anything else, and I was starving.'

'Where are you going?' says Isabella.

'Matthew's taking me for dinner at the Wild Horse. I'd better get a move on. The table's booked for seven.'

'Did you miss lunch?' I say sympathetically.

Georgia gives me an odd look. 'No.' She disappears upstairs.

Isabella doesn't appear to find anything unusual in this exchange. 'I'll show you to your room. Then we can think about dinner. I was going to have that pie, but Georgia has beaten me to it. I don't think there's much else in the house. I meant to go to the supermarket at lunchtime, but our supplier was late, and Abby couldn't wait in for them.'

'We could order a takeaway,' I say. 'I'm paying.'

'I was going to suggest we went to the Red Lion,' she says. 'That way, you can meet some of the locals and get to know them.'

'That would be nice. But I'm just passing through. I'll never see any of them again.'

'Maybe,' she says. 'I need a shower. Shall we leave in about half an hour?'

She shows me to the guest bedroom. I sit on the bed and stare out of the window, thinking about the strange turn my day has taken.

I set off this morning in a functioning car, heading for Dorchester, determined not to think about the past few days. I've ended the day with no car at all, sitting in a strange bedroom, in the house of a complete stranger. And now I'm about to go to the pub to meet the local inhabitants of a village of which I'd never heard until today.

I take a deep breath, trying to clear my mind. I can't allow myself to think about everything that's led me to this point. I came here to escape, to find some peace and quiet. The last thing I need is to get caught up in someone else's drama.

A knock on the door brings me back to reality. Isabella pokes her head around. 'Do you have everything you need?'

'I have, thanks. It's a lovely room. You must let me pay for it.'

'You can buy me a drink and call it even,' she says. 'Are you ready?'

I pick up my bag. 'As I'll ever be. I'm not particularly hungry, but I'm happy to watch you eat.'

'Wait until you've smelled Shelley's game pie,' she says. 'I guarantee you'll be ravenous.'

Chapter Four

The Red Lion is full when we arrive. No one seems to notice I'm here, which suits me fine. I'm only passing through, and I have no desire to learn the names of people I'll never see again. All I want is a quiet dinner and a chance to relax before diving into the comfortable bed in Isabella's spare room.

'I'll get us a couple of menus,' she says. 'You find us a table. There's one over there by the window. Or would you rather eat outside? They have a lovely garden.'

'Good idea,' I say. 'It will be quieter.'

'Don't count on it. Half the dog population of Honeywell is out there at the first hint of a warm evening. Do you mind dogs?'

'I love them. I'll see you out there.'

Isabella's prediction is slightly exaggerated. Most of the outside tables are occupied, but I only count three dogs – an elderly golden retriever who's trying and failing to catch a butterfly, a Jack Russell eating chips off the grass, and a chihuahua scrambling up its owner's leg.

I sit at the last empty table and look around me. The garden is enormous. The part nearest to the building is fenced in, but there's a gate in the fence, beyond which half an acre of rough grass leads down to what I assume is a small river. I can't see the water, but something about the row of willow trees suggests they're growing there for a reason.

Isabella appears and dumps the menus onto the table. 'I don't really need one. I already know what I'm having.'

'The game pie?' I say.

'I wasn't joking when I said it's the best I've ever tasted. Why don't you try it?'

'I had pie for lunch,' I remind her. 'One of the nicest I've ever eaten.'

'But that was lunch,' she says. 'It's half a lifetime ago. Why can't you have pie for dinner too? Is there some new law I haven't heard about?'

'Not exactly a law. But I've heard the Royal family ostracises anyone who dares to consume pastry more than once a day.'

'I don't dare ask what they have to say about cake,' she says.

'Never more than once a week.' I laugh at her horrified expression.

'I considered marrying Prince William when I was younger,' she says. 'I realise now I had a lucky escape.'

She picks up the menus and heads back towards the pub.

'You forgot my card!' I call after her. 'I'm paying for this.'

She waves her hand. 'You can get the next one.'

She disappears before I can protest. I'll have to make a bank transfer or something. There won't be any 'next one'. With any luck, my car will be fixed by tomorrow morning, and I'll be able to resume my journey.

The whole point of my trip is to keep moving and avoid having to think about what's happened, or what my future might hold. Stopping in Honeywell wasn't part of the plan. That isn't too important. I'd have had to stop somewhere tonight, and this seems as good a place as any. But I have no intention of making a prolonged visit. I plan to be away from London for at least a week and to stay in a different place each night. Constant change is the best remedy I know for keeping the mind off difficult subjects. But I'm here for tonight. I may as well make the best of it and treat it as an adventure.

Isabella reappears. 'That was a close call. Matt told me there were only two servings of game pie left. I don't know what we'd have done otherwise.'

'Ordered something else?' I suggest.

She gives me a horrified look. 'I'll let that pass because you're a newcomer. You won't speak so lightly about such things once you've been here for a while.'

'I'm sure I wouldn't. But I'm not a newcomer. I'm a sojourner.'

'A what?'

'A traveller,' I elaborate. 'An out-of-towner, a passer through.'

'I know what it means,' she says. 'I may not be royalty, but I have an excellent vocabulary. However, I'm not sure it applies to you.'

'I'm pretty sure it does. I may have taken a slight detour, but it's only for one night. I'll be on my way tomorrow.'

'But why?' she says. 'Don't you like Honeywell?'

'What I've seen of it looks lovely.'

'It *is* lovely,' she says. 'I often feel sorry for all the people in the world who don't get to live here.'

'That's an awful lot of people to feel sorry for. What's the population of Honeywell?'

'About two thousand,' she says.

'Which makes nearly eight billion people who don't live in Honeywell.'

'Minus two thousand,' she reminds me. 'It *is* an awful lot of people to feel sorry for. Is it any wonder I feel exhausted at the end of each day?'

'I've been living in London for the past eight years,' I say.

'Poor you.'

'I don't see why,' I say. 'I quite like it.'

She gives me a keen look. 'Why do I think that isn't quite true?'

'Because you seem to be some sort of paid brand ambassador for Honeywell?'

'They don't pay me,' she says. 'But wouldn't it be great if they did? I could lie in bed all morning. I *hate* getting up early. After a light lunch, I'd wander around the village for an hour, telling everyone I met what an incredible place Honeywell is. After which, I'd collect my cheque and use it to pay for a cream tea.'

'I thought you owned the Sugarloaf,' I say. 'You don't have to pay for what you eat.'

'But I wouldn't own it if I took on this new job. I couldn't do both jobs justice. I'd have to sell my share of the bakery. Either Lily would buy me out, or I'd have to sell it to some awful London type, who would treat it as a weekend bakery.'

She catches my eye. 'Someone like you, in fact! The locals are always complaining about the horrible Londoners who buy second homes in the village and drive up house prices until no one can afford them.'

'They sound awful,' I say. 'I'd better not to spend any more time here. If anyone hears I come from London, they'll be after me with pitchforks.'

'That depends,' she says. 'Do you own a mansion in Mayfair?'

'Not even a house on Park Lane,' I say. 'We've … I've been renting a flat in Putney.'

Our food arrives before she can comment. Her eyes light up when she sees our plates. 'Take a bite of that and tell me you aren't hungry.'

I dig into the pie, which emits a cloud of fragrant steam. I'm suddenly ravenous. Maybe it's something in the air of this place. Isabella seems to be perpetually hungry.

I take a bite. 'You're right. This is the most delicious pie I've ever tasted. Including the one you gave me this afternoon!'

'I told you so,' she says, pleased. 'I'm not even insulted by the comparison.'

'That's good because, compared to this one, your pie is barely a prototype pie.'

'Hey!' she says.

'It's true,' I say through another mouthful. 'If all the pies in the world were arranged next to each other, yours wouldn't even be on the same continent as this one. The only use people would have for your pies would be as doorstops or weapons in some pie-related combat.'

'Hey!' she says again. 'I made that pie. I helped to make it, at any rate.'

'You told me Abby made it,' I say.

'Technically, that's true. But I was in the kitchen while she was making it. At least, I was for part of the time.'

'That's very impressive,' I say, selecting a chip and dipping it into the gravy. 'It sounds as though you're some sort of patron saint of baked goods.'

'That's an excellent way of putting it,' she says. 'It isn't often I meet someone who gets me like you do.'

'All the more reason for you to stay on as manager of the bakery. Think what a loss it would be to the village if you took up this tourism job.'

She finishes her pie. 'You really do get me! Anyway, I can't consider other employment at the moment. I'm not sure when Lily will be back, so Abby and I will have our hands full for the foreseeable future. I can't leave her in the lurch.'

'I'm sorry to hear Lily's child is ill,' I say. 'How old is she?'

'Almost a year. Her birthday is on June 4th. I'm her godmother, so it's my job to keep tabs on all that sort of information.'

'Don't her parents do that?' I say.

'I have no idea. Lily may have it scribbled down somewhere, but I wouldn't trust Jack to remember anything more important than dinner time. It doesn't matter. That's what I'm here for.'

'What kind of godmother are you?' I say. 'Are you like the ones who turned up at Sleeping Beauty's christening and gave her those gifts of grace and beauty and whatever? Or are you more like the one who sulked because she wasn't invited and came up with all that ridiculous nonsense about a spindle?'

'I'm not like any of them,' she says. 'It would have been a complete waste to give Daisy gifts like beauty and brains. She's the prettiest baby I've ever seen. She's super intelligent too. She knows her godmother already. She calls me Whizzy.'

'It suits you,' I say. 'You don't seem to sit down much.'

'Except for meals,' she agrees. 'She also knows I'm the person who always has cake in their bag. She makes a beeline for it as soon as I walk in the door. She can crawl even faster than I can.'

'Somehow, it doesn't surprise me that you always have cake somewhere about your person,' I say.

She doesn't look insulted. 'Be prepared for anything, my mother always said. She was talking about men, but it applies to cake too.'

She stretches out a hand. 'Are you going to finish those chips? Do you mind if I do?'

I push my plate towards her. 'Go ahead. But save room for dessert.'

She eats the last few chips and wipes her fingers. 'Always. Shall I get us some dessert menus?'

'I was joking. After that pie, I'm not sure I ever want to eat again.'

She stands and brushes pastry crumbs onto the grass. 'You won't say that when you've tasted their crème brûlée. It's amazing.'

'I'm sure it is,' I say. 'You were right about the pie.'

'And I'm right about this,' she says. Without giving me the chance to protest, she disappears inside the pub.

I lean back and let the evening sun soak into me. This is one of the most peaceful places I've ever visited. It isn't only the lack of traffic and hordes of commuters rushing home about this time. It's the village itself. There's something special about it. I can't quite put my finger on what it is. But I'm starting to think Isabella is right to feel sorry for all the people who don't live here.

Chapter Five

Isabella returns a few minutes later carrying two glasses. 'I forgot to mention this pub sells the best local cider I've ever tasted.'

'Is there anything this pub doesn't sell the best of?' I ask, laughing. 'First, there was the game pie, and now the cider.'

'You haven't tasted it yet,' she says, handing me a glass. 'And you haven't tasted their creme brûlée either. I was right about the game pie, wasn't I?'

I take the glass she hands me. 'You were. It was amazing.'

'There you are, then. You have to learn to trust me. Once you've been here for a while, you'll realise I'm an infallible source of information concerning anything edible or drinkable.'

I take a sip of the cider. I don't want to add to Isabella's inflated sense of self-importance, but it's beyond delicious. It's like distilled sunlight. It's as though someone has concentrated the flavour of a hundred different varieties of apples into one glass of sparkling amber liquid.

Isabella is watching me, a gleam in her eye. 'I'm right, aren't I?'

I fling caution to the winds and risk the truth. If her ego explodes, that's nothing to do with me. 'I think I've died and gone to heaven.'

'That's exactly how I felt when I first tasted it!' she says. 'My boyfriend Stephen brought me here, and he said I ought to try it. It was our second date, and I wasn't sure whether to agree to a third one. But this tipped the balance!'

'Does Stephen live locally?' I say, and she laughs.

'He's not my boyfriend now. That was ages ago. About three years, in fact.'

I try to read her expression to see whether this is a painful memory for her. It doesn't appear to be.

'I'm sorry,' I say. There doesn't seem anything else to be said.

'Why?' she says. 'That's all in the past now.'

I take another sip of the cider, wondering whether they sell it in bottles. If they do, I intend to load up the boot of the rental car with as much as it will hold.

'Three years isn't that long,' I say. 'Not after a painful breakup.'

'But this wasn't a painful breakup,' she says. 'We were only together for a few months, and we were completely wrong for each other. It turned out it was Lily he wanted all along, not me.'

'Your partner wanted to be with Lily?'

I don't want to pry, but this sounds as though it could be an interesting story. I can't imagine continuing to work with someone after they'd gone off with my boyfriend.

'That's right,' she says. 'It's how she and I met.'

'Don't tell me. You were busy screaming at her to keep her claws out of your man, and it somehow morphed into a decision to buy a bakery together?'

She finishes her cider. 'Not even close! Stephen and Lily used to date, then he broke up with her. He met me the following year, and we got together, but he decided it had been a mistake to let her go.'

'So, she's with him now?'

She waves an airy hand. 'Oh, no. She's with Jack now, and they have baby Daisy.'

I decide not to pursue this any further. Isabella isn't the most coherent storyteller. A server comes out of the pub, carrying two plates.

Isabella waves. 'Over here, Dave!'

He puts the plates in front of us. Isabella looks delighted. 'Extra-large ramekins, I see.'

'Matt told me who'd ordered them,' he says.

She doesn't look abashed. 'Olivia, this is Dave. He's in charge of …'

'Portion control?' I suggest, and he grins.

Isabella ignores me. 'Dave, this is my new friend Olivia. She's moving to Honeywell, so we need to make her welcome.'

Dave shakes my hand. 'Nice to meet you, Olivia. And welcome to the village.'

'Nice to meet you too,' I say. 'But I'm not moving here. I'm just passing through.'

He gives Isabella a confused look. She picks up her spoon. 'Don't worry about Olivia. She's a little behind the curve, but she'll catch up. See you later, Dave.'

'Try this crème brûlée,' she tells me. 'I'm about to go three for three.'

I don't move. 'Why did you tell him I was moving to the village?'

'Daisy's cold has turned into bronchitis,' she says. 'Lily's had to take her to the hospital. She won't be back in the bakery for a week or two. We'll need an extra pair of hands at the Sugarloaf.'

'But what does that have to do with me?'

She looks exasperated. 'Isn't it obvious?'

'Not to me.'

'Eat your pudding!' she says, sounding like my mother when I was a child and refusing to try a new vegetable. 'It can't be a coincidence that you arrived in the village on the very day we heard Lily would be out for a while.'

'Of course, it can. Coincidences happen all the time.'

'Not this one,' she says stubbornly. 'I knew as soon as I saw you that you were going to be around for a while.'

'I'm sorry to disappoint you, but in this case, your intuition has failed you. I'm carrying on to Dorchester tomorrow. I may come back through Honeywell on my way home. If this crème brûlée is as delicious as it looks, I'll make a point of it. But that's all. You can get a temporary staff member from an agency. You must have had to use one before.'

'I could find hundreds of people,' she says. 'But that isn't the point. I've found you.'

'Technically speaking, I found you,' I say. 'Even more technically speaking, Will found me and brought me here. And he didn't mention there were any conditions attached. He didn't say, "I'll rescue you, but only if you guarantee to spend at least a week in Honeywell." I'd have refused to come with him if he had.'

'You'd still be sitting there,' she says. 'There isn't much traffic along that lane.'

'I wouldn't still be sitting there. I'd have been bound to have been rescued by now. Some handsome farmer would have come along and seen my plight.'

'That would be Mr Marshall,' she says. 'He's in his seventies, and I wouldn't call him handsome. Not unless you have a thing for bloodshot eyes and a threatening manner. Maybe you do. People have different tastes. Far be it from me to judge.'

'It wouldn't have been Mr Marshall,' I say. 'It would have been his handsome young assistant. I'd have helped him to deliver a calf. He'd have been so grateful that he'd have given me a lift to Dorchester.'

'It's mostly sheep in these parts,' she says. 'And they aren't much use to stray travellers. If you have visions of them being trained to rescue passers-by with little kegs of brandy tied around their necks, you can forget it. Sheep are practically untrainable. I ought to know. My uncle has an enormous flock of them, and he ropes me in to help at lambing time. Delivering a lamb in the middle of a field on a freezing February night isn't actually as much fun as you might imagine.'

'But this is May,' I say. 'I wouldn't mind helping to deliver a calf. I've done it before.'

She looks interested. 'Have you, indeed? Was that in pursuit of another handsome young assistant farmer?'

'Not exactly. I'm a veterinary nurse. I was attached to a rural practice during part of my training. I helped out occasionally on the farms.'

'I'm impressed,' she says. 'Is that what you do in London?'

'It's what I've been doing for the past few years.' I haven't decided how much detail to give her about my life. Not too much. I'm only passing through.

'Does that mean you're no longer doing it?' she says.

'You don't have to tell me if you don't want to,' she adds, noticing my expression. 'Lily is always telling me not to be so nosy. I just wondered, that's all.'

I almost take the lifeline she's handed me and change the subject. I'm not sure why I don't. Maybe it's the cider, or maybe it's the strange day I've had. I feel a sudden urge to confide in someone. And who better than a complete stranger, a person I'm never going to see again?

'I resigned last week,' I say.

'Do you have another job to go to?'

'Not yet. I was going to look for work after this trip.'

Her eyes gleam. 'So, you aren't currently employed, and you don't have a new job lined up?'

'There's a vast difference between a veterinary nurse and a baker,' I say.

'A bakery assistant,' she corrects me. 'Abby does the actual baking. We're looking for someone to help in the shop and the cafe. You could do that on your head.'

'That would be a little unorthodox.'

'Then you can do it the right way up. Come on, Olivia. What's stopping you?'

'I have to get back to London,' I say.

'Why is that?'

'Because my life is there. Because you can't up sticks and move whenever the fancy takes you. It isn't what adults do.'

'Plenty of adults do that,' she says. 'My mother was born in Scotland. When she met my father, she upped sticks without a second thought and moved to Little Compton.'

I allow a hint of exasperation to creep into my voice. 'That's different. She had a good reason.'

'And you don't?'

'No, I don't.'

She finishes her pie. 'Working at the Sugarloaf Bakery is a good reason in itself. You're new to the area. You'll learn. But you haven't mentioned any other reason you shouldn't stay here for a while. Are you married?'

'I'm not married, but I've been living with someone for the past five years.'

She arches an eyebrow. 'Again, the use of the past tense. Do I infer you're no longer living with him, or her?'

'I left Charlie a week ago.'

'It's always nice to be the one who does the leaving,' she comments.

'It's nicer to be in the position where you don't want to leave.'

'True,' she says. 'Would you like to talk about it?'

'Not really. But it's the reason I'm taking this trip. I wanted to give him time to cool down in case he was angry.'

'Is he likely to be angry?'

'Who knows? Probably. He's not too keen on other people making decisions.'

'What about your accommodation?' she says. 'Do you have somewhere to go back to?'

'It was Charlie's flat. He bought it before we met, so it's entirely in his name.'

'Better and better,' she says. 'You don't have anywhere to live, you don't have a job, and you're already in the area. What's to stop you adding some extra time to your trip to help out an old friend?'

'You aren't an old friend,' I say without thinking. 'I'm sorry, Isabella. That came out wrong.'

She tries to look affronted but spoils the effect by grinning. 'You can be very harsh at times. Despite that, the job offer is still open.'

I look past her at the meadow leading down to the river. She's being ridiculous. This place is lovely, but it's the sort of place you come to for a holiday, not to stay permanently. It's different if you were born here, as she was.

'I can't,' I say. 'And I'm too tired to argue about it anymore. It's been a long day, and I really need some sleep. Can we get the bill and go?'

'I've already paid for the meal,' she says. 'I'd have done so even if I didn't know you'd be staying here. But I won't bother you anymore.'

She looks at my plate. 'You haven't even tried your crème brûlée. That's a serious mistake. Taste it, at least. If you don't like it, I'll finish it for you.'

'Fine.' I plunge my spoon into the brûlée and lift it to my mouth.

She stops me before I can taste it. 'I said I wouldn't try to persuade you any longer, and I won't. But just remember I was right about the game pie, and I was right about the cider. Two seconds from now, you're going to realise I was right about this too. We don't have to talk right now about you working at the Sugarloaf. But I'm telling you it's a great idea for both of us. Think about it. Remind yourself this strange woman has been right about three things within the space of an hour, so the odds of her being right about a fourth thing are pretty good.'

'Strange woman is right,' I say.

'And you'll think about the other thing?'

'I'll think about it. That's the best I can offer. But don't get your hopes up. It's a ridiculous idea, and I can't see myself changing my mind.'

'That's a deal,' she says. 'Now, get a move on with your dessert. The pub will be closing soon, and I forgot to bring a doggy bag.'

Chapter Six

I sleep surprisingly well. I don't usually enjoy staying in strange places, but no sooner does my head hit the pillow than I'm fast asleep. I don't stir until there's a light tap at the door, and Isabella peeps around it.

'I hate to disturb you, but I'm leaving for work in twenty minutes. I didn't want you to wake up and find yourself all alone in a strange house.'

Does she know I almost cut and ran when I arrived here yesterday? She'd probably find it amusing. She seems to find most things amusing.

'I'm sorry I slept so late,' I say with a yawn.

'It's the country air,' she says. 'It has that effect on me too. I can never get up in the mornings.'

'Aren't you used to the air by now?' I ask, swinging my legs out of bed.

'You'd think! But it doesn't seem to have worn off yet. What would you like for breakfast?'

'Don't worry about that. I rarely eat it.'

Her eyes widen in horror. 'How can you rarely eat breakfast? It's the most important meal of the day!'

'Says who?'

'Everyone! My mother, for one. She told me never to trust a man who doesn't eat breakfast.'

'Is that her criterion for selecting a man?' I say.

'Oh, no! She has a very long list. She made me learn it by heart before she let me date anyone. I'll tell you about it some other time.'

'I'm sure I'll find it very useful,' I say. 'In the meantime, would you mind if I took a quick shower? I was too tired when we got home last night. After that, I'll get out of your hair.'

'Aren't you coming to the bakery with me this morning?'

'A ride into the village would be very welcome,' I say. 'Maybe you can point me in the direction of the garage. Hopefully, the mechanic will have my car ready to go.'

'The mechanic rang about half an hour ago,' she says. 'He says the big end has gone in the engine, and he'll have to order another one, which could take days. He told me to ask whether you'd like him to do that or tell the rental company to send over a truck and tow it?'

I sigh in frustration. 'They promised me it was in great repair and had recently been serviced.'

'Maybe you're a terrible driver,' she says.

'I'm not. I don't drive too often in London, but I passed my test over ten years ago, and I've never had so much as a speeding ticket.'

'Would you like some of mine?' she says. 'My father says if I get any more, he'll remove me from his insurance.'

'Why are you on your father's insurance?'

'It has something to do with the farm,' she says vaguely. 'I do the books for them. As I told you yesterday, I also deliver the odd lamb. Apparently, that makes it ok for my car to be registered as a business vehicle.'

'I'll pass on your very kind offer of sharing your tickets with me. I only have last month's pay cheque to see me through until

I find another job. I can't afford to waste any of it. I shouldn't have taken this trip, but …'

'Of course, you should.' She gives me an encouraging smile. 'And don't forget you've already found another job. It's ready and waiting for you. You only have to say the word.'

I feel my resistance beginning to crumble. 'This is ridiculous. You only met me yesterday. I could be anyone at all. I could be a murderer on the run from justice.'

She looks interested. 'Are you?'

'Not to date, but I like to keep my options open.'

'That's wise,' she says. 'I'm pretty sure murderers are one of the things on my mother's list. In the meantime, while you're waiting to decide whether or not you are, why not come and work with me?'

'I don't have anywhere to stay.'

'You can stay with me until you find somewhere better. This village is absolutely crawling with places to stay. You can't go ten yards down the street without tripping over a bed-and-breakfast or an Airbnb.'

'I haven't brought enough for a long stay,' I protest.

'Did you leave everything at that man's flat?'

'I packed up my clothes and a few belongings. I didn't dare take anything we bought together. Charlie would have gone mad if he'd come home to find things missing. He'd probably have called the police.'

'Didn't you discuss how you were going to divide everything up?' she says.

'We didn't discuss anything. I didn't tell him I was leaving.'

She looks amused. 'It didn't occur to you to mention it in passing?'

'It wasn't like that. It's difficult to explain. Either he'd have been angry, or he'd have talked me out of it.'

'It sounds as though you did the right thing,' she says. 'Did you leave a note?'

'I did. It felt too impersonal to break up by text.'

'Please tell me you pinned it to his pillow,' she begs. 'That's what everyone does in movies. Or they leave an envelope on the dressing table. I've always wanted to do that, but my handwriting is atrocious.'

'Why does that matter?' I say.

'Oh, you know! The heroine writes the man's name on the outside of the envelope in a beautiful flowing script. If I tried that, the man wouldn't know who it was for. He'd find an envelope on his pillow, and he'd have no idea it was intended for him. It would be terribly anticlimactic.'

'I'm pretty sure Charlie would have known the note was for him,' I say, laughing.

'What did it say?'

'Just that things weren't working out, and I'd decided to leave.'

'Short, sweet, and to the point,' she says. 'I approve. After all, what is there to say when you break up with someone? You're telling them you don't want to be with them anymore. There's no real way to sugar coat that. Unless you go down the route of saying it's not you, it's me. And I don't expect it was you.'

'I should have left years ago,' I say. 'I don't know why I didn't. Anyway, all I have with me now is a suitcase of clothes and a few pairs of shoes.'

'What else do you need?' she says. 'I know you brought a toothbrush because I offered to find you one last night and you refused.'

'Maybe I only brush my teeth once a week,' I say.

'No, you don't. You wouldn't have such nice teeth if that was the case. And I wouldn't have offered you the job. I'm extremely hot on dental hygiene for my employees. It's one of the first questions I ask at interview.'

'Really?'

'Not really,' she says. 'I'm also sure you packed deodorant and shampoo. Your hair is clean and shiny, and you smell fine.'

'Is there anything else about my personal appearance you'd like to comment on?' I say. 'Don't be shy. It appears to be *Say what you think* day.'

She looks remorseful. 'I'm sorry, Olivia. I'm afraid that every day is *Say what you think day* for me. I didn't mean to be rude.'

'You weren't,' I assure her. 'On the contrary, you've told me my hair isn't greasy, my teeth don't have bits between them, and I don't smell. That's all very complimentary. I'll be sure to include it in my resume when I apply for my next job.'

'The job after this one,' she corrects me. 'You can look around for vacancies while you're working at the Sugarloaf. I'll even let you leave early for interviews. You can't say fairer than that.'

She looks like an eager terrier waiting for me to tell her where I've hidden its bone.

'I still think it's a ridiculous idea,' I say.

She claps her hands together. 'So, you'll do it?'

I cast around for reasons to say no – unarguable, incontrovertible reasons to which even Isabella must give way. But I can't come up with any. When I left London two days ago, all I could think about was getting away and leaving the past behind me. I didn't want to face dealing with the fallout with Charlie. All I knew was that I wanted a break. I *needed* a break.

So, I jumped on a train and set off. Somehow, without quite knowing how, I ended up here and met Isabella, and she offered me a job. Only a temporary job, but that's fine. I don't want to work in a bakery for the rest of my life. I need to decide what to do next.

But I'm exhausted. Leaving Charlie has taken every ounce of energy I possess, and I'm drained. The idea of returning to London and finding a job and accommodation makes me want to lie down and go to sleep. It will have to be done, but I can't bear to think about it. And the opportunity not to think about it for a while is being handed to me on a plate.

Isabella is offering me the prospect of a few weeks' respite, the chance to consider what I want from my future without having to deal with anyone else's opinions. Why am I resisting it? It's time I made my own decisions and my own mistakes.

The worst that can happen is that Lily comes back to work, and she and Isabella tell me they don't need me anymore. In which case, I can return to London and resume my life there.

I'm not sure what's the best that can happen. It's been so long since I've thought about my future with any optimism. But that won't always be the case. When I left Charlie, it was because I knew it was time to make a change. If I didn't do it now, I knew I never would. This isn't the change I expected to make, but who cares? It's a change, and everyone says a change is as good as a rest. I'm sure that's somewhere on Isabella's mother's list of life lessons.

Isabella is looking at me with a hopeful expression.

Why not?' I say. 'You seem to need some help, and I don't appear to have anything to do for the next few weeks. It's Kismet!'

'You may mock,' she says, 'but I believe in Kismet.'

'You realise it isn't a fancy French pastry?'

'I'm aware,' she says. 'Seriously, Olivia, this is great. I hate taking on temps. It takes longer to explain stuff to them than to do it myself.'

'You have no idea how slow I am to pick things up,' I warn her.

'You'll be fine. You have all the qualifications. You laugh at my jokes, you like my pies, and you brush your teeth. We're going to get along well. Get dressed as quickly as you can, and we'll go to the bakery and get you fitted for a Sugarloaf overall.'

Chapter Seven

Isabella's induction course is short and concise. It doesn't take me long to pick up the essentials. I've used one of these tills before, which she's delighted about.

'I hate having to teach people how to use it,' she says. 'I'm fine with the basics, but I always forget what I'm supposed to do for a refund.'

'Do you have to issue many refunds?'

'The occasional one. You wouldn't believe how fussy some customers can be. The crust is too brown, or too pale, or they told Albert to ask for thin slices, and the ones he brought home don't fit in the toaster, even if you push them hard. I used to argue, but I gave up. It's easier to smile and give them a refund.'

She shows me how to use the coffee machine, which is rather more complicated. She promises to give me a longer lesson this evening. In the meantime, we both agree it would be better not to unleash me onto unsuspecting customers.

'You'll be fine after some more training,' she says. 'I confidently expect you to win employee of the month before you've been with us for a year.'

'I need to win it long before that,' I say. 'I'm here until Lily returns, and then I must move on. I have my entire life to sort out.'

'Of course, you do,' she says reassuringly. 'Daisy won't be in the hospital for long. At least, I hope she won't. I'm going to visit her tonight.'

'In your capacity as godmother?'

'Absolutely!' she says. 'It's one of a godmother's first duties to sneak chocolate buttons into her goddaughter's hospital room.'

'Won't Lily mind?'

'Not if I take her a packet too.'

I give a snort of laughter. 'That's not what I meant.'

The door opens, and Isabella nudges me. 'Your first customer. Remember what I told you – shoulders back, chin up, look them in the eye, and make sure you know how thick they like their slices *before* you switch on the machine.'

I'm about to greet the customer with the mantra Isabella has taught me: 'Welcome to the Sugarloaf bakery. How may I help you?' when I realise it's Will.

'Oh, hi!' I say.

Isabella clears her throat loudly.

'Welcome to the Sugarloaf bakery. How may I help you?' I add.

Will's eyes open in surprise. 'She has you working here?'

I give him a dejected smile. 'I'm afraid so. When she found I couldn't pay for my night's accommodation, she insisted I work it out in indentured labour.'

He grins. 'Seriously, what's going on?'

'I'm thinking of retiring soon,' says Isabella. 'I'm anxious to leave my half of the bakery to someone worthy of the honour. I've tried out several candidates, but terrible things have happened to them. One of them fell into the dough mixer, another ate too many eclairs and exploded, the third one –'

'I get the picture!' he interrupts. 'I suppose Olivia found the final golden ticket in her strawberry tart?'

She looks delighted. 'I love it when people get my literary references.'

'It was very obscure,' he says. 'Luckily for you, I'm extremely well read.'

He turns to me. 'You're my last hope for a sensible explanation. Why are you standing behind the counter, wearing a Sugarloaf overall?'

'I'm sorry about my co-worker,' I say. 'It was a perfectly reasonable question, and I don't know why she was being so evasive. The real answer is that I'm taking part in Secret Millionaire.'

He rolls his eyes. 'Is there any point in me asking for a coffee, or will I get gravy instead?'

'You'll have to ask Isabella,' I say. 'Apparently, I'm not fit to be let loose on the population of Honeywell without extensive further training.'

'I'll bring it over,' says Isabella. 'I'll throw in a cookie for free as an apology.'

'That's very kind of you,' says Will. 'I accept.'

She opens the sliding door behind the counter and picks up a cookie. 'Don't get too excited. They're out of date. I was about to throw them away.'

'By which you mean put them in your bag to take home?' he says.

She hands him the plate. 'Whatever! You say potato ...'

'The mechanic says he can't fix my car today,' I tell Will.

He looks surprised. 'Are you sure? He'd just given it a test drive when I walked past the garage a minute ago.'

'Quite sure,' I say. 'That must have been a different car. He called Isabella this morning and told her he needed to order in a part, which could take a while.'

'It wasn't a different car,' he says. 'It was the one you were driving yesterday. The same number plate and everything.'

I glance over at Isabella, who's turned pink. 'Are you sure you got the message right?

She shrugs. 'Who can say? He said something about cars and parts and fixing problems. I'm not technical. I never pretended to be.'

'Did you tell me he couldn't fix my car so I'd agree to stay longer?' I ask sternly.

She gives me an inscrutable look. 'Or did he make his message confusing because the universe wanted you to remain in Honeywell?'

'I'm betting on the first one,' says Will. 'What do you think, Olivia?'

I ought to be angry, but somehow, I'm not. If anything, I'm grateful to Isabella for buying me enough time to make this decision.

'I'm inclined to go with the second one,' I say.

He smiles. 'So, she's persuaded you to stay with us for a while?'

'Just for a week or two,' says Isabella. 'While Daisy isn't well.'

'That's great,' he says. 'It will be nice having you around. And there are worse places than Honeywell to take an unscheduled hiatus.'

I like that description. I'm not taking an enforced time-out. I'm enjoying an unscheduled hiatus.

'It's time for your break, Olivia,' says Isabella. 'Why don't you sit and chat with Will while I get you a coffee?'

'It's only ten o'clock. Have I been working for long enough to take a break?'

'Of course, you have!' she says. 'I don't want you resigning on your first day due to overwork. I'll make you a latte. I've been trying to do those pictures on the foam. I'm getting much better at them. What would you like?'

'What can you do?'

She considers. 'I can do footballs, netballs, and ping-pong balls. The other day, I managed a very nice balloon.'

'I'm not terribly sporty,' I say. 'Unless you count ice-skating. I love that.'

She frowns. 'I can't do an ice skate, if that's what you're after. I'll tell you what. I'll do you an ice hockey puck.'

'I'm sensing a common theme here,' says Will. 'Are we to understand you've mastered the art of making circles on the foam?'

'That's right,' she says. 'I'm hoping to expand my repertoire to squares soon, but I don't want to run before I can walk.'

She brings me my latte, and Will and I dutifully admire my ice hockey puck. I wouldn't have guessed what it was if Isabella hadn't told me. But it doesn't matter. The latte is excellent.

'You didn't have breakfast!' she exclaims suddenly. 'I'd completely forgotten that in all the hurly-burly of giving you my intensive training course. You must be passing out, Olivia. What can I get you? Will, stand ready to catch her if she faints.'

'He's done enough rescuing of damsels in distress for one week,' I say. 'I'm fine. I rarely eat until lunchtime.'

She shudders. 'Is that a London custom? No wonder I've never wanted to live there. It sounds horrific.'

She makes a dive for the counter and emerges with a cookie on a plate, which she hands to me. I break it in half and hand her a piece. 'I appreciate the thought. I'm not really hungry, but this looks good. Why don't we split it?'

'Isabella doesn't usually share her cakes,' says Will. 'You're a beneficial influence on her already.'

'I'm not sharing,' she says with her mouth full. 'Olivia is. It's a very different thing.'

'Shall I let the mechanic know you're staying in the village and no longer want the car?' he asks me. 'He can arrange for it to be picked up, and you can call and sort out a refund.'

'Thank you. Is everyone in the countryside so helpful and community spirited?'

'He isn't from the countryside,' says Isabella. 'He comes from London, like you.'

'Which part?' Will asks me.

'You can talk about all that later,' says Isabella. 'In the meantime, Olivia's break is over. Can I get you anything else, Will?'

He shakes his head. 'I should get going. I'm driving to Mitcham this morning to take some pictures of the church. The light should be just right. I'll see you both later.'

He gives us a friendly wave and disappears.

'I'm sorry about that,' says Isabella. 'I shouldn't have mentioned you came from London. It isn't anyone else's business.'

'I'd prefer not to talk about my life there,' I say.

'I know,' she says contritely. 'But I'd already mentioned it before I realised. That's why I said your break was over. It isn't really. You have ten more minutes.'

'I don't need ten more minutes,' I protest. 'It's your turn for a break. I can watch the till.'

'If you're sure,' she says. 'I wouldn't mind a coffee. I only had a small one before we left this morning.'

She switches on the coffee machine again. 'Your hockey puck came out so well that I'm going to be daring and attempt a rugby ball.'

Chapter Eight

Isabella hands me a piece of paper the following afternoon.

'I dropped in at the estate agents on my way back from lunch,' she says. 'They have two properties they're trying to rent out at the moment. The only problem is that you'd have to sign a six-month lease.'

'I'm not doing that,' I say. 'Lily may be back at work next week, and where would that leave me?'

'Living in Honeywell,' she says. 'I don't need to remind you it's the best place in the world to live.'

'So you keep saying. But living here with a job is one thing. Living here without one is quite another. It isn't the cheapest of areas.'

'You can stay with me for as long as you like,' she says. 'I don't know when my mum's coming home, and Georgia is almost never there. I'd enjoy the company.'

'Your dad is there,' I remind her. 'At least, you've told me he is. I haven't seen any evidence of it so far. For all I know, he's a figment of your overactive imagination.'

'He is not!' she says indignantly. 'He came in late last night and left early this morning. It's always a busy period on the farm at this time of year. They're muck-spreading this week.'

'Lovely for them,' I say. 'Don't you want to join in?'

'I used to when I worked for them full time. It was more fun than being stuck in the office doing the accounts. But I've stopped doing that sort of thing since we bought the bakery. The customers don't appreciate being served by someone smelling of manure.'

'Even accepting your father exists,' I say, turning the conversation back to the original subject, 'he won't want some complete stranger camping out in his house for weeks. I need to find myself something a little more permanent.'

'There's always Tom and Diane's place,' she says.

'Who are they?'

'They keep a bed-and-breakfast up by the crossroads. It's usually full in the school holidays, but not so much during term time. I expect they'd give you a reasonable rate if you booked a room for a few weeks. And you don't eat breakfast, which means it would be even cheaper! You'd like it there. It's a little run down, but the garden is lovely.'

I resolve to see for myself how run down this place is before committing myself to anything permanent. Isabella seems the sort who would be up for any adventure. But I want to make sure I won't be expected to sleep on bales of straw or use a hand pump to wash each morning.

Still, if it's clean, and I can afford it, it would be nice to find a place of my own. Isabella is lovely, and the bed she's given me is the most comfortable I've ever slept on. But it feels increasingly surreal to be staying with a complete stranger in a place I never intended to visit. I've decided to go with the flow and enjoy my time here, but I'd prefer to do it on my own terms.

The shop bell rings, making me jump. I haven't yet got used to the sharp, jangling noise that warns us of a customer. Maybe when I've been here for a while I'll relax and take the whole thing more in my stride. I look up to see Will standing there.

'Hey, how's it going?' I say.

'Aren't you supposed to say, "Welcome to the Sugarloaf? How may I help you?"'

'Only when Isabella is around. Did you want to see her? She's in the kitchen. I can fetch her.'

'I wanted to see you,' he says. 'How's your hunt for accommodation going?'

'It isn't, but I need to sort out something soon. I can't keep living with Isabella's family forever. Even if they don't know I'm there.'

He raises an eyebrow. 'They don't know you're there? Does she sneak you in through the back door when everyone is at dinner and force you to use the servants' staircase?'

'There's a servants' staircase?' I say.

'There's bound to be. Doesn't she live in the Manor House in Little Compton?'

'Her family lives in the Lodge. Her uncle lives in the Manor House.'

'How disappointing,' he says. 'I was hoping for the grand tour. I thought there might be some historical features I could photograph inside the house. Perhaps there are some in the garden.'

'I don't know. I haven't been up there yet. But there's a sundial in Isabella's garden which is missing the metal bit.'

'Isn't that the most important part?' he says.

'That's what I thought, but Isabella says not. She says it's the perfect height for her morning coffee.'

'Less of a sundial and more of a table?' he says.

'I suppose so. She puts her phone on it, set with an alarm to tell her when it's time to leave for work. Do you think that counts as a time-keeping device?'

'Definitely,' he says. 'But I'm not sure I could persuade my editors to give it a double page spread.'

'That's a shame. There's also a gnome with a broken fishing rod, if that's any help?'

He laughs. 'I appreciate the suggestion, but the editors are distressingly narrowminded. They commissioned this book as a record of the historical features of the New Forest. It would take a better man than me to persuade them that modernised sundials and vegan gnomes would make a suitable alternative.'

'You don't know the gnome is vegan,' I say. 'All you know is that he doesn't eat fish. At least, not fish he catches himself. But that's true of most of us. I love fish and chips, but I prefer someone else to do the work.'

'I'll have to take you to the Red Lion one Friday,' he says. 'They make the best fish and chips I've ever tasted.'

'Not you too! Do you and Isabella have shares in the Red Lion? She's always saying they serve the best food for miles around.'

'I expect she took you there for game pie,' he says. 'She seems to eat her body weight in that when she can get it.'

'Not just the game pie. I had to try their crème brûlée too. And their homebrewed cider.'

Isabella appears, her arms full of loaves. 'Is Olivia giving you what you want?'

'Am I what?' I say.

She waves a hand towards the cakes, almost dropping a loaf as she does so. 'Have you found whatever he came in for?'

'I don't know what he came in for,' I say.

'I'd like a couple of Abby's jam doughnuts,' says Will. 'But I really came to find out whether Olivia has found herself somewhere to stay.'

'She's going to check out Diane and Tom's place,' says Isabella.

'Why would she do that?' he says.

'Because I need a place to stay,' I tell him. 'I thought we'd established that.'

'I don't think you'd be very comfortable there. The guestrooms are in the attic, and the roof has been leaking ever since that hailstorm last month.'

Isabella looks dubious. 'It may not be too bad.'

'My parents stayed there last week,' he says. 'I'd have had them at my place, but I'm only renting the one room. Mum said there were three buckets in their bedroom, and she and Dad had to keep moving them because the leaks couldn't decide where they wanted to settle.'

'Maybe they've fixed it by now,' I say.

'No, they haven't,' he says. 'The insurance company told them there were so many broken tiles on the roof before the storm, it was an accident waiting to happen. So, they're refusing to pay up. Tom was in the Red Lion last night. He says Diane is incandescent. She wants to sell up and move to Southampton. Anyway, you can't stay there, Olivia.'

'She has to stay somewhere,' says Isabella. 'She'd be very welcome at our house, but she doesn't like the idea. And she doesn't want to sign a six-month lease.'

'That's understandable,' says Will. 'That's what I stopped in to tell you. I asked my landlady if she had any ideas, and she said her friend Eleanor across the road is looking for a lodger. Her old one left last week, and she can't afford the mortgage unless she lets out her spare room. What do you say, Olivia? Would you like to take a look?'

'I'd love to,' I say. 'I assume Eleanor's house has a roof?'

'I have a good view from my bedroom window,' he says. 'It appears to have a roof. Otherwise, the chimney pot would have fallen down into the garden.'

'Appearances can be deceptive,' says Isabella darkly. 'So, your accommodation has a roof. Big deal! For all you know, this Eleanor woman has knocked down all the internal walls and put up a giant bouncy castle.'

'In which case, I'll give Olivia my room and move in with Eleanor,' says Will. 'I love bouncy castles!'

'Or she might be a hoarder,' she goes on without listening. 'Olivia won't be able to move without tripping over collections of novelty teapots or antique toasters.'

'Even more reason for me to move in,' he says. 'I love antique toast.'

'Or she might host open mic nights and force Olivia to do comedy routines.'

'I'd come and listen to that,' he says.

'Or keep chickens indoors,' she finishes. 'Olivia won't be able to sleep because of the rooster crowing.'

'But think of having fresh eggs for breakfast every morning,' he urges. 'Seriously, Isabella, why don't you want her to move in with Eleanor?'

'Because it would be a lot more fun if she stayed with me,' she says.

I give her an impulsive hug. 'I love staying with you, but I'd prefer to be independent. If this Eleanor isn't as awful as you think, maybe you could come and sleep over one night.'

'Fine,' she says. 'But only if it's open mic night, and you let one of the chickens sleep in my room.'

I put a couple of doughnuts into a bag and hand it to Will. 'I'm afraid all the strawberry ones have gone. But the raspberry ones are very good.'

'What a coincidence,' he says. 'I believe strawberry is Isabella's favourite flavour.'

She ignores him. 'Can you tell this Eleanor woman we'll be over after work to look at the room?'

'You're coming too?' I say.

'Of course. I want to check out the sound system.'

'I'll find out when she's free,' promises Will. 'I'll give you a call later.'

Chapter Nine

He holds the door open for an elderly man before disappearing out of the shop and striding away down the high street.

'Hello, Mr Mason,' says Isabella. 'How are you today?'

The man gives her a perplexed look. 'Oh, I'm … that is to say …'

'That's good,' she says. 'Mr Mason, I'd like you to meet our newest member of staff, Olivia Sullivan. Olivia, this is Mr Mason. He used to run the Sugarloaf bakery. Lily and I bought it from him when he retired.'

He peers at me over his half-moon spectacles. 'It's very nice to meet you, my dear. I didn't realise Lily and Isabella were taking on any more staff.'

'We aren't really,' she says. 'Lily is out because Daisy isn't well. Olivia has kindly agreed to fill in for as long as she's needed.'

'How nice,' he says. 'I hope Daisy will recover soon. She was named after my wife, you know,' he tells me in a pleased tone.

'That's lovely,' I say. 'It's a beautiful name.'

'What can I get you today, Mr Mason?' Isabella prompts him.

He looks puzzled. 'Get me?'

'From the bakery,' she says. 'Or are you here for a cup of coffee?'

'I'm afraid I don't have time,' he says, looking at his watch. 'I only popped in for a … now, what did I pop in for?'

We regard him with fascinated attention as he frowns and stares into the distance, his lips moving slightly.

'A cob loaf!' he exclaims at last. 'Daisy told me we were almost at the end of ours and asked me to collect one on my way home.'

He catches my eye. 'Daisy my wife, I mean. Not little Daisy, her namesake.'

I keep my face straight. 'I assumed that was who you meant. Although I haven't met little Daisy yet. For all I know, she may be very advanced and write her own shopping lists.'

He frowns. 'I don't think so, my dear. She's only a few months old.'

'She's almost a year old,' says Isabella. 'If you remember, she was born during the final of the New Forest Mix-up.'

'My goodness!' he says. 'Has it been that long?'

'I'm afraid so,' she says. 'They aren't running the competition this year. They said it's because of a lack of funding. But Lily and I are sure that, having seen our entry last year, all the candidates have backed out. We put them all to shame, Olivia. It was a travesty we didn't win. Abby made the most amazing pirate ship.'

'What was the theme?' I ask.

'*I love the New Forest.*'

'Are there many pirate ships in the New Forest?'

'That's what I asked Abby,' says Mr Mason. 'I don't remember what she told me, but I'm sure she knew what she was doing.'

Isabella laughs. 'She did. It's a long story, Olivia. Remind me to tell you sometime. Anyway, we've scared off all our competitors. Hopefully, they'll run it again next year, once people have forgotten how good we were.'

Mr Mason picks up his loaf. 'I must be going. I told Daisy I'd be back before lunch.'

He glances at me again. 'My Daisy, I mean. Not –'

'I understand,' I assure him. 'Enjoy your bread.'

He potters out, and I turn to Isabella. 'Did he really run the bakery before you?'

'He did. Why do you ask?'

'No reason. He seemed a little confused about where he was. I half expected him to ask you for some batteries or a bunch of asparagus.'

'He's always like that,' she says. 'He was exactly the same when Lily started working for him. He'd got rather stuck in his ways, and it was hard to convince him to change anything. I don't think he'd have retired at all if we hadn't offered to buy the bakery. I'm glad he did. He seems very content nowadays. He comes in and tells us everything we're doing wrong. We smile and thank him for his advice and carry on as we were, and everyone's happy.'

'Is baby Daisy really named after his wife?' I say.

She smiles. 'He likes to think so. I suspect it has more to do with daisies being Lily's favourite flowers.'

She looks at her watch. 'How do you feel about holding the fort while I run out for half an hour? Abby's in the kitchen if you get into difficulties.'

'Are you sure I'm ready?' I say.

'Why not? You know where everything is, and you can handle the till. After last night's intensive training session, you're able to make lattes and cappuccinos. You're a lot more ready than I was on my first day here. I dropped one of those giant bags of flour when I was carrying it in from the delivery van. The bag exploded, and the flour went everywhere. It was like a blizzard in here. We were brushing off the customers for hours. We had to give them all free cake to calm them down. And the day we opened the café, I overfilled the milk jug and left the steam nozzle in for too long. It foamed up and went all over the floor. A customer trod on it and skidded halfway across the cafe. I think we gave away that entire day's profits in free cake.'

'I'm feeling more confident already,' I say. 'As long as no one asks me to foam their milk or carry their flour, I should be fine.'

She grins. 'That's the Sugarloaf spirit! I'll be back as quickly as I can.'

She disappears, and I nervously take my place behind the counter. I don't know why. There isn't much that could go wrong. If by some chance I spectacularly mess everything up and lose all the stock or offend a customer, this isn't a career on which I've been staking my entire future. I can apologise and move on, and Isabella can ring the temp agency and ask them for someone more competent.

Anyway, Abby is here. She's making pastries this afternoon, but I'm sure she'd abandon them to their fate and rush into the shop if I screamed loudly enough. I brace myself for an onslaught of customers, but it doesn't come. The bell remains obstinately silent. There are very few people on the high street at this hour. The morning rush has subsided, and the people on their way home from work haven't yet appeared.

I'm startled out of my musings by a commotion at the far end of the street. An elderly woman has crossed the road with her dog, who is now lying on the grass verge. She's dropped her bags of shopping and is kneeling next to him. I look up and down the high street, but no one seems to be around.

'Abby!' I shout. 'Can you look after the shop for a minute?'

Without waiting for her to answer, I dart out of the door and run down the street.

'What happened?' I gasp as I reach the woman. 'Did he get hit by a car?'

She frowns up at me. 'Of course, he didn't get hit by a car! He has excellent road sense. My vet says he's rarely seen a dog with such intelligence.'

I kneel next to her. 'That's a relief. What's happened to him? Does he suffer from fits?'

She gives me an outraged glare. 'My dog has never had a fit in his life!'

'That's good to hear. So, what's wrong with him?'

As if hearing my voice for the first time, the dog rolls over and looks up at me.

'Hello, old fellow,' I say in a soothing voice. 'What's going on?'

As if in reply, he holds up his front paw. I grasp it lightly and inspect it. I gently run my thumb over his pads, and he winces. I look at it more closely. 'What's making you so sore? Oh, I see! Let's get that out.'

I reach into my pocket for a pair of tweezers, but the woman stops me. 'What do you think you're doing?'

'He has a thorn in his paw. I'm taking it out for him.'

'No, you aren't! I'm not having a complete stranger poking around my dog's paw. How do you know he has a thorn?'

I point with the tweezers. 'Because I can see it right here.'

Without waiting for her to answer, I catch the end of the thorn and pull it out. 'There you are, old man. You're good to go.'

The dog rolls over and jumps to his feet. He capers in circles around his owner, while she tries to prevent him from tangling his lead around her legs and pulling her over.

I put a hand on his collar. 'Easy there. I'm glad you're feeling better, but you need to calm down.'

I keep a firm grip on him, hand the end of the lead to the woman, and watch while she untangles herself. She looks up at me with an expression of annoyance and relief.

'Thank you,' she says gruffly.

'No problem.' I ruffle the dog's head. 'You need to look where you're walking.'

He gives me an imbecilic grin and licks my hand.

I suddenly remember where I am and what I'm supposed to be doing. 'I must go! I've left the shop unattended.'

I dash back up the street and into the bakery, where I find Abby standing behind the counter.

'Are you ok?' she says. 'I heard you yell, but you'd disappeared by the time I arrived.'

'I'm fine. I had to rescue a dog. I'd better wash this mud off my hands.'

I return a minute later to find the elderly woman and her dog have followed me into the bakery. The woman is frowning more heavily than ever, and I wonder whether she's come in to complain about me. She didn't seem too happy when I produced my tweezers. But I couldn't leave her dog to limp around with a thorn in his paw. If she wants to complain, she can go ahead.

'There she is!' says the woman, pointing to me.

'Look!' I say with a trace of impatience. 'What did you expect me to do? Your dog was in pain or he wouldn't have been lying down like that.'

'Olivia,' interrupts Abby. 'This is Mrs Ogilvie, one of our regular customers. Mrs Ogilvie, this is Olivia. And this is Bernie. But I don't need to introduce you to him. I gather you've already met.'

'That's right,' I say. 'I saw him lying by the side of the road and went to see what was wrong. Luckily, he only had a thorn in his paw.'

Abby laughs. 'Did he do his full collapse in agony routine?'

She gives Bernie a stern look. 'I've never seen such a drama king in all my life.'

He grins up at her hopefully, and she rolls her eyes. 'Just a small one.'

She reaches into the box next to the counter and hands him a biscuit.

'Should he be having that?' I say.

'We make them for the local dogs, using a recipe the vet suggested. We bake a variety of flavours.'

She doesn't appear to be joking, so I decide to leave it.

'May I buy you a cup of coffee?' says Mrs Ogilvie.

For a moment, I think she's talking to Bernie, and I open my mouth to protest. Dog biscuits are one thing. Coffee is quite another. Then I realise she's addressing me.

'That's very kind of you,' I say. 'But there's really no need. And it isn't my break time.'

'It is,' says Abby. 'I've finished the pastries. I was coming through to tell you to have some lunch. I'll make your drinks.'

Mrs Ogilvie sits at the table by the door. Bernie obviously knows the bakery well because he's already lying under the table, chewing his biscuit.

I sit down at Mrs Ogilvie's table, and Bernie gives my ankle a welcoming lick.

'He seems quite happy now,' I say.

'Yes, he does,' says Mrs Ogilvie. 'It occurs to me I forgot to thank you.'

She says it rather stiffly, but with obvious sincerity. I'm pleased she's dropped her hostile attitude.

'You're very welcome,' I say. 'I've taken a lot of thorns out of dogs' paws over the years.'

'Do you have a dog of your own?' she says.

'I've been living in London for the past few years,' I say. 'Our tenants' association doesn't allow pets. I'd love a dog of my own, especially one like Bernie. I'm fond of cavoodles. They're a lovely breed.'

She unbends further. 'I've always kept cavoodles. They're very intelligent. And they make excellent watchdogs.'

I look at Bernie, who's dropped his biscuit and doesn't seem to have realised it's stuck behind his ear. He's staring around the shop as though suspecting one of the customers of having abstracted it when he wasn't looking.

'They are wonderful,' I agree.

Clearly, this dog is the light of her life, and she won't take kindly to any criticism of him. Besides, she's right. Bernie may not be receiving his invitation from Mensa any time soon, but he obviously has a lovely temperament. I've been around enough dogs to tell at a glance which of them are highly strung and need extra care. Bernie appears to have been passed over when they were handing out high strings.

I remove the biscuit from behind his ear and hand it to him. He snatches it from me with evident delight, then drops it on the floor and rolls over on it. He looks at me with the patient air of a dog accustomed to being handed treats that promptly grow legs and has become resigned to it.

'You'll figure it out,' I tell him.

Mrs Ogilvie takes a sip of her tea and gives an approving nod. 'They make a very nice cup of tea here. I never drink coffee in the afternoon. Some people do, but I don't understand why.'

I take a sip of my latte. 'I'm sure tea is much better for you, but I still prefer coffee.'

'How do you know so much about dogs?' she says.

'I'm a veterinary nurse.'

She looks surprised. 'What are you doing working here?'

'That's an excellent question. I'm not quite sure. My car broke down a few miles from here, and the man who rescued me brought me to Honeywell. I only meant to stay the night, but Isabella talked me into staying for a few weeks.'

Abby looks up from the coffee machine. 'Lily's little girl isn't well, Mrs Ogilvie. Lily has taken some time off to look after her.'

'I'm sorry to hear that,' says Mrs Ogilvie. 'I hope it isn't too serious.'

'I talked to Lily last night,' says Abby. 'She expects to bring Daisy home in a few days. But she won't want to return to work until Daisy is recovered. Olivia is kindly helping us out until then.'

'I should get back to work soon,' I say. 'It would be a good idea to rub some antiseptic ointment into Bernie's paw when you get home, Mrs Ogilvie. Keep an eye on it for a day or two. Puncture wounds can become infected. But this one was superficial. I'm sure Bernie will let you know if it gets worse.'

Abby winks at me. 'He'll let the whole village know. You saw him in action today.'

Mrs Ogilvie ignores her. 'We must be getting on. We have to call in at the post office before it closes, and you know what a chatterbox Mrs Jayson can be.'

She clips Bernie's lead to his collar, and he jumps up and sprints towards the door.

'Haven't you forgotten something?' I ask him, pointing to the place where he was lying.

He skips back, grabs the last piece of biscuit, and disposes of it in two noisy crunches. Clearly, he doesn't want to risk it growing legs again and trotting off to hide in a dark corner.

Mrs Ogilvie gives me a gracious inclination of the head as she leaves.

'You've made a hit, Olivia!' says Abby as the door closes behind her.

'How so?'

'I've never seen her offer to buy someone a coffee before. She must like you.'

'I think she likes her dog. She looked terribly upset when he was lying there. That's why I thought something more serious had happened to him.'

'That's why Bernie does it,' she says. 'If you knew the number of biscuits he'd conned her out of with his dying swan act …'

'She said he was very intelligent,' I agree. 'She could easily have removed the thorn herself. I'll show her how the next time I see her.'

'She comes into the bakery several times a week,' she says. 'You're bound to see her again soon. Wait until Isabella hears about this! Seriously, Olivia, you have no idea what a hit you must have made. Isabella told me Mrs Ogilvie refused to learn her name for more than a year. Even now, she occasionally refers to her as Imogen.'

I laugh. 'I'll have to remember that one.'

'It's as if you'd saved the life of the son of a Mafia boss,' she pursues. 'You'll probably find the villagers doff their caps as you pass by. The word will go round that anyone who lays a finger on you will be answerable to Mrs Ogilvie. Your money will no longer be good in any of the shops on the high street.'

'Which would suit me fine,' I say. 'I have about twenty-five pounds to last me until payday, and I'm looking at a room this evening. If I take it, the landlady will want a deposit.'

'Don't worry about that,' she says. 'Mrs Ogilvie will beg you to stay with her for free and offer to make you an allowance.'

'Sounds good,' I say. 'In the meantime, Isabella's car has pulled up outside. It seems to me this is the perfect time to strike while the iron is hot and demand a raise.'

Chapter Ten

Will calls me just before closing time and tells me Eleanor will be home this evening and is happy for me to drop around whenever I like.

'Unless you've seen the room by then and decided you want it,' I say.

He laughs. 'I'll admit I was temporarily seduced by visions of antique teapots and free-range chickens. But I'm happy where I am, thanks. The room's all yours if you want it.'

Isabella pulls a face when she hears this. 'I still think you ought to change your mind and stay with me. But I'll come along with you this evening. I'm sure I can find a few flaws and point them out to you.'

We drive back to Honeywell after dinner. A middle-aged woman opens the door to us.

'Is one of you Olivia?' she says. 'Will said you might drop around this evening.'

'That would be me,' says Isabella. 'I have to warn you I'm very picky, and I drive a hard bargain. I've turned down hundreds of rooms already.'

The woman looks at her more closely. 'You're Isabella Campbell, aren't you? Don't you work at the Sugarloaf bakery with Angela Carson's daughter?'

'Run!' Isabella hisses in my ear. 'She's onto us.'

I give her a quelling look. 'I'm Olivia, and you must be Eleanor. Please ignore my friend. She's had a difficult day.'

I turn to Isabella. 'Would you like to wait in the car?'

'No, I promise I'll behave.' She grins at the woman. 'Sorry about that. I've been trying to persuade Olivia to stay with me, but she insists on looking for her own place. I'm doing my best to put her off.'

Eleanor doesn't look put out. 'Are you both coming in?'

Isabella gives her a contrite look. 'I'll take my shoes off.'

'No need,' says Eleanor. 'It's all hard floors downstairs.'

'Even more reason to take them off,' says Isabella. 'I can slide around in my socks. On second thoughts, perhaps it would be better if I went across the road to visit Will. Come and find me when you're ready, Olivia.'

'Great idea,' I say, relieved.

'Olivia is an ideal tenant,' she tells Eleanor. 'She's tidy and quiet, and she doesn't hog the bathroom for hours.'

'I'm sorry about Isabella,' I apologise as Eleanor leads me into the house.

'No problem,' she says. 'I like people with a sense of humour.'

Is she saying I don't have a sense of humour? Should I do a dance or tell her a knock-knock joke to prove what a riot I am?

'She's very nice,' is all I can think of to say.

Eleanor opens the nearest door. 'This is the living room. It faces west, so it's lovely in the evening. The dining room is through those double doors. There are French windows leading out to the garden.'

I look around appreciatively. The living room walls are painted a pale lilac, which sets off the honey-coloured wood of the floor. There are two comfortable looking sofas, a coffee table covered in newspapers, and several bookcases filled to overflowing with books.

This is my kind of room. Charlie is obsessed with neatness and would hate everything about it, which only makes me like it the more. He'd be horrified by the newspapers thrown down at odd angles, and the non-matching sofas.

There's a vase of flowers on the mantlepiece, the delicate scent of carnations mixing with the crisp bouquet of freshly cut roses. The afternoon sunlight dances in waves across the room, creating a ripple effect on the floor. I take a deep breath and feel my entire body relax for what seems the first time in weeks.

Eleanor leads me down the hallway. 'That's the kitchen. There are three bedrooms upstairs. The smallest one is barely a bedroom, and I use it as a study. I have the largest bedroom with the ensuite. My lodgers have the middle room and use the main bathroom.'

The bedroom she shows me is lovely. I'm thankful to see it's at the back of the house, facing out over the garden. I'm not sure which way Will's bedroom faces, but it would have been embarrassing if both our bedrooms were at the front. I'd have had to keep my curtains closed at all times.

Eleanor's voice breaks into my musings. 'What do you think?'

'It's perfect!' I say with enthusiasm. 'When can I move in?'

'Don't you want to know how much I'm charging?' she says, looking amused.

'Will mentioned that when he called. The only problem will be finding a deposit. The rent is no problem, but it may take me a while to sort out my finances.'

I feel my face flame. 'They're … tangled up with someone else's at the moment. It could take a while to untangle them.'

'It's difficult when that happens, isn't it?' she says. 'I'm happy to waive a deposit, especially as Will tells me this is a temporary thing for you. How long are you staying in the area?'

'I have no idea. It could be a couple of weeks, or a couple of months.'

'No problem,' she says. 'If you pay each week in advance, that works for me.'

'Are there any house rules I ought to know about?'

'Lodgers must be in their rooms by nine o'clock each night,' she says. 'No gentlemen visitors at any time. Any other visitors by negotiation. But only once a week, and they must bring their own toilet paper and soap. I'm not running a hotel here.'

She sees my face and bursts out laughing. 'Olivia, I'm kidding! Just behave like a reasonable human being, and I'll be happy. I'll do my best to do the same. I've got on fine with all my lodgers so far. I don't imagine things will be any different with you.'

She smiles. 'That friend of yours won't be visiting, will she? I couldn't cope with that.'

'Isabella? Not if you don't want her to. But she's lovely when you get to know her. And she's been very kind to me.'

'I'm kidding,' she says. 'Ask anyone you like. This is your home too for as long as you live here.'

I laugh. 'Sorry, my sense of humour needs some work. I've been living with someone who had lots of rules, but he wasn't joking.'

She pulls a face. 'That's not good.'

'No, but it's my fault. I should have left a lot sooner.'

'Don't think like that,' she says. 'It can take a while to realise what people are like. Years, sometimes. I should have divorced my husband long before I did, but I got tangled up in the fallacy of sunk costs and kept telling myself I had more to lose than gain. It wasn't until I'd left him that I realised quite how bad things had got. And he didn't have any weird house rules.'

'That's exactly it!' I say. 'By the time I'd been with Charlie for several years, it felt as though there was too much history to throw away without a far better reason than I could come up with. Whenever I tried to discuss my concerns with him, he had a way of pushing them all back on me and making me think everything was in my head. I thought I was losing my mind.'

'I'm sorry,' she says. 'No one should have to live like that. Have you left him permanently?'

'I hope so. I told myself it was only for a week or so because that was the only way I could get up the courage to leave. This job came up at the perfect time for me, although I didn't realise it at first. I'm hoping it will give me some space to think things through and put some distance between me and everything that's happened. I'm still not sure whether I've made a mistake.'

She looks at my flushed face. 'I don't know you, and I don't know what's been happening in your life over the past few years. But I'm a great believer in instinct, gut feelings, intuition, whatever you want to call it. I suspect when you've had time to settle down and think, you'll realise you did the right thing.'

'I don't feel able to think clearly about anything at the moment.'

'So, don't!' she says. 'You've been given an unexpected opportunity to take some time for yourself, away from whatever's been going on. Take it! You have a job, which ought to keep you busy. If you're working with Isabella Campbell, I doubt your days will be too dull. You've found yourself somewhere to stay and, despite what she hinted just now, your landlady really isn't the boarding house supervisor from hell. Honeywell is a lovely village, and the New Forest is beautiful in the summer. I suggest you make the most of it and don't worry too much about the future.'

I follow her downstairs, and she hands me my coat.

'Can I move in tomorrow night?' I ask.

'Move in whenever you like,' she says. 'I'll give you my phone number, and you can call me directly instead of going through Will.'

'Good idea. I'm very grateful to him for mentioning this place. Do you know him well?'

'Not really,' she says. 'He hasn't been in the village for long. He seems like a nice guy.'

'He is. That's twice he's come to my rescue. First, he picked me up when my car broke down and brought me to Honeywell. And now he's found me somewhere to live.'

'Is that right?' she says with a smile. 'They say the third time's a charm.'

I don't know what she means by this, and she doesn't elaborate.

'See you tomorrow, Olivia,' she says and closes the door.

I look across at Will's house. There's a light on in the downstairs front room, but none upstairs, so he and Isabella probably aren't up in his room. Not that it's any of my business.

I set off down the garden path, wondering what I'll find when I arrive. If Will's house has wooden floors like Eleanor's, I'll probably discover him and Isabella skidding around the living room in their socks.

Chapter Eleven

Mrs Ogilvie turns up at the bakery a few days later with Bernie in tow. He races in and leaps up at me, trying to lick my face.

'Stop that at once, Bernie!' she says. She gives me an apologetic smile. 'He doesn't usually do that. I think he recognises you and is saying thank you.'

'No need,' I say, catching Bernie's paws and putting him back on the floor. 'Judging by the speed at which he charged in here, he hasn't suffered any ill effects.'

'None at all,' she says. 'I applied some of the ointment as you told me, and I kept a close eye on him, but he seemed fine. I would have taken him to the vet at once if he had been limping.'

'Good idea,' I say. 'Any advice I gave you was in a purely advisory capacity as a private citizen. I'm not qualified to diagnose or prescribe or anything like that. If in doubt, always call your vet.'

'Oh, I do!' she says. 'He loves Bernie, and he's always delighted to see him, even if it turns out there's nothing much wrong. And Bernie loves Dr Marsden, don't you, darling?'

Bernie grins up at her and wags his tail.

'Dr Marsden says Bernie is one of the most intelligent animals he's ever had to do with,' she tells me proudly.

I don't mention that vets say that about all their patients. I've seen one tell a young boy that his goldfish displayed remarkable skill and dexterity in dodging through the weeds and avoiding crashing into the toy castle in his tank.

But it would be unkind to remark on this. Mrs Ogilvie is obviously besotted with Bernie, and he seems very fond of her. He must be good company for her. I'm not sure what her personal circumstances are, except that Isabella mentioned she was a widow. Whatever their situation, most people benefit from having a pet.

'He looks very alert,' I say.

Bernie promptly collapses under the nearest table, rolls onto his back and starts to snore.

'I hope you've come in for a drink,' I say. 'Bernie doesn't look as though he intends to make this a brief visit.'

She pulls out her purse. 'I'd like a cup of tea please, and a slice of Battenberg.'

'Coming right up.'

She watches me carefully as I make her tea. I hope I'm doing it properly. It isn't as complicated as using the coffee machine, where I have to remember whether or not the customer wants caffeine, and whether they've requested extra-hot, extra-strong, or extra foam. And that's before we get onto the question of which milk they require. All I have to do with the tea is to pour in boiling water and make sure the cup isn't chipped.

Mrs Ogilvie takes a sip and nods. 'Very nice. The last girl who was here used to make it far too weak.'

'You mean Lily?'

She shakes her head. 'Lily makes a nice cup of tea. I'm talking about Alice. She wasn't here for long. She was a pleasant enough girl, but she could never learn to warm the pot, and she had no idea how many tea leaves she was supposed to use. Why don't you join me?'

I look at my watch. 'I'm due for a break in five minutes. As long as Isabella is here by then, I'd love to.'

For a wonder, Isabella arrives four and a half minutes later. She pulls off her coat and gives me a cheerful smile. 'You must be impressed by my punctuality. I had to run the last quarter of a mile. It's all your fault. You weren't there to wake me up this morning.'

'What about your alarm?' I say.

'I believe it rang once or twice,' she says. 'The second time it rang, I swiped at it, and it crashed onto the floor. I didn't hear a thing from it after that. I'll have to buy a new one.'

'Or you could use your phone,' I say.

'No, I couldn't. The last time I did that, I was so startled that I made a grab for it, knocked it halfway across the room, and smashed the screen. I'm not risking that again.'

'Maybe Georgia could wake you up?' I suggest.

'Fat chance! My sister wouldn't wake up if a bomb went off. When she was younger, I used to pour cold water on her, but even that didn't work. She used to mutter and grumble, then roll over and start snoring again. The only thing that's ever been known to wake her is the smell of frying bacon. One hint of that, and she's out of bed in a flash.'

'Couldn't you go downstairs and fry bacon each morning?' I suggest.

'What would be the point of that? I'd have to be awake to do it. Then I wouldn't need Georgia.'

'Someone ought to invent an alarm clock that pumps out smells instead of screeching in your ear,' I say. 'I'd love to wake to the scent of freshly baked bread each morning.'

'You spend your entire day smelling freshly baked bread,' she says. 'You should come up with something more original.'

'Popcorn,' I say after a moment's thought. 'I love the smell of buttered popcorn. It always reminds me of going to the movies with my parents when I was a child.'

'It certainly beats bread,' she says. 'I'm not sure what I'd programme my alarm to smell of. I'll have to give it some thought.'

'And wait until someone's invented it,' I say. 'Is it ok if I take my break now that you're here?'

'Of course.' She drops her bag behind the counter. 'Hello, Mrs Ogilvie. How are you today?'

Her eyes fall on Bernie. 'Is he asleep, or is he pretending to have hurt himself in the hope we'll ply him with one of Abby's biscuits?'

'Bernie would never do that,' says Mrs Ogilvie. 'He's an exceptionally brave dog. It worries me sometimes how little fuss he makes. He might not let me know if something was really wrong with him.'

Isabella's lips twitch. 'I don't think you need worry about that too much. I'm sure he'd let you know.'

'He's extremely intelligent,' I say, shooting her a warning glance.

I make myself a coffee and sit down at Mrs Ogilvie's table. Isabella looks surprised, but she doesn't comment.

We chat about Bernie for a few minutes, and I hear his entire life history. How he came to live with Mrs Ogilvie just before her previous cavoodle, Maisie, died. What a joy he's been to her, and how many tricks he's learned.

'I've never seen him do any tricks,' says Isabella. 'What can he do?'

'Bernie doesn't like to perform in public,' says Mrs Oglivie. 'He's an extremely shy dog.'

'Do you live in Honeywell?' I ask her.

She nods. 'Bernie and I live in one of the cottages down by the water meadow.'

'I'm renting a room in Cherry Street,' I say. 'Do you know it?'

'I know all the roads in Honeywell,' she says. 'I've lived here since I was five years old.'

'Goodness! So, you're the person I should come to if I want to learn anything about the village?'

'I can tell you all about its history,' she says. 'But I don't know as many people as I used to. Plenty of them have moved on since I arrived here, particularly the younger ones. There isn't much work in the area, and house prices have risen a lot.'

'Have you lived in your cottage for long?'

'Since Edward and I were married,' she says. 'That was almost sixty years ago.'

Her mouth tightens. 'He left me six years ago. He had a heart attack. One day he was there, and the next day he wasn't.'

'I'm so sorry,' I say with genuine sympathy. 'I can't imagine losing someone after spending so long together.'

'I had Bernie,' she says. 'Edward and I had only just got him. I don't know how I would have managed without him. He gave me a reason to get out of bed each morning. Gradually, it became a habit, and things got back to normal.'

'Not quite normal,' says Isabella gently, and Mrs Ogilvie shrugs.

'Perhaps not, but it happens to us all in the end. You're still young, so you won't understand that.'

'I haven't lost a husband, but both my parents died when I was eighteen,' I say. 'So, I understand a little of what you went through.'

To my surprise, she stretches out her hand and gives mine a squeeze. 'You poor thing. That's a terribly young age to lose your family.'

'It is,' says Isabella in a low voice. 'I'm so sorry, Olivia.'

I take a sip of my coffee before answering. 'It was pretty rough. They died in a car crash during my first year of university. But I got through it because I had to, much like Mrs Ogilvie says. Only I didn't have a beautiful cavoodle puppy to distract me. University halls don't allow pets.'

'You must get a dog as soon as you can,' says Mrs Ogilvie. 'I always pity people who don't have dogs.'

'Some people are allergic to them,' says Isabella. 'My sister Georgia knows at once when there's a dog or a cat in the vicinity. Her eyes stream, and her face breaks out in hives.'

'Cavoodles are hypoallergenic,' says Mrs Ogilvie primly.

'So is Georgia, but that doesn't stop me from having an adverse reaction to her now and then,' says Isabella. She grins at us and disappears into the kitchen.

'That young lady is entirely too fond of a joke,' says Mrs Ogilvie.

'She's great fun,' I say. 'I'm enjoying working here.'

Bernie stirs and sits up. He looks around him, blinking.

'He's hoping for a dog biscuit,' says Mrs Ogilvie. She hands me her credit card. 'I wonder whether you would mind fetching one for him.'

'I'd be delighted. Does he have a favourite flavour?'

'He enjoys them all,' she says. 'He's a very polite dog.'

'I can see that.' I choose the largest biscuit and hand it to Bernie, who falls on it in delight.

I sit down again. 'I have five minutes left of my break, and I intend to take all of it. It's taking me a while to get used to standing all day, and my legs don't appreciate it. I thought I had a busy job as a veterinary nurse, but I was moving around rather than standing behind a counter. I'm making the most of these few minutes. Why don't you tell me some more about the village?'

She considers. 'I'm not sure where to start. I moved here with my parents when I was five years old, nearly seventy-five years ago. We moved into the cottage the day before my birthday. I remember I was terribly excited to have a party in the garden. Before that, we lived in the flat over my father's shop in Christchurch.'

'What kind of a shop was that?'

'It isn't there now,' she says. 'He ran the ironmongers. We sold a bit of everything. I used to love to spend the morning in there with him when my mother had to go out. It was convenient for him to live over the shop. But it didn't pay, and it closed down when I was five. So, we moved to Honeywell, and my father became a farm labourer. That row of cottages was tied to the farm. They aren't now, but that's why they were originally built.'

'So, you celebrated your fifth birthday party in your new house?' I say.

She gives me an unexpectedly sweet smile. 'It was a wonderful day. I was always glad my birthday was in August because it was the middle of the school holidays. We invited the entire class, and almost all of them came. We played pass the parcel and musical chairs, and my mother made a beautiful chocolate blancmange in the shape of a rabbit. It was the best birthday I could have imagined.'

'You said your family moved to that house nearly seventy-five years ago,' I say. 'I don't want to be rude, but does that mean you'll soon be eighty?'

'I will,' she says. 'But I'm far too old to be making a fuss about birthdays. They're for children, not for old women.'

'Nonsense!' I say. 'Bernie is neither a child nor an elderly woman, but I'd be willing to bet you celebrate his birthday.'

Is that a pink flush on her cheeks? 'Just a small celebration to mark the occasion.'

'When is it?' I ask.

'As it happens, it's the same day as mine. At least, I think it is. We didn't get him until he was nearly a year old. The person who adopted him became ill, and Edward and I took him in. We asked the date of his birthday, but they couldn't remember exactly. All they knew was that they had taken him home when he was eight or nine weeks old, so he must have been born sometime in the middle of August. Edward said he and I should have a joint celebration. And so, we did. It was great fun. We made a maze for him to run around in the garden, and he had his favourite biscuits.'

Her face looks animated as she thinks back to Bernie's puppyhood. 'We had no idea Edward wouldn't be there for

Bernie's second birthday. I bought Bernie a cake that year, but I didn't have the heart to do more.'

'But eighty is a pretty special birthday,' I say. 'Surely, you plan to celebrate?'

She shakes her head. 'It's a lot of nonsense. Bernie will have his cake, as usual. He would never forgive me if I forgot his birthday. But that's all.'

'Do you have any family in the area?'

'No family,' she says. 'And very few friends. I have a sister who lives in Australia, but I don't hear from her often.'

'What a shame,' I say. 'How old will Bernie be this year?'

'He'll be seven years old!' she says proudly. 'The vet says he has the energy of a dog half his age.'

'He has a great zest for life,' I agree. 'I expect he keeps you busy.'

Isabella comes back into the shop. 'I hate to disturb you, but I have to run out for a few minutes. The supplier has forgotten our dried fruit, and they aren't answering their phone. Abby was supposed to be making Eccles cakes today, and she's stomping around the kitchen in a blind fury.'

'I've never seen Abby stomp,' I say. 'Neither have I seen her furious.'

'Possibly not,' says Isabella. 'But I could swear someone in the kitchen was.'

She catches my eye and laughs. 'All right, it was me. I love Abby's Eccles cakes. Anyway, I have to pop over and threaten to sue our suppliers or withdraw our custom or something. Will you be all right on your own?'

'Of course.'

Mrs Ogilvie clips Bernie's lead to his collar. 'We must be going too. Thank you for a pleasant chat.'

'I've enjoyed it,' I say. 'I'm looking forward to hearing more about Honeywell. I've never been in this part of the world before, and it's wonderful to have a walking encyclopaedia to consult.'

She looks pleased. 'Bernie and I will pop in again tomorrow. He loves the walk up here.'

Bernie jumps up and licks my face before I can stop him.

'Naughty boy,' says Mrs Ogilvie in an indulgent tone.

She gives us both a gracious wave and follows Bernie out of the shop.

Chapter Twelve

Isabella calls round to see me the following evening.

'I thought I should come and check out your new place,' she says as soon as I answer the door.

'You saw it when I came to look at it.'

'Only from the outside,' she says. 'You made me leave before I'd seen the bouncy castle. Is it all you dreamed it would be? Is there a rota, or can you use it whenever you like?'

'I'm sure there would be, if we had one.'

'Don't you?' she says, disappointed. 'Not even a tiny one in the garden?'

'I've inspected every inch of the place, and I haven't been able to discover so much as an inflatable air bed in the garden shed.'

'You should have stayed with me,' she says. 'My uncle opens up his gardens one weekend each summer to everyone in the village. He gives all the children pony rides in the paddock behind the house.'

'That sounds rather strenuous for him,' I say.

She sighs. 'You don't know the first thing about country life, do you? We use an actual pony. It's a kind of small horse.'

'Thanks,' I say. 'My training didn't cover anything bigger than a hamster.'

'I thought that would be the case,' she says. 'Which is why I filled you in. Feel free to ask me anything you want about animals. We could have an animal of the week at the bakery and learn all about them. We'd start small and work up to the large ones, like elephants. I vote we begin with sheep. I know lots about those. More than I care to, if I'm honest.'

'You're too kind,' I say, ushering her inside. 'What were you saying about ponies?'

She slips off her shoes. 'I'd better not annoy your landlady any more than I already have. Oh, yes. My uncle's open day. They serve tea in the rose garden, and the children have pony rides. And he puts an enormous bouncy castle on the lawn. It's my favourite weekend of the year. They don't come to take it away until the following morning, so I get it all to myself for the night. I bet you're kicking yourself now, aren't you?'

I follow her into the living room. 'I'm devastated. But it would be bad manners to walk out on Eleanor before I've been here for a week, so I'll have to live with it. Besides, I'm not likely to be here in August. Lily will be back at work long before that, and I'll be on my way.'

'Where to?' she asks. 'You don't want to go back to London. Why not stay around here?'

'I'll think about it. Would you like a drink?'

She sinks into the sofa. 'I thought you'd never ask. I've had a long journey to get here, and I'm parched.'

'Did you walk over to Honeywell?'

'No, I drove. But you have an exceptionally long garden path. I wasn't sure I'd make it.'

Are you in Honeywell to see me, or did you drop in on your way to see Will?'

'To see Will?' she says. 'Am I supposed to be meeting him tonight?'

'I have no idea. I thought maybe you and he were …'

She gives a snort of laughter. 'I'm sorry. It's just the idea of me and Will.'

I'm surprised to hear her speak so decisively. He's an attractive guy, and the pair of them seem to get on well.

'I didn't mean to offend you,' I say. 'I just wondered whether …'

'Not even close,' she says. 'Will's great, and I really like him. But I haven't considered him as boyfriend material.'

I feel almost offended on Will's behalf. He isn't here to defend himself, so maybe I should.

'I don't see why,' I say. 'He's a good-looking guy, and he's thoughtful and kind, which you can't say about everyone.'

'He *is* good-looking,' she agrees. 'I wonder why I've never thought of it before. It's strange, when you come to think of it. But he still isn't my type.'

'What is your type?'

'It's hard to say. I've dated plenty of men you'd have said were nothing like each other. But they must have been my type, one way or another. I'm not sure what the connecting factor is. It isn't colouring or body type. I've dated blonds and brunettes. And there was one man who was completely bald but who made all the men around him look as though they were trying far too hard with their ridiculous heads of hair. I really liked him.'

'What happened?' I say.

'Oh, he had to go to Alaska or somewhere with his job, and I didn't fancy it.'

I have a vision of a Bear Grylls type striding across the Alaskan Tundra. 'What did he do for a living?'

'He was an actuary,' she says. 'Maybe it was Alabama or Africa. It was definitely somewhere that began with an A. Altrincham, perhaps?'

'And you still didn't fancy it?'

'I like to travel,' she says. 'But I like this place too. And Lily and I were in the middle of buying the bakery. The timing was wrong.'

'That's a shame. Maybe he'll move back here sometime, and you can reconnect.'

'I doubt it,' she says. 'He messaged me a few months later to say he'd met someone, and he was getting married.'

'I'm sorry.'

'Don't be. There are plenty more fish in the sea, even around Honeywell.'

'But not Will?' I don't know why I'm pursuing the subject. It's nothing to me what two complete strangers choose to do. I'm just intrigued.

'Not remotely,' she says. 'He's all yours.'

I jerk upright. 'What makes you say that? I told you I've just come out of a difficult relationship. I'm not thinking about another one for a long time, if ever.'

'My mistake,' she says. 'Are you going to give me the grand tour?'

I show her the rest of the house. She surveys my bedroom thoughtfully. 'It's rather bare, isn't it?'

'I told you I didn't bring much with me when I left. Most of the things in Charlie's flat were there when I arrived. And the things we bought together aren't mine.'

'They aren't his either,' she says.

'But he isn't the one who called it a day and left.'

She sits on the end of my bed and regards me thoughtfully. 'You're allowed to decide a relationship isn't working for you.'

'But you usually do the other person the courtesy of discussing it first.'

'Why didn't you?' she says.

I'd decided not to think about Charlie for a while, but the temptation to discuss him is too much. Isabella is a sympathetic listener, and I doubt she'll try to persuade me I've made a mistake.

'Don't talk about it if you'd rather not,' she says. 'It's your own business, no one else's.'

'I'm not sure where to begin. And I'm scared that if I start talking, I'll never be able to stop.'

'I know the feeling,' she says.

'That's different. You love the sound of your own voice.'

'True,' she agrees. 'But I'm also able to shut up for a while and listen to a friend. I won't comment if you don't want me to. Despite my undeserved reputation for chatter, I'm excellent at keeping secrets. I found out Lily was pregnant before Jack did, and I never said a word.'

'How did you find out?' I say. 'Godmotherly second sense?'

'It could also have something to do with the fact she turned a delicate shade of green one morning and rushed out of the shop. I remembered she'd gone off her favourite cookies, and I put two and two together.'

'Trust you to notice that,' I say.

'The point is that I didn't breathe a word to Jack when he came into the shop later that day.'

'There isn't much to tell,' I say. 'I've been living with Charlie for the past four years. We met at university and dated on and off for a while. I wasn't sure about moving in together, but he was adamant it made sense. He'd bought himself a flat, and he said it was ridiculous for me to keep paying rent on my studio flat when I could move in with him. He said we could put my rent into a savings account and use it to buy somewhere bigger when we started a family.'

'I can see that makes financial sense,' she says. 'But you weren't sure about it?'

'It was just cold feet. He was right to say we should give it a try. I moved in, and I've been living there ever since.'

'Saving your rent money?' she says.

'I believe so.'

'What do you mean? You must know whether you've been saving it.'

'I'm sure we have. Charlie is weird with money. He's always moving it around and changing accounts to get better interest rates. I couldn't keep up. It seemed easier to leave it to him. He's better at that sort of thing than I am.'

'But it's your money,' she says.

'I said that once, but he pointed out I would have been paying rent anyway, so it didn't make much difference to me.'

She doesn't look convinced. 'I wouldn't let anyone tell me what I could and couldn't do with my own money.'

'It wasn't like that. He liked to be in charge of the day-to-day logistics, and I wasn't too bothered. He must have been investing it well because he told me a few weeks ago we had enough for a deposit on a house. With the sale of his flat, he said we'd be able to afford a three bedroom outside London.'

'Is that what you wanted?' she says.

'I thought so. But now I'm not so sure.'

'Did you tell him that?'

I think back to the row Charlie and I had the evening he told me we could finally afford to move house. He was right to be confused and upset. I'd been happy to go along with all his plans until then. I don't know why I suddenly raised objections. He didn't speak to me for a couple of days, which is always the way he handles disagreements. He says it's better than constant arguments. But I hate it. I'd far rather discuss things rationally and come to some sort of compromise that works for us both.

'I told him I didn't feel ready,' I say. 'He was pretty upset, as you can imagine. First, he said I'd wasted six years of his life and treated him like a fool. Then he said I'd used him for cheap rent. But that wasn't true. I offered to pay half of his mortgage from the day I moved in, but he refused. He said he was easily able to afford it himself, and it made much more sense to put my money into high yield deposit accounts, so that's what we did. I paid him the same amount as I paid my old landlord.'

'But without being on the deeds,' she says. 'I don't think much of that.'

'Charlie said it didn't matter. He said when we bought a house, it would be a joint purchase because I'd be putting my money into it too. I can see his point. When I first moved into the flat, I hadn't put anything into it, so there was no reason for me to have a share in it.'

'Did you split the other bills?' she asks.

'I bought most of the food, and I paid the utility bills. Charlie never wanted the heating on, and I hate being cold, so it was only fair that I paid.'

'Let me guess,' she says. 'You cooked and cleaned too?'

'Only because he worked longer hours than me. It would have been unreasonable to expect him to come in from a long day at work and start cooking and cleaning when I'd only been at work from nine to five. Anyway, that's how we saw it.'

'It sounds idyllic.' She sees my expression and sighs. 'I'm sorry, Olivia. I won't say any more. If it worked for you, it worked for you. Why did you hesitate when he started talking about moving somewhere bigger?'

'I have no idea. Charlie told me I was panicking because I'm not good with change. He was great about the whole thing after he'd calmed down. He said he knew what I was like, so he should have broached the subject more carefully with me. He promised not to mention it again for a week to give me time to get used to the idea.'

'And did you?' she says.

'Almost. I persuaded myself I was being immature and panicking about nothing. Charlie was right to say this was something we'd discussed several times over the years. How was he to know I'd react like that?'

'You realise you're allowed to react in any way you like?' she says.

'Maybe. But I'd go to bed each night convinced this was what I wanted, and that everything was fine. Then I'd wake up each morning in a cold sweat, wanting to run away. None of it was Charlie's fault. It was my fault for being miserably indecisive.'

I look past her out of the window. The elm trees at the bottom of the garden are in full leaf, and a nuthatch is swooping in and out of a hole in the tallest one, its beak full of fluff. It seems to have no difficulty in making a home for itself and starting a family. I doubt it had to spend the winter months being persuaded by its mate that now was the perfect time to find a bigger hole and make it their forever nest. I don't know why I'm less decisive than a nuthatch.

'What happened next?' Isabella prompts me. 'Did you decide one way or the other? Given that you're sitting on a bed in Honeywell talking to me, I assume you must have done.'

'Not really. I got up one morning and went to work and gave in my notice. It felt as though I was on autopilot. I half hoped my boss would persuade me to stay. But she accepted my resignation at once and even offered to waive my notice period. I thought she must have someone else she wanted to bring in, but I don't think so. I heard her on the phone to the temp agency that afternoon, and I know how much she dislikes having to use temps. It's a lot of extra work for her.'

'That was nice of her,' says Isabella. 'Not many employers would be so understanding.'

'Especially when there was nothing to understand,' I say. 'As far as she was concerned, an employee who had been with her for several years had decided to move on. I almost asked her about it, but something stopped me. I was too relieved to want to rock the boat.'

'How did Charlie react to the news you'd quit your job?'

'I didn't tell him. I have no idea why. He would have been delighted. He was always telling me I should cut down my hours to give me more time to look after things at home. He said he was earning enough to support us both, and it would be good practise for when we had children.'

'When was this?' she says.

'Last week. I didn't go in to work the following morning. Instead, I waited until Charlie had left the flat, threw my clothes into a suitcase, and called a taxi. I took the first train to Southampton, picked up a rental car, and set off. The rest is history.'

She squeezes my hand. 'Good for you. Is this a temporary thing, or is it permanent?'

'I don't know. I had this overwhelming feeling I needed to escape. I wasn't sure from what. I haven't allowed myself to look more than a couple of days ahead.'

'That's wise,' she says. 'For what it's worth, I don't think you have a problem with change. Look how well you've settled into Honeywell.'

'But that's only temporary. It feels like an extended holiday. Buying a house and settling down is a different thing entirely.'

She jumps off the bed. 'Perhaps. But it isn't always a good idea to accept what other people tell us about ourselves. Are you hungry?'

'A little. Why?'

She pulls me to my feet. 'I've remembered the kitchen at the Red Lion stays open late on Thursdays. I haven't had a thing to eat since this afternoon. What do you say to walking down to the pub to see whether there's any of Shelley's game pie left?'

Chapter Thirteen

Isabella doesn't mention Charlie again, for which I'm grateful. There's nothing to say. I've left, even if I'm unable to articulate why. I'll have to talk to him at some point, but I'm not ready to do that yet. Maybe I won't have to. He may be so angry with me for what I've done that he won't want to see me or speak to me again.

It's a pleasant thought, but I doubt it. Charlie has always expected me to come around to his viewpoint and accept I was in the wrong. And I'm definitely in the wrong this time for leaving him without a word. I'd be devastated if someone did that to me. Nevertheless, I keep his number blocked and don't check any of my emails. I'll have to contact him sometime, but not now.

I'm having a great time in Honeywell. Not only is it a lovely village, but I'm enjoying working in the bakery. Isabella and Abby are friendly and uncomplicated, and I don't reach the end of each day feeling as though the weight of the world is on my shoulders and crushing the life out of me. It's been too long since I took a holiday. Charlie hates being away from home for more than a few days at a time, and I've never yet booked somewhere with which he hasn't found fault.

I don't know what he'd think of Honeywell, but I suspect he wouldn't be too impressed with it. Not that it matters, as there's very little chance of him arriving on my doorstep. I haven't told anyone where I am, and Honeywell is the last place he'd think to look.

There are no cinemas or theatres here, and the closest thing to fine dining is the Red Lion. The food there is excellent, but it doesn't have any Michelin stars, which is the yardstick by which Charlie measures any new place.

I finally meet Lily, the co-owner of the bakery, and Isabella's business partner. She comes into the bakery one afternoon while I'm serving there alone. It's Abby's afternoon off, and Isabella is in the office doing the accounts.

I greet her politely when she comes in. 'Good afternoon. How may I help you?'

'You must be Olivia,' she says.

'That's right.' I study her carefully, but I'm sure I haven't met her before.

'I'm Lily,' she says, holding out her hand. 'I expect Isabella's mentioned me.'

'She has!' I say. 'How's your little girl doing?'

'Much better, thanks,' she says. 'She's coming out of hospital tomorrow morning.'

'What a relief for you.'

She nods. 'It's been awful. It's the first time she's been properly ill. I feel as though I haven't slept in weeks. Daisy's dad is great, and my mum has been wonderful, but Daisy has wanted me with her all the time. I'm exhausted.'

I look at her more carefully and see she's telling the truth. She's pale, and she has dark circles under her eyes.

'Lots of the customers have been asking about her,' I say. 'Everyone seems to know her.'

'My mum often brings her in here. She looks after her three days a week, and they come in to choose something to take home for tea. It's Daisy's favourite place in the whole world. Have you met Bernie yet?'

'Several times,' I say. 'He's gorgeous, isn't he?'

'He's lovely. Daisy adores him. She runs over to give him a hug whenever she sees him. He's very gentle with her. He licks her face, but he doesn't jump up at her.'

'He doesn't afford me the same courtesy,' I say. 'He launches himself at me whenever he sees me and tries to knock me over.'

'I take it you've met his owner too?' she says.

'I have. She's rather sweet.'

Lily gives me an awestruck look. 'If there's one word I never expected to hear applied to Mrs Ogilvie, it's sweet.'

'She has a brusque manner,' I agree. 'But she's devoted to that dog. It's a rule with me that anyone who loves animals can't be all bad.'

'True,' she says. 'It took her a while to warm up to me, and I'm not convinced she's quite got there with Isabella. But I'm glad you've been getting on with her all right.'

'So far,' I say. 'Did you know it's her eightieth birthday in August?'

'How do you know?'

'She told me recently. We were talking about the history of the village, and she mentioned she moved into her cottage when she was five, almost seventy-five years ago.'

'Goodness!' she says. 'That's quite an achievement. How is she celebrating?'

'That's the thing. I don't think she is. She said she'd be getting a cake for Bernie, as usual, but nothing more. It seemed a little sad. In fact, I was wondering ...'

Isabella appears behind us. 'Hi, Lily! I didn't hear you come in. How's my favourite goddaughter?'

'That depends,' says Lily. 'How many do you have?'

'Only the one at present,' says Isabella. 'Unless you have something to tell me?'

'Decidedly not!' says Lily. 'And can you be a godmother to more than one child in the same family?'

'Just watch me!' says Isabella. 'How's she doing?'

'Much better,' says Lily. 'The doctor says we can bring her home tomorrow, all being well.'

Isabella hugs her. 'That's wonderful! You must be so relieved.'

'And nervous,' says Lily. 'I've hated her being in hospital, but I've felt safe while she's there.'

Isabella gives her a reassuring smile. 'You'll be fine. Jack will take the pair of you straight back if anything changes. Or your mother will. If they're both too drunk, you only have to call me, and I'll be there in three minutes.'

'How about if you're drunk?' says Lily.

'I'm never drunk,' says Isabella. 'And I shall make it a point not to have more than one small glass of cider until I'm sure Daisy doesn't need me.'

'You had four the other night,' I say, and she frowns.

'I don't think you can be right. A responsible godmother is always available, always sober, and always prepared.'

'Like a girl guide?' I say.

'Exactly! I was a guide for almost six weeks.'

'What happened?' asked Lily. 'Didn't you like it?'

'I loved it,' says Isabella. 'But the leaders told my mother there were only two of them, and I required a whole leader all to myself. So, they had to respectfully decline the honour of my continued presence.'

'What did you do?' I ask, fascinated.

'Exactly what I was supposed to,' she says. 'I was almost halfway through my helpfulness badge, which was annoying. I only had a few more deeds of kindness to perform. After that, I wanted to try for my fishing badge.'

'I'd love to hear the leaders' side of it,' says Lily.

'So would I,' says Isabella. 'But my mother advised against it. I don't know why. She was probably worried they would realise their mistake and be upset. Anyway, that's all in the past now. Is Olivia looking after you?'

'I haven't had the chance,' I say. 'I was about to ask what Lily would like when you came through and distracted us with tales of your childhood exploits.'

'The exact word my guide leaders used,' says Isabella. 'How odd!'

'I'm a little disappointed to see you've lowered the standard of staff training,' says Lily. 'When I first started working here, I had to say, "Thank you for visiting us at The Sugarloaf Bakery. I hope your experience was everything you hoped for," whenever a customer left.'

'But you haven't left yet,' says Isabella. 'How do you know Olivia wouldn't have said it when you'd finished?'

'I stand corrected,' says Lily. 'I came in to collect Mum's wholemeal loaf before you sell out. She and Dad have gone to Southampton for the day, and she was worried she wouldn't be back before the bakery closed. I told her I'd drop it on her doorstep on my back to the hospital.'

'I've already put one aside for her,' says Isabella, handing her a wrapped loaf. 'And what can I get for you?'

'I'm fine, thanks,' says Lily. 'I had lunch at home.'

'Nonsense,' says Isabella. 'You have to keep your strength up at times like this. Don't forget you're eating for two.'

'I most certainly am not,' says Lily. 'The only person eating for two around here is you.'

I stifle a laugh, and Isabella gives me a wounded look. 'You aren't supposed to take her side.'

'I'd better get going,' says Lily. 'I told Jack I'd be back at the hospital ten minutes ago.'

Isabella drops a couple of brownies into a bag and hands it to her. 'Please give these to my goddaughter. Tell her that Whizzy sent them.'

'She can have one bite,' says Lily. 'Jack and I will eat the rest. Nice to meet you, Olivia. Thanks for standing in for me at such short notice.'

Isabella nudges me in the ribs. 'Olivia, our customer is leaving,' she says in an encouraging tone.

'What?' I say. 'Oh, yes! Thank you for visiting us at The Sugarloaf Bakery today. I hope … I'm sorry, I've forgotten the rest.'

Isabella tuts. 'So much for my intensive staff training. You see how it is. This younger generation won't be taught.'

'I'm twenty-nine,' I say.

'Then there's no hope for you. Please excuse her, Lily. I'm sure your experience today was everything you hoped for and more. I'll come over to see Daisy this evening if that's ok?'

'Are you sure?' says Lily. 'She'll be out tomorrow morning.'

'Quite sure,' says Isabella.

She watches Lily leave. 'There's a rather nice cafe in the hospital foyer that stays open until seven. They reduce their prices around six thirty. It would be a pity not to visit it one last time.'

'And you might pick up a nice doctor while you're at it,' I say. 'Your eyes will meet over the one remaining slice of reduced-price banana bread. You'll both reach out for it at the same time, and …'

'If he thinks I'm going on a date with him after that, he can think again!' she interrupts. 'So much for the healing profession.'

'Have fun, anyway,' I say. 'There was something I meant to mention to you before I left. I started talking about it with Lily, but you interrupted us. Did you know Mrs Ogilvie is about to turn eighty?'

'I had no idea,' she says. 'She does pretty well for her age, doesn't she? She's always out and about with Bernie.'

'She told me the other day she isn't celebrating it,' I say. 'I thought that was rather sad.'

'How can you not celebrate your eightieth birthday?' she exclaims.

'That's what I thought. But I barely know her. It isn't my place to say anything. You know her much better than I do. Maybe you can persuade her it would be a shame not to celebrate such a milestone birthday. She says she doesn't have any family around here, but she must know plenty of people if she's lived here all her life.'

'I never see her with anyone,' says Isabella. 'But she must have some old friends living here.'

'I was wondering whether we could throw a small party for her at the Sugarloaf?' I say. 'She seems to be a regular customer.'

'That's a great idea!' says Isabella. 'Do you mean a surprise party?'

'I don't know. Do you think Mrs Ogilvie is a surprise party sort of person?'

'Why not?' she says.

'Some people don't like surprises. I'm not too keen on them myself.'

'I'd love one,' she says. 'But I'm not Mrs Ogilvie. Could you talk to her and find out?'

'Ask her whether she'd like a surprise party? Wouldn't that give the game away?'

'We'll have to find out some other way,' she says. 'Who does she know who comes in here?'

'I have no idea. I've only met her a couple of times.'

'There's Mr Mason,' she says. 'The pair of them used to be sworn enemies, but they get on a lot better now. I could ask him what he thinks.'

'The man who owned the bakery? He seems a little indecisive. And forgetful. Do you think he'd be able to keep it a secret?'

'Maybe not,' says Isabella. 'But I'm glad you mentioned it. I'd hate to think of her celebrating her birthday all by herself. Besides, it's about time the Sugarloaf held a party. We had one when we re-opened, but that was ages ago. I'll mention it to Lily tonight. I can't imagine she'll have any objection. Assuming she's on board with the idea, you and I should start organising it at once.'

Chapter Fourteen

Will comes into the bakery the following morning.

'Hi, Olivia,' he says when he sees me. 'Just the person I was hoping to bump into.'

'The odds were pretty good,' I say. 'I'm here every day except Wednesday and Sunday. How can I help you?'

'I was wondering whether you'd like to come to Harfield with me tomorrow,' he says. 'Tomorrow being Sunday, one of the days I'm reliably informed Isabella won't have your nose to the grindstone.'

'What's at Harfield?' I say.

'There's an old water mill I've been wanting to photograph for the past week. Every time I start off in that direction, the sky clouds over. I was thinking about going first thing tomorrow and taking a picnic. The forecast is good. You haven't seen much of the area, so it would be a chance to remedy that.'

Isabella comes into the shop, carrying a ledger. 'Hi, Will. What are you doing here?'

He frowns as though in concentration. 'Now, what would I be doing in a bakery? Oh, yes, I remember. I've brought my dry-cleaning in. Olivia says it will be ready tomorrow.'

'Don't mess with me,' she says. 'I'm not in the mood. I'm off to see our accountant. I always have the most dreadful fear he'll discover I've been cooking the books and report me to the Inland Revenue.'

'Have you been cooking the books?' he asks with interest.

'Not to the best of my knowledge,' she says. 'But you never know. It's the sort of thing that might happen when I'm distracted. I'd be off to prison before I could say chocolate éclair.'

'Which would probably be the thing that distracted you in the first place,' I say.

'Very true. I'd better get going. It would look suspicious to be late. He'd be bound to think I had something to hide.'

'Will asked me whether I'd like to see Harfield water mill tomorrow,' I tell her. 'Will I be safe?'

She stops with her hand on the door. 'With Will? I'd say the chances are slightly better than even, but don't hold me to that.'

'At the mill, I mean. Is there likely to be a landslip that tips us both into the mill stream?'

'Hard to say,' she says. 'But you should go. My parents used to take me and Georgia there when we were younger. We fell into the stream once, but it wasn't because of a landslide.'

'And I wasn't there to take the blame,' says Will. 'What happened?'

'Georgia was being even more annoying than usual,' says Isabella. 'I forget why. Got to go!'

She rushes out and jumps into her car, and we watch her drive away.

'I hope you feel reassured by that,' says Will. 'You should be safe as long as you're not too annoying.'

'It sounds like fun,' I say. 'Did you say you wanted to take a picnic?'

'I did. But I'll sort that out.'

'No need. Isabella lets me have anything I want once it's past its sell by date. If you can put up with stale sandwiches and yesterday's brownies, we'll be fine.'

'If you're sure,' he says. 'I'll bring something to drink. I'd offer to pick you up, but you live opposite me. Shall we aim to leave around nine o'clock tomorrow morning?'

I remember what I discussed with Isabella last night. 'Do you have a moment?'

'I have nothing but moments,' he says. 'That's the beauty of being on assignment. There's no one to check up on you.'

'Until they ask for your portfolio,' I remind him.

'True, but they won't do that this week, so I'm fine. Is there something you want to discuss? If so, may I have a cappuccino? Have you mastered those yet?' a

'If you don't mind the foam being somewhat uneven,' I say. 'And if you aren't expecting elaborate art.'

'Something simple like the Sydney Opera House will be fine,' he says. 'Can I buy you one too? You could gulp it down between customers.'

'I'm allowed as much coffee as I can drink,' I say. 'It's one of the many perks of this job.'

'What are the others?' he asks.

'I've already told you about the cakes. I can't remember the rest of them right now, but I know Isabella enumerated them at length on my first day here. I seem to recall one of them was her sparkling conversation and inexhaustible supply of trivia.'

'I hope she pays you well,' he says, sitting at the table next to the door. 'Before you say anything, I'm aware this is Mrs Ogilvie's table. I'll move the second I see her sailing down the high street.'

'It's more Bernie's table,' I say. 'Isabella gave me strict instructions that he's only allowed to sit at the table by the door. He isn't allowed to rampage all over the shop. He doesn't strike me as much of a rampager, anyway. He knows where the basket of dog biscuits is kept, and he likes to stay within striking distance.'

'He's a bright little fellow,' he agrees.

I hand him his cappuccino, and he peers at the surface. 'I thought I requested the Opera House.'

'I'm more of a fan of portraits,' I say. 'This is modelled on one of Picasso's more famous works.'

'Which one?'

'I have no idea. But if you squint hard, that blob looks like a nose.'

'It looks nothing like my nose,' he says. 'Or yours either. But the clump of chocolate powder next to it looks rather like an eyebrow, so I'll give you the benefit of the doubt.'

He takes a sip. 'It tastes fabulous, which is the main thing. I'd never have known you hadn't been doing this for years. You're wasted as a veterinary nurse.'

'I mix up an excellent solution of glucose and vitamins too,' I say.

'I'll try that next time I'm in,' he says. 'You said you had something you wanted to talk about?'

'It's about Mrs Ogilvie. I was chatting with her the other day, and she mentioned her eightieth birthday is coming up soon. At least, she was talking about how long she'd been living in her cottage, and I did the maths. She isn't planning to celebrate it, so I thought it would be nice to throw her a small party at the bakery. Isabella and Lily like the idea. But it was my suggestion, so I should do most of the work.'

'It's a great idea,' he says. 'I'll be happy to help out in any way I can.'

'I'm glad you said that. It makes it less awkward to ask you for a favour. I wondered whether you might be the official photographer.'

'You *are* pushing the boat out,' he says. 'How big will this party be? Do I need to run up to London to fetch my tux?'

'That's up to you. It won't be a fancy party, but it struck me we have a professional photographer right here in the village, so we should make use of him. Will you still be here in August?'

'I should be,' he says. 'I'm happy to take photographs for you. Let me know if there are any other ways I can help. I really should get going now. I promised my landlady I'd help her to put together a bookcase this afternoon. Apparently, her husband hasn't got around to it, and she's getting desperate. She may regret her impatience when she sees what kind of a job I do. Flat pack furniture is not my forte.'

'I'll remember that if I decide to put up an awning for this party,' I say. 'We don't want it crashing down on the customers' heads.'

'It would make a wonderful picture,' he says. 'I could sell it to the tabloids for millions and never have to work again.'

'But they'd sue the bakery, and Isabella wouldn't like that. Maybe we should stick to balloons.'

'We can discuss it properly tomorrow,' he says. 'See you at nine o'clock, Olivia.'

Chapter Fifteen

Will is waiting by his car when I arrive the following morning.

'It's a lovely day,' he says. 'I ought to get some good shots of the mill.'

'How far is it?' I ask, climbing into the car and dumping my bag of food onto the back seat.

'About forty-five minutes if the traffic isn't too bad. We'll head towards Lyndhurst, then turn off towards Harfield.'

He sets off in the direction of the high street.

'Do you want to stop and get a coffee for the road?' he asks as we approach the Sugarloaf.

'Absolutely not! This is my day off. If we go into the bakery, Isabella is bound to discover there's somewhere she needs to be, and I'll end up covering for her. Keep driving. If she comes out of the bakery, pretend not to see her, and put your foot on the accelerator.'

'I'm not sure I like this attitude,' he says. 'As a new employee, I'd have thought you'd be only too pleased to make a good impression.'

'A new and extremely temporary employee,' I say. 'That makes all the difference.'

'You can't be all that temporary,' he says. 'You've promised to organise a party in August.'

'I know, and I'm already regretting it. That's more than two months away.'

He glances over at me. 'Don't you like Honeywell?'

'I love it. But it isn't real. I keep expecting to wake up in my bed in London.'

'Which part of London?'

I wish I hadn't mentioned London. It's the last thing I want to talk about.

He notices my hesitation. 'I only asked because that's where I've been living for the past few years. I have a flat in Hammersmith.'

'I was in Putney,' I say reluctantly.

'Honeywell is a bit of a change from either of those,' he says. 'I've been having a great time down here. I'm spinning it out for as long as I can.'

'How long is your assignment?' I say, happy to move on to safer ground.

He shrugs. 'It's a bit of an open question. I've been working for a commercial photography company for the last few years as a semi-permanent freelancer.'

'That seems a bit of a contradiction in terms,' I say.

'I suppose it does. I'm not a permanent employee, and I don't want to be. But they give me enough contracts that I may as well be. They had someone lined up for this job, but it fell through. I happened to be free, so I agreed to take it on.'

'But it can't make financial sense for you to spend longer on it than you need to,' I say. 'All the freelancers I know are racing to line up their next contracts as quickly as possible.'

'That was me until recently,' he says. 'But I realised that wasn't how I wanted to live. The company have offered me a permanent position, and I'm considering it. But I'd already decided to take a few months off before this job came up, and this seemed an ideal opportunity.'

'Is there a deadline for publication?'

'September,' he says. 'It's coming out at Easter, and they want the photos well before then. It shouldn't be a problem.'

I want to ask him why he needs this time off, but I don't dare. He would probably tell me, but he'd be bound to ask questions in return, and I'm not ready for that.

He reaches into the glove compartment. 'I don't have the half bar of chocolate I hear is the basic requirement for any journey over three miles, but I have a tin of travel sweets if you'd like one.'

I take a sweet and hold out the tin to him. He doesn't take his eyes off the road. 'I'd like a red one, if there are any.'

'I just took the last one,' I say apologetically. 'I'm sorry. They're my favourite.'

'How about an orange one?' he says.

I relax, realising my shoulders have tensed up and my heart has started to race.

He glances at me. 'You aren't feeling carsick, are you?'

I shake my head. 'I don't get carsick. I'm fine, thanks.'

I drop the sweet into his outstretched palm and take a few deep breaths to steady myself. I must learn not to overreact in this sort of situation. So, I took the last red sweet without thinking. Big deal. But it takes me a couple of minutes before I feel completely calm.

I sense Will turning his head to look at me a couple of times, but he doesn't speak until we reach the turning.

'We head west along here for a few miles, then turn off towards Harfield,' he says. 'We can get a coffee there without running the risk of anyone asking you to stand in for them.'

'Didn't you bring a flask? You're supposed to be in charge of drinks.'

'My landlady didn't have one,' he says. 'I settled for a bottle of wine instead. It seemed a reasonable substitute. I even brought my penknife with the bottle opener attachment.'

'Red or white?'

He gives me a smug look. 'I wasn't sure which you preferred, so I went for rosé.'

'Still or sparkling?' I say, and he laughs.

'Is it a dealbreaker?'

'Not at all. I just wanted to worry you.'

'Would you have demanded I took you home if I'd brought the wrong one?' he says.

'Maybe.'

'I knew it! "Now, there's a woman who's difficult to please," I said to myself the first minute I saw you.'

'Is that what you really thought of me?'

'No. What I really thought was, "Now, there's a woman who has terrible taste in cars." Why do you ask?'

'No reason,' I say. 'It's just something someone used to say to me quite often.'

He shoots me a quick look. 'Someone important?'

'I thought so.'

'But you don't still think so?'

'Probably not.'

'Good,' he says. 'No one needs that sort of negativity in their life. Do I take the first or the second left on this road?'

I look at the GPS and guide him for the next few miles.

He pulls up at last outside a small row of shops. 'This is Harfield. At least, I hope it is. Shall we find ourselves some coffee before we set off for the mill?'

I look around. 'I don't see any mill.'

'That's because it's a couple of miles from here,' he says. 'But this is as far as the road goes.'

'There isn't even a track?'

He smiles. 'I should have said this is as far as I'm prepared to take the car. She doesn't like bumping and jolting along stony tracks.'

'Now, there's a car who's difficult to please,' I say, and he laughs.

We set off ten minutes later, clutching our cups of coffee and the picnic basket.

'When you say two miles, do you really mean five?' I ask.

'Not if the map is correct,' he says. 'Don't you like walking?'

'I love walking. I'm less keen on getting lost. Particularly after my recent experience.'

'I can understand that,' he says. 'But look how well it turned out. You were rescued almost at once, and you started a whole new life.'

'I don't know why everyone keeps saying that! I haven't started a whole new anything. All I'm doing is taking some time off while I decide what to do next. It isn't much different from what you're doing, and no one tells you that you've started a whole new life.'

'You may be right,' he says. 'But it feels different. I'm just taking a few months off from a job I love.'

'How do you know I don't love my job?' I say.

'I don't. Do you enjoy it?'

'I do, although I'm ready for a change. I've been working for a practice in Wimbledon for the past six years.'

'Are you going back after your break?'

'I don't think that's a good idea,' I say. 'Not because of the job itself, but there are other things …' I'm not sure how to finish the sentence. No matter how hard I try to avoid the subject of my past, it keeps sneaking up on me regardless.

'There must be a lot of that sort of work around Honeywell,' he says, not appearing to notice my confusion.

'I like small animal work,' I say. 'I haven't had much experience with rural practices. Just the odd cow and sheep during my training, but nothing since then.'

'London probably isn't overrun with people keeping sheep and cows in their high-rise flats,' he says.

'You'd be surprised what some people consider as pets. But you're right. Our practice mainly treated cats and dogs and rabbits and hamsters.'

'No snakes?' he says.

'A few. Don't tell me you're a secret snake lover and keep a pet boa constrictor in your Hammersmith flat? What have you done with it while you're down here?'

'I brought him with me,' he says. 'Haven't you noticed him wandering around the front garden each morning, enjoying the sunshine?'

'I must have missed that. I have extremely early starts at the bakery. Do you really keep a snake?'

'Absolutely not!' he says. 'I'm terrified of them.'

'Even little ones?'

'Particularly little ones. At least, with the big ones you know where they are. The small ones could be anywhere, and you'd never know.'

'You'd better watch your feet,' I say. 'There are adders in the New Forest. They're fairly rare, but we might spot one.'

'Not this year,' he says. 'They've been banned. I checked before I agreed to come down here.'

'Banned?'

'That's right. My manager assured me there would be no snakes in the area for the entire duration of my visit.'

I burst out laughing. 'If it makes you feel better to feel they've been banned this year, I'll go along with it. Is it just snakes you don't like? How do you feel about spiders?'

'They're even worse,' he says with a shudder. 'Snakes tend to live outside. Spiders have no such boundaries. There was one in the bath the other day, and I had to go downstairs in a towel and ask my landlady to remove it.'

'What was it doing in the bath?' I ask.

'I didn't look too closely. The back crawl, I think.'

'Next time you find a spider in the house, and the landlady isn't around, you can call me,' I say. 'I can be there in twenty seconds.'

'What if you don't answer your phone?' he says. 'Could I throw stones at your window?'

'My landlady is very nice, but I expect she'd draw the line at that.'

'Is your bedroom at the front of the house?' he says.

'It's at the back. Why do you ask?'

'Because mine's at the front. We could have set up a signalling system with candles. One flash for a house spider, two for a tarantula, three for a very small snake, and four for a python.'

'My landlady may think you're trying to proposition her.'

'The phone, it is,' he says. 'But please keep it on you at all times.'

'Is that the mill over there?' I point towards a clump of trees. I can just see the outline of a roof behind them.

'Let's have a look at the map.' He waves his phone around. 'There doesn't seem to be any connection.'

I watch him, amused. 'Why does everyone do that? Do they think there are stray telecommunication waves floating around, and all they need to do is catch one?'

'I don't know what else to do,' he says. 'Except for climbing up a very high tree. That seems to work in movies.'

'I'm happy to watch you try,' I say. 'Are we at least going in the right general direction?'

He switches off his phone. 'I thought we were. But this path keeps twisting and turning, and I'm losing track.'

'In which case, we should definitely head for that building over there. There may be someone we can ask.'

I strike off up the side path towards the clump of trees, and Will follows me.

'Can you hear something?' I say.

'What sort of something?'

I point towards the trees. 'I thought I heard voices.'

'Are you sure it isn't music?' he says.

'You may be right. Come on, there's bound to be someone who can tell us which way the mill is.'

We quicken our pace and head up the slope towards the trees. The bursts of noise and laughter grow louder as we approach.

'Do you think they're having a rave?' says Will.

'It would be a strange time to have one. Don't they usually take place in deserted warehouses in the middle of the night?'

He raises an eyebrow. 'You seem to know an awful lot about them. I'll defer to your superior knowledge.'

'That's the only thing I remember. I'd be willing to bet Isabella knows a lot more about them than I do. You should ask her if you want more information. She's probably the local organiser.'

'It wouldn't surprise me,' he says. 'The noise seems to be coming from the other side of the trees. Maybe they'll invite us to join them. I'm glad I brought that bottle of rosé now. It's like currency in those places. It should stop anyone from attacking us.'

A movement among the trees catches my eye. A moment later, a man appears. He's dressed in a full-length leather apron and is holding what looks like a large hammer.

I take an involuntary step backwards, and Will laughs. 'He's a blacksmith. He's probably working on one of the farms around here. He's bound to know where we are.'

The man sees us and waves. We walk towards him. I keep a wary eye on his hammer, but he doesn't seem as though he's about to swing it at us.

'Hi!' calls Will when we come within earshot. 'We were hoping you could tell us where we are.'

The man stops and considers. 'You are in the fair vale of Mitcham.'

'Where?' says Will. 'We're trying to find the old water mill. Is it somewhere around here?'

'There is a water mill yonder,' says the man, pointing. 'Master Twyford built it nearly two score years ago, and a great wonder it is.'

I glance at Will, who looks as puzzled as I feel.

'I'm not talking about a modern building,' he says. 'We're looking for the water mill. My GPS says it's in this general direction, but there's no signal, and we're lost.'

'GPS?' says the man.

'Satellite,' I explain. 'I should have brought the map from the car, but I thought we'd have enough connection if we got lost. Evidently not.'

'Your cart?' he says. 'Where is it?'

'Car,' says Will. 'We left it in the village.'

'Which was unwise,' says the man. 'There are thieves in that village. Nothing is safe.'

Will looks startled. 'Car thieves? Perhaps we'd better …'

'It's fine,' I say. 'I saw you lock it, and it has an alarm. I'm not walking all the way back there to check on your precious car.'

He doesn't look convinced, but I'm rapidly losing my patience. 'I mean it, Will. I want my lunch. Let's find this mill and have something to eat.'

'An excellent idea,' says the man. 'Make your way through yonder thicket, and you will find all the food you want.'

'Another village?' says Will.

'Exactly!' says the man.

He turns and strides off the way he came, beckoning to us to follow.

I hang back. 'I'm not going with him. He seems a little strange. Maybe we should head back to the village after all and check your car. Someone there is bound to have a map we can use.'

A look of comprehension flashes over Will's face, and he grins. 'I think we'll be fine. Come on! He's almost out of sight.'

He takes my hand and starts jogging along the path after the blacksmith. I almost pull away and turn back the way we came. But his hand feels oddly comforting. He's tall and strongly built. He can probably cope with most things. As long as the blacksmith doesn't start waving his hammer around. Will's penknife may not be a match for that, even with the bottle opener attachment.

We weave through the clump of trees and stop dead. Below us is a large field with hundreds of people in brightly coloured clothes milling around. Several men on horseback are playing what looks like a game of polo. Scores of tents are spread across the field, and the sound of music and laughter rises up to meet us.

A woman carrying a large bundle is climbing the hill towards us.

'Welcome, strangers!' she calls when she sees us. 'I did not think to see so strangely clad a couple on this fine June morning.'

'Sorry about that!' says Will. 'We didn't expect to be here today, or we'd have made more of an effort.'

'And speaking such a strange tongue,' she says. 'Are you from foreign parts?'

'If London counts,' he says.

'A foreign place, indeed! Still, if you are loyal servants of the crown, I bid you welcome.' She wanders over to talk to a nearby group of people.

I stare at the scene in front of me. 'Have we stumbled into Brigadoon?'

'Wouldn't that be something?' says Will. 'The real explanation is rather more prosaic. I remember seeing a flyer when I was in Lyndhurst last week. It's the annual medieval fair.'

'That's a relief! I thought for a moment the blacksmith was about to murder us both.'

'He may still plan to,' he says. 'But on the off chance he's forgotten about us and found himself another victim, shall we go and explore? It would be a shame not to take a look now we're here.'

'Fine,' I say. 'But just in case that blacksmith is still hanging around, you can go first.'

Chapter Sixteen

I follow him down the hill towards the field.

'I feel rather underdressed,' I say. 'Or overdressed. I'm not sure which.'

'You're fine,' he says. 'That summer dress isn't vastly different to what some of the women here are wearing.'

'Thank goodness I'm wearing a long dress. Can you imagine what they'd call me if my knees were showing?'

'I'm not worried about my knees,' he says. 'These jeans cover them. But I feel I'm lacking something regarding the rest of my outfit.'

He looks at a group of men standing by the entrance to a nearby tent. 'They knew how to do sleeves in those days. Those shirts make me feel distinctly underdressed.'

'There aren't too many T-shirts around,' I agree.

'Maybe I can buy myself something to wear.'

'Are you serious? We'll only be here for an hour or so.'

He looks around him. 'There seems plenty to see and do.'

'They won't throw you out because you've turned up in a Hugo Boss T-shirt.'

'Selfridges,' he corrects me. 'My mother gave me a voucher for my birthday last month. I thought I'd better spend it before I lost it, which is what I usually do with vouchers. If I'd known I was coming here, I'd have spent it on something more appropriate.'

'I don't think puffy sleeves and leather jerkins are in this year.'

'You're wrong,' he says. 'They were all over the catwalk in Milan. And those long, pointy shoes were everywhere. If I'd had the forethought to buy myself a pair, I wouldn't be sticking out like a sore thumb right now.'

'Despite the jeans?'

He gives me a reproving look. 'These aren't jeans. They're cotton hose.'

'I stand corrected. Shall we stand here all day arguing about fashion, or shall we see what's going on?'

'Give me a moment to stash this picnic basket behind a tree, and I'm all yours.'

We wander around the field, watching the performers walking on stilts and juggling. One man is playing a lute badly, but at least he's trying.

'I can't make out whether that's supposed to be Greensleeves or Ticket to Ride,' whispers Will.

'Shhh! He'll hear you. I know the Beatles are timeless, but they weren't around in medieval times.'

'True,' he says. 'I think he's actually playing That'll be the Day. He's obviously a Buddye Hollye fan.'

'I like it,' I say. 'And he looks as though he's having fun. He isn't bothered by what other people think, which is a good thing. I wish I could be more like that.'

'Are you bothered about what people think of you?' he asks.

'Yes.'

'You shouldn't be.'

I give a fake start. 'My goodness! Why hasn't anyone told me that before? This is life-changing information!'

He smiles. 'Fair enough. But it's a shame to waste our lives trying to be what we think other people want us to be, when we're fine as we are.'

'What if we aren't?'

He shoots me a quick look. 'Are you asking generally or specifically?'

'I don't know. A bit of both.'

'I'd give you the same answer either way,' he says. 'We're all of us fine, just the way we are.'

'What if we burgle houses or hack into nuclear facilities and steal the codes?'

'That's oddly specific,' he says. 'Do you make a habit of doing either of those things?'

'No, but it's a cliché to say everyone is fine just the way they are. It's patently obvious that's not true in a lot of cases.'

'You've got me there,' he says. 'But my point still stands. What do you think is so wrong with you?'

'I'm not talking about anything in particular,' I say. 'But you hardly know me. You've met me a couple of times in the bakery, and we've been for a walk and got lost. It isn't nearly enough to make a judgement about what kind of person I am.'

'Maybe not,' he says. 'But if you look at it the other way around, I don't know anything bad about you. Time for a different judgement when I discover you're a cat burglar who targets antique snuff boxes.'

'That also seems oddly specific,' I say. 'Is that what you get up to when you aren't in Honeywell?'

'Nothing so exciting,' he says. 'I work, I go home and I make dinner. I forget to water my plants, then realise they're plastic, so it doesn't matter. Occasionally, I play tennis. It may not be everyone's idea of fun, but it suits me, so I'm sticking with it. How about you? What do you like to do in your spare time?'

'I never seem to have any. I go to work. I come home and clean the flat.'

'That can't take long,' he says. 'It won't get too messy if you're out at work all day.'

'No, but my … flatmate was quite fussy about how it was done. He worked longer hours than I did, so it seemed only fair for me to take care of things at home.'

He pulls a face. 'I wouldn't house share with someone who told me what to do with my spare time. Especially when it's something as boring as housework. Why didn't you tell them where to go?'

I don't meet his eyes. 'It was more complicated than that. When I say housemate, I mean partner.'

'Ah,' he says. 'That makes a difference. But not a huge one. Is that what you're going back to when you leave Honeywell?'

'No. At least, I don't think so. I left him last week.'

'That sounds like an excellent decision to me,' he says.

'Maybe.' To my dismay, I feel my eyes filling with tears, and I turn away before he can see.

He squeezes my hand. 'There's no need to talk about it now. Look at us – we're as far away from real life as it's possible to be. We're living in Mediaeval England. It would be a pity not to make the most of it.'

I smile back at him. 'You're right. This is fun. I saw a stall selling what looks like pies. Shall we contribute to the local economy and try a couple?'

He reaches into his pocket. 'Always assuming they accept modern doubloons.'

'Aren't those Spanish?'

He opens his wallet. 'Who knows? It may be too much to expect them to take Ye American Expresse. But with any luck, they'll change some of these coins into shillings and sixpences for us. Don't let's stand around talking any longer. Let's go and negotiate with the peasants.'

Chapter Seventeen

We find a stall selling pies, and Will buys two.

'We could have stayed in Honeywell and eaten these,' I say.

The stallholder overhears us. 'I know not of this Honeywelle, but I doubt they could compete with our pies, which are known the length and breadth of the kingdom. We have sold them to noblemen and commoners, as far away as London Towne.'

'I must remember to take a look next time I'm in Starbucks,' says Will.

We sit on the grass a little way from the stall to eat our pies.

'Aren't you hungry?' asks Will. 'I thought you were eager to get to the mill so we could have our picnic.'

'I'm ravenous,' I say. 'But I'm waiting for you to try yours first.'

He gives the pie a dubious poke. 'What do you think is in it?'

'How should I know? But you're about to find out.'

'Funny,' he says, 'I had the exact same idea.'

'You won't win this argument,' I say, 'so you may as well give up now. This is the age of chivalry. I'm looking to you for gallantry and courteous behaviour and all the rest of it. That means being the first to try that pie and letting me know whether it's safe.'

'Fine!' He takes an enormous bite and chews.

'Well?' I say.

'Interesting,' he mumbles. 'Definitely a hint of some small mammal, but I can't place it. Rat, perhaps? And there's something slimy. I suppose it could be a frog? It's difficult to tell. The bones are a little crunchy, but the overall flavour isn't too bad.'

He sees my instinctive recoil and laughs. 'You deserved that for making me eat it first. It's very nice. I think it's lamb. And there's some sort of spice I can't place. It's quite pleasant.'

I pick up the pie and take a tentative bite. 'It's lovely!'

'I imagine they're here to make a profit,' he says. 'I expect they get some local bakery to deliver them, then add a few doubloons to the price.'

'Farthings,' I remind him.

'Inflation means we're way past farthings,' he says. 'Sovereigns, perhaps, or guineas. It's a good thing I brought some money with me.'

'I have about ten pounds in my purse,' I say. 'Enough to buy us a drink, at least. Unless you want to retrieve your bottle of wine?'

'Absolutely not,' he says. 'They didn't have supermarkets in mediaeval times.'

'You don't know that for sure. You're a photographer, not a student of mediaeval history. I bet they did have supermarkets. They'd have called them things like Ye Olde Cooperative or Sainsburyshire's. They'd have people standing at the ends of the aisles, handing out free samples of potions.'

'And the shopping baskets would be made of chain mail,' he says.

'And there would be express checkout lanes for knights and lords.'

'Don't be ridiculous!' he says. 'They would have sent their jesters and fools to do their menial work.'

'Not if they wanted to get exactly what they'd written on their list. Noblemen wouldn't allow for random substitutions. I wonder whether they had mediaeval loyalty cards.'

'Probably,' he says. 'They would periodically receive an illuminated piece of parchment, telling them that armour polish was on special that week. You were so quick to assume modern day society was superior. And all along, people in the Middle Ages were having a wonderful time.'

'If they spent all their time wandering around fields and eating pies and jousting, they must have had lots of fun,' I agree.

'Have you finished your pie?' he says. 'Would you like something else?'

'I wouldn't mind something to drink. I don't suppose there's any chance of finding a coffee around here?'

He pulls me to my feet. 'I doubt it. I seem to remember that coffee didn't arrive in the country until about the sixteenth century.'

'Even in the supermarkets?'

'We didn't learn about those in our history lessons, so I can't help you. I can see what looks like a beer tent over there.'

'Even better!' I say. 'I assume mediaeval beer is similar to ours? It doesn't have frogs' legs floating around in it, or anything equally horrible?'

'Only if you pay extra.'

'I'm not doing that. I don't want to run out of doubloons too quickly.'

'You aren't a pirate,' he says. 'How many times do I need to remind you?'

'Arrr!' I hop ahead of him towards the beer tent.

The man serving behind the makeshift bar greets us pleasantly. 'Good morrow, friends. How may I be of service to thee?'

'We're looking for beer,' I say, adding without thinking, 'Prithee.'

I catch Will's eye and laugh. 'You order, if you think you can do any better.'

'Not at all. You have it covered.'

The bartender smiles at me. 'For thee, my lady, I recommend small beer.'

'Why?' I say. 'Don't you know that women drink pints these days?'

'You misunderstand,' he says patiently. 'Small beer is that which is brewed to be less intoxicating, and so may be consumed in greater quantities without ill effect to man or woman.'

'Sounds good to me,' says Will. 'I'll have a gill of that. Or a flagon, or whatever you use to serve it.'

'How about a skip?' I say. 'Do you serve anything besides this small beer?'

'Assuredly,' says the man. 'We serve the finest ale in all the county.'

'I'll have a barrel of that,' I say. 'I think it's best that my friend here sticks to small beer. He doesn't have a strong head.'

'Ale sounds good too,' says Will. 'Maybe I'll try both.'

'We are also serving mead,' says the man. 'Brewed with the honey from Master Lovelock's bees. The finest bees in all of Hampshire, and singularly free from plagues and agues.'

'I'm delighted to hear it,' I say. 'I'd love to try some mead. I've read about it, but I've never tasted it.'

'You're in for a treat,' says Will. 'I had some last year at a Christmas fair, and it was Ambrosia.'

'In which case, you were honoured above the lot of mortals,' says the man.

'Sure,' says Will. 'Lucky me! Ok, that's two flagons of your finest mead, please. What is that? A farthing?'

'Alas,' says the man, 'the taxes on grain have been such this year that prices have risen beyond belief. The King is determined upon war with France, so the taxes continue to rise.'

I hand him a ten-pound note. 'How much will that buy?'

He hands us both a tankard of mead. 'As it happens, the amount you offer is almost correct. Be not alarmed, for a tithe of the merchants' profits goes to the local infirmary for the young.'

He points to a sign pinned to the flap of the tent, proclaiming in heraldic script, *This Mediaeval Fair supports Reardon Children's hospital.*

'That's great,' I say.

'Indeed it is, fair maid. Therefore, reach deep into the recesses of thy pockets and spend freely as you go about.'

'That's pretty much all the cash I have,' I say. 'Unless you take debit cards.'

'I myself do not,' he says. 'But I have heard tell of others present here today who dabble in the witchcraft of magical waves throughout the ether.'

We finish our mead, which is, as Will predicted, delicious. It tastes like the essence of sun-kissed meadows, with bees drifting lazily through the wildflowers.

I take a deep breath. 'If there's a definitive description of liquid gold somewhere, this would be it.'

I follow Will out of the tent, where we almost bump into a woman juggling flaming torches.

'Do you fancy a go?' says Will.

'Not after that mead. I'd burst into flames as soon as I breathed.'

'It was strong, wasn't it?' he says. 'But it beats my bottle of rosé hands down. Why is that man waving at me?'

'I think he wants to fight you.'

'What?' he says, startled.

'He's waving a stick at you. What else could that mean?'

'Maybe he thinks he's a wizard?' he suggests.

'Anything's possible. Why don't we ask him?'

The man waves again. 'A joust, young master, a joust! Cry not craven before thine fair companion.'

'I can't ride a horse,' says Will.

'Tis of no matter, sire,' says the man, taking his arm. 'For this is merely tilting at the quintain. A practice beloved of all young knights in training.'

'There you are,' I say with an encouraging smile. 'It's only tilting. Off you go! I'll stand here and applaud.'

'Why don't you do it if you're so keen?' asks Will.

'I'm a woman!' I say in a shocked tone. 'I'd be put on the ducking stool if I tried something like that.'

'Only sixpence a try,' says the man. 'The successful tilter wins a ribbon for his lady.'

'You can't buy too many ribbons for sixpence,' says Will.

'Five pounds in modern money, sire. But what is that against the chance to impress the fair maiden and win her heart with your skill and daring?'

Will sees my quick grin and sighs. 'If I must. Do you take debit cards?'

'No problem, mate,' says the man.

He hands Will a stick. 'At thine own pace. The target is yonder. Run fast and strike it true, then quicken thine pace so as to avoid the sandbag which pursues thee.'

Will looks alarmed. 'No one said anything about being hit with a sandbag.'

'Cry not craven!' I remind him. 'Besides, we've already donated to the hospital. I mean, the infirmary. I'm sure they'll be only too happy to patch you up.'

He gives me an ironic look but picks up a stick. With a doubtful glance at the target, he sets off towards it at a quick trot, waving his stick wildly. A man standing near the target, chatting with a woman on stilts, jumps out of the way.

Will hits the target right in the centre. He gives a jubilant shout, which is cut off a split second later as the sandbag swings around and hits him in the back of the head, sending him flying. He lies on the grass without moving, and I run towards him.

He rolls over, groans, and sits up. 'What happened?'

'You forgot about the quicken thine pace bit,' I say.

He rubs his head. 'Is that what he meant? He could have made it clearer.'

I help him to his feet. 'I don't see how. He was speaking the King's Englishe to you. It isn't his fault you weren't listening properly.'

He returns the stick to the man, who smiles. 'A valiant attempt. Wouldst thou perchance wish to essay the task once more? Tis only another sixpence.'

'There's no perchance about it,' says Will. 'I'm not tilting at another target as long as I live.'

The man shrugs. 'As you wish. 'Tis not the spirit the King would wish to see in his yeomanry, but no matter.'

I interrupt before Will can make an unpatriotic remark about King Richard, or whoever is supposed to be on the throne right now.

'He hit the target right in the middle,' I say. 'Doesn't that mean he wins a ribbon?'

'Naught but a broken head,' says the man. 'The rules are very clear.'

'Not even a little one?' I plead. 'You've already flouted about ten health and safety regulations in running this so-called game.'

He sighs. 'That one so young should descend to blackmail and extortion. I shall not yield to base threats. Yet, for the sake of thy bright eyes shall I let thee choose a riband for thy wrist.'

'That's more like it,' says Will. 'Which one would you like, Olivia?'

'The maiden art named after a future Lord Protector of England,' says the man. 'Thy patriotism shines like a light in a dark world.'

'I'm not sure you're supposed to know about Cromwell yet,' I say. 'You'd better not mention it again or you'll be accused of witchcraft. I'd like a yellow one, please.'

He hands me the ribbon, and I tie it around my wrist as we wander towards the next tent.

'Are you going to win me a whole rainbow of ribbons?' I ask Will.

'Not a chance. They'd probably make me eat a live frog to get the green one. You'll have to be happy with the one you have.'

A man sitting behind a stall runs out as we pass. 'Good morrow, fair strangers. I am Frances Whytleafe. I am able to take thy likeness in fewer than fifteen minutes of the clock.'

I look at the easel standing next to his stall. 'A cartoonist! Can I pay for him to draw you, Will?'

'Not a hope,' he says.

'Oh, go on. It would be fun.'

'How if I should make a likeness of you both together?' suggests the artist. 'It would be both a memento and an economy. I shall remove twenty-five percent from the final reckoning.'

'I hate having my picture taken,' I say.

'But you're happy enough for me to have mine done,' says Will. 'And it isn't a photograph. Cameras weren't invented in mediaeval times.'

'How do you know?' I grumble. 'Did they teach you that in your history of cameras class at photography school?'

'No, but we covered it in magical inventions of the future,' he says. 'Otherwise known as digital technology.'

'I still think you ought to have your picture done while I watch.'

'And I don't,' he says, grasping my wrist and leading me towards a chair.

'Wonderful!' says the man. 'I shall create a portrait of thee both to gladden thine hearts and remind thee for many years to come of this day.'

'As long as you make it quick,' I say.

'And what are thine interests and dispositions?' he enquires. 'Thy passions and daily pursuits?'

Will and I look at each other.

'He's a photographer, and I'm a veterinary nurse,' I say. 'But I'm working in a bakery at the moment.'

'And how dost thou utilise thy spare time?' he enquires.

'What *do* you do in your spare time?' I ask Will. 'Apart from driving that red car around the countryside rescuing people.'

'Indeed?' says the man. 'A knight errant, I perceive.'

'Otherwise known as a driver with a map,' says Will. 'Olivia's rental car had broken down, and I happened to drive past and see her. That's how we met.'

The artist nods. 'And how does the young maid employ her spare hours when not attending to her livestock?'

I open my mouth to answer, then shut it again. I don't want to tell him I have no hobbies or interests. Or rather, I don't want to tell him that in front of Will. How did that happen? I used to have hundreds of hobbies. Why did I stop doing them? I grew up, I suppose. Most adults don't have time for hobbies. At least, responsible, mature adults don't.

'No matter,' says the man when I don't answer. 'I have already seen into the depths of both thy souls and shall create a likeness accordingly.'

He directs Will to sit next to me, produces a pack of pastel crayons, and starts to sketch.

'Why did I let you talk me into this?' I mutter to Will, trying not to move my lips. I realise this is ridiculous. We aren't having our photo taken, where there's a risk of camera blur. The artist already knows what we look like, and the odds of the final image being in any way recognisable are slim. If he were a proper artist, he wouldn't be wasting his Saturday afternoon touting for business at a mediaeval fair.

'Because it's fun,' Will murmurs back. 'There's nothing wrong with having fun.'

'I'll take your word for it.'

The man draws for ten more minutes, humming a madrigal to himself as he sketches. At last, he lays down his crayon. 'Before I show thee the result, I shall require payment.'

I'll bet he does. I knew he'd be terrible. If he allows us to see the picture first, he knows we won't pay.

'Here you go,' says Will, tapping his card on the reader.

He looks at the paper the man hands him and laughs. 'And you said no one had ever taken a good picture of you, Olivia!'

I peer over his shoulder and burst out laughing. 'That's amazing!'

The man gives us a modest smile. 'You are too kind, my lady.'

'You must be a professional artist in real life,' I say.

'I work in a gallery in Bournemouth. I show my work there occasionally.'

'What brings you here today?' I say. 'You don't appear to have many customers.'

'Because I enjoy it,' he says. 'I come here every year. I love it.'

'You mean, like a hobby?'

'Exactly.' He switches back into character. 'I thank thee for thy custom. Shouldst thou encounter other young couples amidst the throng, who would be glad of this experience, please mention my name and direction unto them.'

'We aren't a couple …' I begin.

'We'd be delighted,' says Will.

Chapter Eighteen

It isn't until we see one of the stallholders taking down their tent that I realise how long we've been here. After having our portrait done, we went to the crafts tent and tried our hand – unsuccessfully – at pottery. Will's attempt was more recognisable as a vase than mine, but I couldn't advise him to give up the day job on the strength of it. After a brief stop to sample the spiced gingerbread, we watched a wedding reenactment which would have put many of today's bridezillas to shame. Somehow, the afternoon seems to have got away from us, and it's now early evening.

'Do you know what time it is?' I ask Will. 'I don't wear a watch, and my phone's out of power again.'

'We could find ourselves a sundial,' he says. 'If only you'd had the forethought to steal Isabella's while you were living with her.'

'It was broken. The only thing it was useful for was to tell her when it was time for her morning coffee.'

He pulls out his phone. 'It's six thirty! How did that happen?'

'Is there anything else you wish you'd done while you had the chance?' I ask. 'There's still time if we hurry. How about another tilt at the quintain? I'm sure your abject failure has been niggling at you all afternoon.'

He smiles. 'Not even a bit.'

'But I want a pink ribbon,' I complain.

'So, go to a craft shop. They'll sell you metres of the things. I've done everything I want to. It's been a wonderful afternoon.'

'Hasn't it?' I say. 'I'm sorry about the mill. You'll have to come all the way back another day, assuming you can work out where it is.'

'Shall we see whether our picnic bag has survived or been discovered by marauding peasants and auctioned off to the highest bidder?'

'Do peasants maraud?' I say, following him up the hill to where he left the bag.

'If they catch sight of day-old cakes and bottles of sparkling rosé, they do.'

He reaches the tree and looks behind it. 'Lucky for us, they didn't find it. Let's get out of here before anyone sees us and gives chase.'

'Do you think we'll find the village again, or are we doomed to wander in circles all night?' I say as we emerge from a thicket of trees.

'I'd give us pretty good odds,' says Will. 'Although it may take a while. Are these the same trees we walked through this morning – where we met the blacksmith?'

'They look the same. They have trunks and leaves.'

'It's a good start,' he says. 'But somehow, I don't think it's enough. What a pity we're city dwellers. I'm not sure I can tell an oak from a rowan.'

'The trees this morning were right on the top of a hill,' I say. 'These are halfway up the slope. I'm not even sure it's the same hill. Someone seems to have moved it.'

Will squints at the sky. 'The sun appears to be going down over there – although I wouldn't trust it not to change its mind at the last moment. If it continues in the same direction, that means we know which way is west.'

'Great!' I say with enthusiasm, adding more uncertainly, 'How does that help us? Is the village due west from here?'

He grins. 'You've put your finger on the problem. It's definitely west of somewhere, but I have no idea where. That's my bright suggestion down the drain. It's your turn. Can't you retrace our tracks from this morning? There's bound to be a trail of pastry crumbs.'

'Wouldn't the birds have eaten them by now?'

'I don't know,' he says. 'Do birds eat cake? I thought they lived on berries and worms.'

'London birds eat cake. I've seen them hanging around picnickers in the park, finishing their sandwiches and biscuits and anything else they can get their beaks on. I don't suppose country birds are any fussier.'

'There's nothing for it,' he says. 'One of us will have to pick a direction and see where it takes us. I'd prefer it to be you. If it goes wrong, I'd prefer to blame you than have you blame me.'

'Don't you have a sixth sense of where your car is?' I say. 'You seem very attached to it. Listen closely. It may be calling to you.'

He tips his head on one side. 'Either it's asleep, or it's got fed up waiting for us and headed home.'

'It's this way!' I say with false confidence, pointing to a narrow track.

'Are you sure?'

'Not in the least. But it's either that or going back to the fair.'

We follow the track for half a mile without any sign of the village.

'We'll give it five more minutes, then it's your turn to choose a direction,' I tell Will.

'Fine, but I don't think I'll need to. I have a good feeling.'

'Is the car calling to you?'

'You misunderstand the nature of my relationship with that car,' he says.

'You don't love it beyond sense or reason?'

'Oh, that! You may be right.'

'I've never considered keeping a car in London,' I say. 'The public transport is so good, and then there's the congestion tax.'

'I don't keep a car in London,' he says. 'This is a rental car. I thought you realised that.'

'A rental car? Like mine?'

'Not exactly like yours,' he says. 'My car goes.'

'Fair enough. But my car went fine until it didn't. How was I to know it was possessed of evil intent? The rental agent didn't issue me with a bell, book and candle and a handbook for performing an exorcism.'

'That's true,' he says. 'But the name of the company ought to have tipped you off. *Econowheels!* It doesn't exactly inspire you with confidence.'

'On the contrary,' I say. 'It exudes solid, reliable efficiency, combined with laudable thrift. Essential in these difficult economic times.'

'Personally, I like a car I can drive for more than thirty miles before it packs up.'

'Each to his own. So, your sports car doesn't belong to you? I had an image of you zooming down from London, forcing all the pedestrians to leap into hedges as you passed, while you yelled, 'Poop, poop!"

'I'm sorry to disappoint you,' he says. 'But I'm not Mr Toad.'

'It must be costing you quite a bit.'

'An allowable extravagance,' he says. 'I'm not taking a holiday this year. I was supposed to be going to Greece, but that didn't work out. I'm treating this assignment as my annual holiday, so I thought I'd splash out.'

'Honeywell is quite a change from Greece,' I say. 'What made you change your plans?'

He doesn't answer, and I glance at him to see his face has settled into a masklike expression.

'I'm sorry,' I apologise. 'It's none of my business.'

He shrugs. 'It's fine. I was going there with my girlfriend Melissa, but we broke up about six months ago. We'd already booked the holiday, so she went with her new boyfriend instead.'

'Ouch!' I say sympathetically. 'How long have they been together?'

'About seven months.'

It takes me a moment to digest this. 'Ouch!' I say again. 'I'm sorry I asked.'

'No, it's fine. At least they had the decency to refund my deposit, so I decided to use it for something fun.'

'That's a good idea. A red sports car may not be my idea of fun, but we're all different. I hope it's everything you ever dreamed of.'

'And more!' he says. 'It's a real babe magnet.'

'Is that right? I've seen you driving around the village, but I've never noticed anyone in the passenger seat. Do you make them lie down on the back seat and hide until you're out of view?'

'No, but that's a great idea. Anyway, how can you say you've never seen anyone in the passenger seat? I drove a beautiful woman through the village only this very morning.'

I make a gagging sound, and he laughs. 'I'm winding you up. And I don't actually refer to women as babes.'

'I should hope not.'

'We've established what I do for fun,' he says. 'I drive fast cars around the countryside to fulfil my childhood Wind in the Willows fantasies. How about you? What constitutes your idea of fun? It obviously isn't driving a functioning car, so what is it? What makes Olivia Sullivan tick?'

I try to answer lightly. 'You know what I do for fun. I look after animals, and I serve annoying customers in the bakery.'

'You've only been doing that for a week,' he points out. 'What did you do until now?'

'I've been busy with work.'

'You said you worked regular hours,' he reminds me.

'What are you, a high court judge?'

He looks surprised. 'I'm sorry. I didn't mean to upset you.'

'I know you didn't. I'm sorry if I over reacted. It's a touchy subject, and I'd rather not talk about it now.'

'No problem.'

We walk in silence for a few more minutes. Is he angry? Is he upset? I can't tell, and my entire body is tensing up in response. It's a familiar feeling and one I'd hoped not to have to feel again. This silence is worse than anything.

'Will,' I say hesitantly.

I'm surprised to see his answering smile. 'Yes?'

'I'm sorry I snapped at you. I was out of order.'

'You had a perfect right not to answer,' he says. 'What you do in your spare time is your own business. You don't have to tell me just because I asked. I have a pretty good idea what it is, anyway.'

'You do?'

'Yes. You teach monkeys to water ski.'

The knot in my stomach unclenches. He doesn't look angry, more amused.

'Close, but no cigar,' I say. 'I'm actually a part-time snake-charmer.'

I see his instinctive flinch and laugh. 'I've taken my preliminary certificate, and I'm almost ready for the advanced one.'

'No details, please!' he says in a faint voice.

'But you asked,' I say. 'And I rudely cut you off. Now I'm making it up to you with a full and frank description of my course. First, we learned how to hypnotise a tiny garden snake by singing it a special lullaby. After that, we moved on to garter snakes. We taught them how to retrieve small objects from our bags. Then it was onto the medium-sized snakes. They were far more difficult.

But we eventually trained them to arrange themselves to spell different words.'

'I'm sure you were an apt student,' he says. 'But you should know I'll have nightmares tonight after this conversation.'

'I can't imagine why. Anyway, having passed my level one snake-handling exams with flying colours, I'm planning to tackle level two. It will take an enormous amount of work, but it will be worth it. You can come and watch the final exam if you like.'

He turns pale. 'How much would it cost to persuade you to give me the wrong date?'

'Why would I do that? You'll love it. First, our snakes have to navigate an intricate maze. After that, it's the dance off. They have five minutes to perform the rumba, the tango, and contemporary freestyle.'

'No jazz?' he enquires.

'It used to be on the curriculum, but the trainers felt it wasn't taxing enough. The snakes were simply phoning it in because they knew no one could tell the difference. It's just like playing it. All you have to do is produce a jumble of notes and claim it's improvisational jazz.'

'Shows what a lot you know about jazz music,' he says.

'I know it's cheating when it comes to snake dancing,' I say. 'Don't tell me you're a jazz aficionado?'

'I've been to the occasional concert,' he admits. 'Thankfully, I've never seen a snake there.'

'That's because they're at the bar, downing snake bites.'

He gives a shout of laughter. 'You win! I wouldn't –'

He breaks off and points. 'Would you believe it?'

'What?' I stop dead too. 'Is that …?'

'It must be,' he says. 'Isn't that always the way? As soon as you stop looking for something, it appears right in front of you.'

'That also happens when you bring a map,' I say, speeding up to keep pace with him.

He isn't listening. 'It's beautiful. What a magnificent setting!'

'Master Twyford knew what he was doing when he built it,' I agree.

'Master who?' says Will. 'Oh, him! He most certainly did.'

Chapter Nineteen

The path drops steeply in front of us, and we follow it down to where the mill stands by the stream, bathed in the early evening sunlight. It couldn't have found itself a more perfect setting, surrounded by trees and hidden from view until the very moment passers-by stumble across it. I wouldn't be surprised to hear it only appears on sunny evenings, or in the depths of winter when the moon is full and the owls set out on their nightly hunting sprees.

The mill seems to have stood there for so long that it's become a part of the scenery. It appears to have grown out of the surrounding landscape, rather than having been built. The wooden paddle is intact and looks as though it could move at any moment. But the stream flows past and around it without it appearing to notice. It's a mill in retirement, determined not to be sucked back into the workaday world.

'I'm so glad we found it,' I say, dropping my bag on the bank of the stream and sitting down. 'You'll know where to look for it when you come back.'

Will opens his bag and pulls out his camera. 'Come back?'

'I thought you wanted to get a picture of it in the sunshine.'

'I did, but this is even better. Look at that sky.' He gestures to where the setting sun has turned a lilac bank of cloud into flame.

'Don't the publishers tell you exactly what they want?'

He screws a lens onto the camera. 'Sometimes. But this brief was fairly generic.'

I pull out my phone. 'I want a picture too. It won't be as good as yours, but my phone camera isn't too bad.'

'I'll take one especially for you,' he says. 'It's the least I can do after dragging you all over the countryside today.'

'I've had a great time. I'd love you to take a photograph for me, but I'll take one of my own too. I want to remember today through my own eyes as well as yours.'

He takes a few steps backwards. 'I'll take a couple of preliminary shots to test the light. Do you mind if I use you for scale?'

'As long as I don't end up in the book. I've told you. I look awful in photographs. No one has ever taken a good picture of me. And don't tell me that's because you've never taken one of me. I've heard it all before.'

'I wouldn't dream of saying anything of the kind,' he says. 'I'm perfectly willing to accept that every image anyone has ever taken of you is hideous.'

I laugh. 'Except for the picture that man drew of us at the fair. I liked that.'

'So did I. From now on, you should stick to having your caricature drawn and avoid all cameras for fear of breaking them. In the meantime, I'll take a couple with you in them to assess the composition. You don't have to look at the camera. You can turn your back if you like. I need a figure. Anything would do – a deer, a fox, a badger. As there don't seem to be any of those around at the moment, I'll have to make do with you.'

I gaze out over the water, feeling self-conscious. It's one thing to accept I look horrible in photos, despite the photographer's best efforts. It's another to know Will is taking pictures of me, secretly expecting them to turn out wonderfully so he can demonstrate his superiority with a camera. He'll have a shock when he sees them later, but there's no use trying to persuade him. He'll have to find out for himself.

'That's great,' he says a couple of minutes later. 'I'd like to get some from the far side of the stream. I want to catch the way the evening sun strikes the grey stones. Are you coming?'

'I'll stay here and guard the picnic and the rest of your camera equipment,' I say. 'Take your time. I'm enjoying the break.'

He disappears around the bend in the stream. He reappears a minute later on the far bank and starts to photograph the mill from different angles. I watch him for a while. It's interesting to see this side of him, no longer light-hearted and full of jokes, but serious, absorbed, completely lost in what he's doing.

After a while, I stop looking at him and become lost in my own thoughts. I don't know why I've been feeling the need to rush back to London so quickly. There's nothing for me there. It's strange to think I've spent nearly a decade of my life in the city and left no lasting impression. I've made very few friends, built nothing, and had my confidence ground down by staying in a relationship I should have known a long time ago was wrong for me. I can't blame Charlie for everything. I saw very early that it was his way or nothing, and I should have got out then. I'm not sure why I didn't.

He was so supportive after my parents died, and I clung on to that. I had no wider family in the area, and I was grateful when Charlie took on the role of being my support, my guide, and my rock. I hardly noticed when that morphed into him becoming my mentor, the person who always knew better than me and was sure of the direction I should take. By the time I emerged from the emotional vacuum into which I'd been flung when my parents died, Charlie and I had settled into a pattern, and it was less exhausting to accept it than break out of it.

I'm not going back to him. I wasn't sure of that when I left London, but after a couple of weeks in Honeywell, things have become clear. Charlie may be right for someone, but that person isn't me. It's time for me to take responsibility for myself and pick up the reins of my life that I dropped when my world fell apart. I'll be turning thirty next year, and now seems as good a time as any to stop and take stock. I don't want to reach Mrs Ogilvie's age and realise I'm still contracting out my life and my decisions to someone else.

She's half a century ahead of me, which seems like forever. For all I know, she may wake up each day wondering where those fifty years went, and what happened to that thirty-year-old woman who looked forward to her life with such hope. I hope not. I hope she looks back and is happy with the choices she made. I hope I'll be able to do that too when I'm her age. But that won't happen if I continue to allow other people to tell me what to do.

I'm so grateful to Isabella for finding a way to stop me in my tracks and keep me in Honeywell for a while. I'll never know how she knew what I needed. But somehow, she did. In her usual impulsive way, she reacted without stopping to consider all the things that could go wrong. Of all the people in the world I could have met on the day my car broke down, I'm so lucky I met her. And Will too. He was the catalyst, and I'm grateful to him for that.

His voice breaks into my musings. 'I'm pretty much done here. Would you like to stay here for a while longer or try to find the car?'

'It's so beautiful here, so calm and peaceful,' I say. 'I feel as though I could stay all night. But perhaps we'd better try to get back to Harfield. Do you have any idea where it is?'

'I'm pretty sure it's over there,' he says, pointing. 'Do you see those roofs and the church spire? That looks like Harfield. It also makes sense when I think about the direction we were supposed to take to get to the mill this morning. When we started along the path behind the church, we should have taken the right-hand fork rather than the left. That would have brought us almost directly to the mill. We couldn't see it from the village because it's in this hollow. Instead, we took the left hand fork and ended up somewhere completely different.'

'I'm glad we took the wrong turning,' I say. 'Otherwise, we wouldn't have found the fair, and I've had a wonderful day. And it all worked out in the end. We found the mill, and you got your pictures. With any luck, we may even locate the car again before dark.'

He zips his camera into its bag and slings it over his shoulder. 'I agree. It's been a lot of fun. Thanks for coming with me, Olivia. I hope you have enough energy to walk back to the village. I'd offer to fetch the car and attempt to drive across country to you, but I'm not convinced I'd ever find you again if I did.'

'We should stay together,' I say, following him across the grass to the stony track. 'There's no guarantee your car will be there, even if we do find Harfield. Remember what the blacksmith told us about the gangs of marauding thieves stealing carts from the surrounding villages?'

'If it isn't there, we'll have to take the mediaeval equivalent of an Uber, whatever that turns out to be.'

'It depends on your income,' I say. 'If you're wealthy, you send a carrier pigeon ahead, and your carriage will be waiting for you when you get to the village. If not, you have to use Dial a Donkey and hope for the best.'

'Both of those sound fun,' he says. 'But I can see the village street now, and my car seems to have successfully evaded the bands of thieves. Unless you're dead set on that donkey, how about I drive you home? Maybe we can stop for dinner somewhere on the way. It's a long time since we ate that pie.'

Chapter Twenty

Isabella greets me eagerly the following morning. 'How did it go?'

'It was great,' I say. 'We had the most amazing day.'

'I knew you would! I'm so glad you two have got together.'

'Got together?' I say. 'What are you talking about? I went to keep him company while he took some photographs, that's all.'

Her face falls. 'I thought you had an amazing day.'

I open the till and check we have enough change to start the day. 'We did. But people can have a wonderful time without it meaning anything more than that. Will and I are just friends. That's all we'll ever be.'

'I don't see why. He's a great guy.'

'He is,' I say. 'And he's single. As are you. Which makes you perfect for each other.'

She pours us both a cup of coffee. 'That's ridiculous. Plenty of people are single. It doesn't mean I have to get together with them just because I'm single too.'

'Exactly,' I say.

She laughs. 'Point taken. But I didn't think you'd be good together because you're both single, although that obviously makes it a lot easier. I thought it because you get along so well.'

'As do you,' I point out.

'But I've already told you I'm not interested in him.'

'And now I'm telling you that neither am I. Poor Will. How is he going to cope?'

The doorbell jangles, and I spin around to see who it is. It would be just my luck for Will to be standing there, having overheard my last comment. But it's a woman I haven't seen before.

'Hello, Mrs Carson,' says Isabella.

The woman beams at her. 'How are you today, my dear?'

'Very well, thanks,' says Isabella. 'How's Daisy?'

The name Carson rings a bell. This must be Lily's mother. She catches sight of me and beams again.

'You must be Olivia! It's lovely to meet you. Lily told me you're kindly helping out while she's away. Daisy is much better, thank you, Isabella. I'm about to pop over to see how she and Lily are doing after their first night at home. I thought I'd pick up a little something to take with me. What do you suggest?'

'As her godmother, I can tell you Daisy loves our brownies,' says Isabella. 'So does Lily. I'd better give you a boxful in case Jack is around too.'

'I think I'll take one of your apple turnovers,' says Mrs Carson. 'Daisy loves those. She gets the cream everywhere, but I always clean her up before Lily gets home, so she's none the wiser.'

'Daisy is lucky to have a godmother and grandmother who understand her so well,' says Isabella.

'And how are you settling into Honeywell?' Mrs Carson asks me. 'Please let me know if there's anything you need.'

'I'm not exactly settling in,' I say with a glance at Isabella. 'I'm only here temporarily. But thank you for the offer.'

'You're staying with Eleanor Marsh, aren't you?'

'That's right,' I say. 'How did you know?'

'Angela knows everyone in this village,' says Isabella. 'How long have you and Martin lived here?'

'Thirty-five years,' says Mrs Carson. 'I was expecting Ben when we moved in, and the sale was delayed several times. The lease on our rental house was running out, and I told Martin I half expected to give birth in a tent. But everything turned out for the best. We moved in a few weeks before he was born, and we've been there ever since.'

'I can't imagine living anywhere for that long,' I say. 'It sounds rather nice. I was talking to Mrs Ogilvie the other day, and she told me she'd been in the village for seventy-five years.'

'Is that right?' she says. 'How marvellous! I know her a little, but she keeps herself to herself. I was pleased when I heard she'd started coming to the bakery more regularly. It must be good for her to see different people and have a bit of a chat.'

'Olivia wants to throw her a party,' says Isabella. 'She's turning eighty in August, and she has nothing planned.'

'What a lovely idea!' says Mrs Carson. 'I'm sure Mrs Ogilvie will be delighted.'

'Isabella and I aren't quite so sure,' I say. 'What if she doesn't like surprises? What if she doesn't like parties?'

'Everyone likes parties,' she says. 'Where were you thinking of holding it?'

'At the bakery.'

She frowns. 'Isn't that rather small? You can only seat fifteen people.'

'I don't think that matters,' says Isabella. 'She may not know fifteen people.'

'Planning it is proving more difficult than I thought,' I tell Mrs Carson. 'It's supposed to be a surprise party, so I can hardly ask Mrs Ogilvie for a list of guests. But I don't know anyone in the village, so I'm not sure where to begin.'

'Leave that to me!' she says. 'I can find out who her friends are and invite them if you like.'

'That would be wonderful,' I say. 'If you're sure you don't mind.'

'Not in the least. I'd enjoy it. It will give me the chance to catch up with people I don't see regularly. I'll make a start this afternoon. What were you planning to do about food?'

Isabella waves towards the counter. 'We can manage sandwiches and sausage rolls and baked goods. Abby has offered to make a birthday cake for Mrs Ogilvie and Bernie. It seems they share a birthday, so we can make it a joint celebration.'

'As long as it isn't a pirate ship,' says Mrs Carson, and they both laugh.

'I must hear that story sometime,' I say. 'Everyone seems to know it but me.'

The doorbell jangles again, and Will walks in. Isabella gives me a meaningful look, which I ignore.

'Hi, Will.' I say. 'What can we get for you?'

'One of your chicken pies, please. I'm off to Overton today to photograph the inside of a Norman church. Hello, Mrs Carson. How are you?'

'I'm very well,' she says. 'It's lovely to see you again, Will.'

She lowers her voice and addresses me. 'Does he know about the *p a r t y*?'

'He does,' says Will, his eyes alight with laughter. 'He can also spell.'

She laughs. 'I'm sorry. I'm so used to being with my granddaughter. We have to spell out all sorts of things now she understands words like cake and ice cream and bath and bed.'

'It's a great idea,' I say. 'Abby and I have to do that when Isabella's around or she discovers the fresh batches of cakes before the customers can get near them.'

'The joke's on you,' says Isabella. 'I only pretend not to understand you.'

'I must be going,' says Mrs Carson. 'I'll let you know how I get on with the guest list.'

She gives us all a cheerful wave and trots out.

'Mrs Carson seems very nice,' I say.

'She is,' says Isabella. 'She's one of those people who can only see the good in others. The strange thing is, it seems to make everyone around her nicer. Even me!'

'If you weren't already perfect,' I say.

'That's true. But you know what I mean.'

'Very rarely,' I say. 'Just the chicken pie, Will?'

He looks at the counter. 'Perhaps I'll take one of your *c o o k i e s* as well.'

Isabella picks up an empty pallet. 'I've already told you that trick doesn't work with me. Anyway, I sold the last cupcake this morning, so you'll have to make do with a cookie instead!'

She gives him a satisfied smile and marches out to the kitchen.

Will watches her go. 'Do you think she's really illiterate?'

'She's running a business fairly successfully,' I say. 'I expect she'll be fine.'

I hand him the two paper bags. 'Are you sure I can't get you anything else?'

'I'm good for now, thanks.'

He pauses by the door. 'Am I officially allowed to know about the *p a r t y*?'

'The cat seems to be out of the bag now,' I say. 'And it wouldn't be a smart move to keep the official photographer in the dark about the arrangements.'

'That's what I wanted to talk to you about,' he says. 'I wasn't sure what to give Mrs Ogilvie for a birthday present.'

'You're taking the photographs. Isn't that her gift?'

'In doing that as a favour for you,' he says. 'For all I know, Mrs Ogilvie may be like you and hate having her picture taken.'

'I'm starting to wish I hadn't told you that. But I haven't thought about a present. I suppose we ought to get her something. I have no idea what.'

'I was thinking about it last night,' he says. 'And I remembered how much she loves that dog of hers. Do you think she'd like a professional portrait of him?'

'That's a wonderful idea!'

'I'm glad you like it,' he says. 'But I can't work out how to take the pictures without her knowing. The pair of them are always together.'

'That's true. It's one thing to grab your phone and take a quick picture of Bernie. It's another to pull out that huge camera of yours and start clicking away. She'd be bound to suspect something.'

'That's what I thought,' he says. 'It will take some thinking about. I'll need your help if you're up for it.'

'I'll help in any way I can,' I say. 'But I know nothing about photography.'

'Not to take the actual picture. But you could be useful in diverting her attention.'

Isabella returns carrying a fresh palette of loaves. 'Diverting whose attention? Not mine?'

'Not this time,' he says. 'Although I wish it were. I have a feeling it would be exceptionally easy.'

'I'd only have to dance around, waving a cake,' I say. 'You'd get as many pictures as you wanted in no time.'

'I'm sorry,' says Isabella. 'You lost me at waving a cake. What are we talking about?'

'What we're giving Mrs Ogilvie for her birthday,' I say. 'Will suggested a portrait of Bernie, but we can't think how to separate him from Mrs Ogilvie without her suspecting.'

'You could try that cake thing,' she says.

'And if that doesn't work?' says Will.

She bites her lip. 'I'm not sure. But I expect I'll come up with lots of good ideas if you give me a day or two.'

'Great,' he says. 'I'll leave it to you two to form a plan. I should get going.'

He hands me a large envelope. 'I've taken a picture of this for my records, but I thought you should have the original.'

'What is it?' asks Isabella when he's left.

'I have no idea.'

'Are you sure?' she says. 'It looks official. Did you and he get married while you were out yesterday?'

'I think I'd remember something like that.'

'Not necessarily,' she says. 'It's the kind of thing that could slip anyone's mind if they were busy. If it isn't a marriage certificate, what is it? Your letter from Hogwarts? An invitation from NASA to head up their next space mission?'

I undo the clasp and ease back the flap. A piece of paper slides out. It's the picture Will and I had done at the fair.

'Let me see!' urges Isabella. She turns over the paper and bursts out laughing. 'This is wonderful! Where did it come from?'

'It's a long story,' I say. 'Will and I ended up at a mediaeval fair yesterday afternoon. There was an artist there doing caricatures. He asked us how we met, and this is what he came up with.'

'We'll have to frame it,' she says. 'We'll put it up behind the counter so everyone can see.'

I remove it from her grasp. 'We'll do nothing of the kind.'

'But it's amazing.' She studies the picture more carefully. 'It's exactly like you. It's a good picture of Will too. Doesn't he look dashing on that white charger?'

'Are you changing your mind about him now you've seen him in a whole different light?'

'I wavered for a moment,' she says. 'But the maiden he's rescuing isn't me. It's you. Look at you, sitting on the grassy bank, making a daisy chain. "He loves me, he loves me not, he loves me …"'

'Whereas in real life, I was setting off to save myself,' I say.

'But look at him in his shiny suit of armour,' she says. 'He wants to rescue you.'

'Not everyone wants to be rescued,' I say rather tartly.

'But it's nice to have friends who look out for you. You can save him the next time, if you like. Anyway, it's a lovely picture.'

'I like my dress,' I say. 'It looks like a nightmare to wash, but it's beautiful.'

'It is,' she agrees. 'That embroidered bodice is gorgeous. I expect mediaeval peasants spent most of their money on dry-cleaning.'

'I'm not a peasant,' I say. 'If I were, a knight would never have stopped for me.'

'Will might,' she says.

'He'd be a rubbish knight if he did. He'd get drummed out of the guild.'

'It's a lovely picture,' she says. 'If you won't hang it in the bakery, frame it and hang it in your room. I told you it was looking rather bare. Now you have something personal to put on the wall. I'm willing to bet you'll have plenty more before you leave Honeywell.'

Chapter Twenty-One

Mrs Carson appears the following morning looking pleased with herself.

'I've been talking to Mavis, and she's helped me to make a long list of people to invite,' she announces as she bursts into the bakery.

'Hello, Mrs Carson,' I say. 'Who's Mavis?'

She looks surprised. 'I thought everyone knew Mavis Sotherby. You must have met her by now.'

'I don't think so. Most customers don't tell me their name. They just tell me what they want.'

'Oh, Mavis would have introduced herself,' she says. 'She'd want to find out everything about you. She has a mind like a computer hard drive!'

'Is that so?' I say, amused. 'I didn't realise you were interested in technology.'

'I go to her class each week,' she says. 'She teaches us all about files and folders and Office, and I don't know what. What that woman doesn't know about computers isn't worth knowing.'

'I wish she'd teach me how to install my new book-keeping program,' says Isabella, emerging from the office with her arms full of files. 'I've seen our accountant, and he insists we move to something more standardised. Apparently, this is the latest program, and it will practically do my books for me. I'm all for that, but it's no good if it won't install.'

'Would you like me to have a look at it for you?' says Mrs Carson. 'We learned all about installing programmes last week.'

Isabella looks alarmed. 'I'm fine, thanks. You have enough to do without worrying about our computing system.'

'If you're sure,' says Mrs Carson. 'But you only have to say the word, and I'll ask Mavis to pop in and sort you out. She'll have it up and running for you in minutes. She'll do the accounts too, if you ask her nicely.'

Isabella looks even more alarmed. 'I'm sure I'll be fine.'

'Mrs Carson says she's already sorted out the guest list for the party,' I tell her.

'Aren't you a marvel?' says Isabella. 'How did you manage that?'

'It was simple,' says Mrs Carson. 'I told Mavis all about it at last night at our class. She talked to the members and told them about the plan. It's surprising how many of them know Mrs Ogilvie, at least by sight. Mavis looked through the list of previous attendees and promised to call them too.'

'I hope Mrs Ogilvie isn't one of them,' I say.

'We're safe there,' says Isabella. 'Can you imagine her in a computing class? She'd insist on bringing Bernie, and he'd have all the wires tangled up before Mavis could blink.'

'Pets aren't allowed,' says Mrs Carson. 'Mavis is very strict on that point.'

'There you go,' says Isabella. 'So, all we have to worry about is one of the members mentioning the party to Mrs Ogilvie.'

'Mavis swore us all to secrecy,' says Mrs Carson. 'I'm sure no one would want to spoil the surprise.'

'With any luck, most of them will have forgotten all about it by next week,' says Isabella.

Mrs Carson gives her a reproving look. 'That's not very nice, dear. Several members of the class may be elderly, but there's nothing wrong with their memories. I think it's admirable they're getting out there and learning new technologies. Mr Pollard learned to put his digital photos into a zip file last night and attach them to an email to his daughter in Hong Kong. We all gave him a round of applause when we saw it had been delivered.'

'You're quite right,' says Isabella. 'I shouldn't be making jokes about the Silver Surfers. I'm the one who can't install this program. Maybe I should ask Mr Pollard to give me a hand.'

'The important thing is that we have some guests,' I say. 'I was beginning to think it would be just us and Mrs Ogilvie, which wouldn't have been the greatest surprise party.'

'Don't worry about that,' says Mrs Carson. 'Everyone thought it was a wonderful idea. There may be too many people to fit into the bakery, but Mavis and I have had some ideas about that.'

'We'll need rough numbers soon,' I say. 'I need to know how many we're catering for.'

'I'll let you know in good time,' promises Mrs Carson. 'I must go now. I promised Lily I'd watch little Daisy this morning while Lily gets her hair cut. It will do her good to get out on her own for a while. Maybe she'll pop in here for some lunch when she's done. Tell her there's no need to rush home. Daisy and I will be pressing flowers this afternoon.'

'Can I send something for your elevenses?' says Isabella. 'On the house, naturally.'

'I wouldn't dream of it,' says Mrs Carson, pulling out her purse. 'What would your accountant say if he found out you were giving away the stock for free? Now, what would Daisy like?'

She leaves a few minutes later, clutching a box filled with goodies.

'I wish my grandmother had been like that,' says Isabella. 'Mine always told me little girls should be seen and not heard. And not seen too much, either.'

'You must have been the ideal granddaughter for her,' I say. 'Tidy, polite, restrained, always happy with a piece of embroidery …'

'I wouldn't know one end of an embroidery needle from another,' she says. 'Although I was planning to do my needlewoman badge when I was a girl guide.'

'What were you going to sew?'

'A cushion or something? I'm not sure what people make nowadays. But my friend Suzanne was taking hers, and I didn't want to be left out. I wonder if they offer an accountancy badge? That should be doable with a little effort. I should check whether Honeywell still has a guide troupe. It may not be too late.'

'They won't know what's hit them,' I say. 'In the meantime, how about working towards your party planner's badge? I could do with some help. I haven't organised anything like this before.'

'You'll be fine,' she says. 'Angela is doing the guest list, Will is doing the photography, and Abby will end up doing most of the food. All you have to do is make a few banners, buy some balloons, and organise a few games.'

'Games? It's an eightieth birthday party!'

'So what?' she says. 'I'd want games at my eightieth party.'

'Like what? I can't imagine sending everyone off to play hide-and-seek around the bakery or organising a game of musical rocking chairs. And before you suggest a pie-eating competition, I'd have to buy in a ton of indigestion tablets. Besides, you'd almost definitely win, which wouldn't be fair.'

'Fine,' she says, 'But I'm having that for my eightieth. Not only pies. Sausage rolls and doughnuts too.'

'We still have to think how to get this picture of Bernie,' I say. 'Mrs Ogilvie is always with him. Do you have any good ideas?'

'For kidnapping her? I'm sure I can come up with some.'

'I was thinking of something less drastic,' I say.

'Then, no!'

'I expect Will can think of something,' I say. 'We only need Bernie for a couple of minutes.'

'Doesn't that depend on what you plan to do with him?' she says. 'What sort of picture does Will have in mind? Is he planning an action shot or does he prefer the stiff, royal type of portrait, with Bernie in a ruff, looking annoyed?'

'Who wouldn't look annoyed if they had to wear a ruff? I'm leaving it up to Will. He's the expert.'

'Does he do many portraits?' she asks.

'I don't know. I haven't asked him much about his job. But how different can it be from photographing a building or a person? Doesn't the camera do most of the work?'

'Don't ask me,' she says. 'All the pictures I take with my phone come out blurred.'

'That's because you never stand still long enough.'

'Bernie won't stand still for long either,' she points out. 'At least, not as long as the Eiffel Tower or the Empire State Building.'

'That's Will's problem,' I say. 'This was his idea. I'm only his helper.'

'He'll probably want you to dress up as something bizarre to distract Mrs Ogilvie,' she says.

'He'd better not. But if he does, you can help him. I suspect you'd enjoy dressing up as an elf or a plumber.'

'What a strange idea you have of me,' she says. 'Anyway, this party is your thing, so you're the one who has to organise it. Abby and I are just providing the food and the premises. We're far too busy for anything else.'

Chapter Twenty-Two

Lily comes into the bakery the following morning with her daughter. It's the first time I've met Daisy, and I'm amused to see she's a tiny replica of her mother – small and slight, with straight fair hair and dimples.

'This is my friend Olivia,' says Lily when she sees me. 'Olivia, I'd like you to meet my daughter.'

She says it with such obvious pride that I smile. I'd feel exactly the same way if I had a mini-me as cute as Daisy. She's wearing a blue pinafore dress with a white daisy print, and a matching Alice headband.

'It's lovely to meet you,' I say, coming around the counter and bending down to talk to her.

Daisy sticks her thumb in her mouth and looks up at me with huge blue eyes.

'Can you say hello to Olivia?' prompts Lily.

Daisy removes her thumb and stares up at me. 'No.'

'I'm sorry,' says Lily. 'She'll warm up to you when she knows you better. She isn't good with strangers.'

'That's fine,' I say. 'I like a woman with a mind of her own.'

'Would you like a babyccino?' I ask Daisy. Isabella has taught me how to make those, so I imagine Daisy has come across them before.

She removes her thumb again and beams at me. 'Yiss!'

'Yes, please,' Lily corrects her. 'You couldn't have offered her anything she'd like better, Olivia. Mum always buys her one when they come in. They sit at that table over there with their drinks and chat about everything that's going on. At least, Mum does. She's a great talker. And Daisy says, "Yiss," and "No," and occasionally, 'More!"'

'It sounds as though she's developed all the most important vocabulary,' I say. 'I hear she can also say, "Whizzy."'

Daisy's eyes light up. 'Whizzy?'

'She'll be back in a few minutes,' says Lily, carrying her over to the nearest table.

'She's adorable,' I say. 'I don't know much about young children. I'm more used to kittens and puppies. She seems pretty healthy now.'

'She's much better,' says Lily. 'She gets tired a little earlier than usual, but she's picking up fast. Children bounce back far more quickly than we do. I'm exhausted from spending a week on a camp bed in the hospital. The nurses came around every couple of hours to take Daisy's temperature. She slept through the whole thing, but I didn't.'

'I remember that from when I had my appendix taken out a few years ago,' I say. 'I used to roll over and groan and try to hide under the pillow, but the nurse wasn't having any of it. She shone the torch on my face until I allowed her to take my temperature and check my pulse. I'm not sure which of us was more relieved when the doctor said I could go home.'

'I know how pleased I was,' says Lily, taking the two mugs I hand her – one adult-sized mug, and one tiny mug with pink rosebuds that match the pink marshmallow I've balanced on the saucer.

She hands the smaller one to Daisy. 'Remember to sit up straight and hold your cup carefully, just like Grandma showed you.'

Daisy buries her face in the mug, emerging a second later with foam around her mouth and a dab of chocolate powder on her nose.

Lily picks up a napkin and wipes her face. 'Good try. We'll have you trained in no time.'

Daisy snatches Lily's spoon and bangs it on the table.

'Careful with that!' says Lily, taking it away from her.

Daisy is about to protest when the shop door opens and Isabella walks in.

'Whizzy!' shouts Daisy.

'Dizzy!' says Isabella, catching her up in her arms and swinging her into an enormous hug.

'I've asked you not to call her that,' says Lily, but without much hope.

'She's my goddaughter,' says Isabella. 'All godmothers have pet names for their godchildren.'

'But she's starting to call herself that too,' says Lily. 'One of the doctors at the hospital was quite alarmed when she said it last week. They made her sit down.'

Isabella laughs. 'I should teach her to say something useful like, "Low blood sugar!"'

She puts Daisy back in her chair and sits next to her. 'Are you hungry?'

'Yiss!' says Daisy joyfully.

'It's almost lunchtime,' says Lily. 'Grandma is making us toasted sandwiches. We only popped in to give Olivia this note.' She hands me an envelope.

'Is it from Will?' says Isabella, and I'm annoyed to feel myself flush.

'It's from Mum,' says Lily. 'Were you expecting something from Will?'

'Of course not,' I say.

She and Isabella exchange the briefest of glances as I tear open the envelope and scan the contents.

'That's kind of your mother,' I tell Lily. 'Can you tell her I'd be delighted?'

'Delighted about what?' says Isabella.

'Mum's invited Olivia and Will to tea on Wednesday,' says Lily, and she and Isabella exchange another quick look.

'Only because we're trying to photograph Bernie,' I say before Isabella can say anything.

'Mum's invited Mrs Ogilvie too,' explains Lily. 'She thought it would be an excellent opportunity for Will to be around Bernie without raising Mrs Ogilvie's suspicions.'

'I'm the decoy,' I say. 'My job is to distract Mrs Ogilvie so Will can get a picture of Bernie.'

'She could have asked me,' grumbles Isabella. 'I'm far more distracting than you are, even when I don't mean to be. I'd be bound to trip over something or break a cup or pour tea into someone's lap. It would give Will the perfect opportunity to take as many photos as he wanted.'

'We'll keep you in reserve for next time,' I promise. 'We don't want to bring out the big guns until we need them. Anyway, you're working on Wednesday. It's my day off.'

Isabella grins. 'I'm only teasing. You don't want me playing gooseberry.'

'Time we were going!' says Lily before I can answer. 'See you on Wednesday, Olivia. I'll tell Mum you'll be there.'

She lifts a protesting Daisy off her chair and straps her into her stroller. 'Say goodbye to Olivia and Whizzy, sweetheart.'

'Bye, Whizzy! Bye, Wovy!' shouts Daisy.

We watch them set off down the high street.

'I hope I didn't go too far,' says Isabella as they disappear around the corner.

'You always go too far,' I say. 'But I'm used to it.'

'Good. You turn such a lovely fiery red when I tease you about Will. It matches your hair.'

'Whereas you say the most outrageous things without turning the faintest pink.'

'Long years of practise,' she says. 'You'll get there if you persevere.'

She picks up the mugs. 'I see you've put my training to good use. Daisy loves her babyccinos.'

'I'm not sure she drank much. Most of it went on her face and over the table.'

'As I say, practise is the key,' she says. 'I'm preparing her for the day when she can drink the real thing. It's basic godmother stuff. Anyway, I must get back to the accounts. I've installed the program now, which is a step in the right direction. But the columns keep on jumping around. No wonder Mr Mason stuck to pencil and paper for all those years.'

I don't see Will until Wednesday afternoon. He texts me on Friday to ask whether I'd like to go to Whitfield Castle with him on Saturday, but I have to tell him I'm working. I feel a pang of regret that I have to refuse. I had such a good time with him last Sunday, and I'd love to do it again. But I have no intention of starting anything with him. In which case, it's better not to go out with him too regularly, fun though it might be.

It's nothing personal. I have no intention of starting anything with anyone for a long, long time, if ever. I haven't yet worked out why I stayed so long in a relationship that caused me to lose myself so entirely. Until I've done that, I'm in danger of repeating the whole thing with someone else. On the face of it, Will is nothing like Charlie. But the Charlie I met and fell in love with was nothing like the man he eventually turned out to be. And I didn't see the signs until it was almost too late. Better to stay away from men altogether than to sleepwalk into another disaster.

Anyway, I have no reason to think Will sees me as anything other than a friend. If my first instincts were right, he may be interested in Isabella. It appears she isn't interested in him, but he doesn't know that. And I refuse to be anyone's rebound if I ever reach the stage of considering a new relationship.

I sleep late on Wednesday morning. I no longer wake each morning at daybreak, trying and failing to doze off again. These days, I'm asleep almost as soon as my head hits the pillow, and I don't wake up until my alarm rings. Isabella is convinced it's the Honeywell air. She says she's lived in this area for her entire life and has always slept like a log, so that proves it.

I suspect she would sleep beautifully anywhere. I've never met someone as full of energy and life. She has the enviable quality of being comfortable in her own skin. She's happy with who she is, without being in the slightest conceited or self-satisfied. She enjoys life and all it throws at her, and she loves people.

I can't imagine her ending up with someone like Charlie. She would have pushed back at the first sign of his trying to control her, and he would have backed off. Whether he would have changed is another matter. Probably not. The more I see of people, the more I sense they're unlikely to change in anything but their outward behaviour. By the time they reach their thirties, most people's characters are fixed.

I'm aware that I follow this pattern too. I am who I am, and I have to find a way of coming to terms with that. I can't beat myself up forever for ending up in a relationship like the one I had with Charlie. But I should work out why I did what I did and try to change that pattern before it leads me into permanent disaster.

Chapter Twenty-Three

I arrive at Mrs Carson's house at three o'clock on Wednesday. I almost texted Will to ask whether he wanted to walk over there together but decided against it. I don't want to look as though I'm unable to do anything for myself. And I'd prefer not to give the slightest impression that I think this is a date. I don't know why I'm being so touchy about this. Will hasn't indicated he sees me as anything more than a friend, even though he's had several opportunities to do so.

That evening at the mill could, in retrospect, have been one of them. It was a romantic setting, with the sunset and the ancient building, steeped in the history of centuries past. It was so quiet and secluded that it felt as though we were hundreds of miles away from any other living thing, despite being only half an hour from civilisation. If someone were planning a romantic evening, which we weren't, they'd need to go a long way to beat it.

Instead of which, Will told me I was nothing more than a substitute for a badger or a fox, left me alone while he wandered around taking pictures, and didn't even open the bottle of wine he'd brought. That may have been because we'd already been drinking mead and he was driving. But the point is that he showed no sign of being affected by the romantic setting, which means I have nothing to worry about and no complications ahead of me.

Mr Carson answers the door. He's a jolly-looking man of about sixty with a salt and pepper beard and twinkling grey eyes.

'I'm Martin,' he says. 'And you must be Olivia. My wife's in the back garden. Would you like to use the side gate? It's quicker than going through the house.'

I follow him around the side of the house, where we find Mrs Carson sitting on the patio, chatting with Mrs Ogilvie.

She jumps up when she sees me. 'Olivia! How lovely. Thank you for coming.'

'It was kind of you to invite me,' I say. 'Good afternoon, Mrs Ogilvie.'

I look around the garden. 'Where's Bernie?'

It hadn't occurred to me he might not be here. I hope Mrs Ogilvie hasn't taken him to the vet or left him with the dog groomer for the afternoon. That would shatter all our plans.

Mrs Carson ghosts me a wink. 'He's somewhere at the bottom of the garden, playing with Will. I suggested they had some fun together while Mrs Ogilvie had a rest after her hot walk over here.'

'What a good idea,' I say. 'Shall I see how they're getting on?'

'Why not? Tell Will we're having tea around four o'clock, but I can delay it if he and Bernie are busy.'

I set off down the garden in search of Will. With any luck, he'll have taken several pictures by now, and we can select the best one later. I reach the end of the lawn and see a small shrubbery on one side, hidden from the house. As I expected, Will and Bernie are here. But Will isn't crouching down, snapping away in his best professional photographer manner. He's sitting on the grass, ruefully surveying his camera.

'What happened?' I say.

Bernie rushed over to me and leaps up to lick my face.

'Gently!' I say. 'It's nice to see you too, but I washed my face only this morning.'

Will looks up from his camera. 'I almost had it! He was sitting on that clump of grass, grinning at me. I crawled towards him and was about to take the shot when he noticed me and jumped up. He raced over to lick me, and I dropped the camera. I've broken the lens!'

I take an instinctive step back. 'I'm so sorry, Will. I really am.'

He looks surprised. 'It's fine. It isn't the first time. It's a hazard of the job. It's a little inconvenient because I've left my spare lens at home.'

'Is it insured?'

'All my camera equipment is insured,' he says. 'Are you ok, Olivia? You look quite pale.'

'Do I? I'm upset for you. You must be so annoyed.'

'With Bernie?'

'I suppose so, although it isn't his fault. But it's made things difficult for you. You have every right to be annoyed.'

He looks puzzled. 'I don't see why. It's not the end of the world. I've broken a lens. So what? I have other lenses. I'll fetch the other one later.'

He gets to his feet and snaps his fingers at Bernie, who's trying to dig up the nearest bush. 'Come on, mutt! Mrs Carson won't love you any more if she sees you doing that.'

I follow him back up the garden to where the two women are sitting, deep in conversation.

Will greets them cheerfully. 'Bernie's had a good run around. Now he's ready for a nap, aren't you, old man?'

Bernie promptly collapses at Mrs Ogilvie's feet and starts snoring.

'Isn't he a wonder?' says Mrs Carson. 'You'd almost think he understood what we were saying.'

'He does!' says Mrs Ogilvie. 'My vet says Bernie is the most intelligent animal he's ever come across.'

'That doesn't surprise me,' says Mrs Carson. 'He's a lovely dog. So well-behaved and docile.'

Will and I glance at each other and look hurriedly away. Mrs Ogilvie doesn't appear to notice.

'I'll pop the kettle on, shall I?' says Mrs Carson. 'I'm sure we're all ready for a cup of tea.'

I follow her into the house. 'Can I help you with anything? I brought a box of cakes from the bakery.'

'You didn't need to do that!' says Mrs Carson as though I've trekked across the Antarctic to bring her favourite walrus steaks instead of picking up a few cakes and cookies from my place of work.

'And Will brought us a bottle of wine!' she says. 'The pair of you are spoiling us. I popped it into the fridge to get cold. It's a lovely bottle of sparkling rosé. Just the thing for an afternoon in the garden. So thoughtful of him.'

I'm glad someone's getting use out of the wine. I smile as I remember the glasses of mead we drank. It was an unforgettable experience.

'You look pleased about something,' she says. 'Did Will get some pictures of Bernie?'

I come back down to earth. 'I'm afraid not. He was about to, but Bernie jumped up at him at the last minute, and he dropped his camera. I'm afraid he's broken his lens.'

'How annoying for him,' she says placidly. 'I hope he has another one.'

I'm taken aback by her response. First, Will didn't seem put out, and now Mrs Carson says it's merely annoying. I thought one of them would recognise the gravity of the situation. However, it's not my business if Honeywell inhabitants do things differently.

'Maybe he can pop home in a while and pick up another one,' she suggests.

'That's what he said.'

'Marvellous!' She hands me a plate of scones. 'Would you mind taking that out to the garden? I'll bring the tray of tea things.'

I find Will chatting with Mrs Ogilvie about gardening. I give him a meaningful look as I put the scones on the table.

'Didn't you say you needed to run home for a few minutes to fetch something you'd forgotten?'

He gives me a bland smile. 'I was telling Mrs Ogilvie I'd like to take some pictures of the flower beds, but I don't have the correct lens with me.'

'A macro lens!' Mrs Ogilvie informs me.

'Do you know about photography?' I say, surprised. I half expect her to tell me she used to do it as a child. But she would have been using a Brownie, and I doubt they had macro lenses.

'Will has been telling me all about the different lenses he uses,' she says. 'It's fascinating. My husband used to dabble in photography. He set up a dark room in his shed, and he developed his own pictures. I didn't like the smell, so I didn't help him. I used to send our holiday snaps to Boots, and they sent me back a packet of photographs by return post. Will doesn't even do that. He says it's all on his computer.'

She looks genuinely interested, and I wish I had something intelligent to add to the conversation. I haven't asked Will much about his work. This is partly because I've been avoiding reciprocal questions. But partly it's because I've been too wrapped up in myself and my own troubles to take much interest in what anyone else is doing. I don't even know what his next project is, or where. For all I know, he may be off on assignment to Cairo soon to photograph the pyramids.

Mrs Carson appears with the tea tray. 'Help yourself to scones! I baked them this morning. Did I hear someone mention computers? Were you talking about the Silver Surfers?'

'What's that?' says Mrs Ogilvie.

'Mavis Sotherby organises it,' says Mrs Carson. 'She teaches the older generation how to get the most out of their computers.

It's a wonderful idea. I pop along whenever I can. I've learned all about attachments and files, and I don't know what else! Martin is most impressed. I showed him how to back up his digital photos yesterday, and he said the end times had come.'

'Would you like to attend the classes, Mrs Ogilvie?' asks Will.

'They aren't for people like me,' she says. 'I don't own a computer.'

'Of course, they're for people like you!' exclaims Mrs Carson. 'Everyone should know how to use one. They're an essential part of modern life.'

Mrs Ogilvie doesn't look convinced. 'Aren't they terribly expensive?'

'They can be,' says Will. 'But a basic second-hand laptop doesn't cost much.'

I hope he doesn't push this. I don't know how much money Mrs Ogilvie has. For all I know, she may spend all her spare income on Bernie instead of putting the heating on or eating properly.

'I don't have one either,' I say, taking another scone and spreading it thickly with jam.

'Really?' says Will.

'I had a PC in London. But it was in my flat, and I've moved out.'

He shoots me a quick look but doesn't comment.

'But you have a phone,' Mrs Ogilvie surprises me. 'I've seen you using it to look things up.'

'True. I'd be lost without my phone.'

'And sometimes you're lost with it,' says Will. 'The first time I met Olivia, her car had broken down. She couldn't get any phone connection, so she didn't know where she was.'

'How dreadful!' says Mrs Carson. 'So, that's how you ended up in Honeywell?'

'Pretty much,' I say. 'If Will hadn't been living here for the summer, he'd have given me a lift to somewhere else, and I'd never have met you all.'

'These things are meant to be,' she says. 'I've always thought that.'

'I almost didn't agree to stay,' I say. 'It seemed so ridiculous to arrive out of the blue and end up working here. If this were a Hollywood movie, I'd say it was too far-fetched for words.'

'If this were a Hollywood movie,' says Will, 'you'd have been a criminal running from justice. Or an innocent tourist who gradually became aware of spooky goings on in the village. At first, you'd have thought it was idyllic, but you'd have started to notice strange happenings. No one would be who they seemed. Everyone would have a secret to hide. By the end of the movie, you'd be running for your life through the forest, armed only with a torch with a failing battery. To make matters worse, you'd have absolutely no phone connection!'

'My goodness!' says Mrs Carson. 'You do have a vivid imagination, Will. I'm sure it would have been nothing like that. If Olivia were in a film, she'd be the beautiful heroine in search of adventure. She'd arrive in Honeywell and meet the love of her life. She wouldn't know he was the love of her life to start with. No one ever does. She'd meet three young men and have to choose between them.'

'I hate making choices,' I say. 'Couldn't someone do it for me?'

'Oh, no, my dear! That isn't how it works at all. We all have to choose our own path in life. Isn't that right, Will?'

'I'm sure it is,' he says.

'Who are these men I'm going to meet?' I say.

She gives me a slight smile. 'That isn't for me to say. That's for the scriptwriter.'

'They need to hurry,' I say. 'I'll be leaving Honeywell soon, and I haven't met many people at all.'

'There was the blacksmith,' Will reminds me.

'I'd forgotten him,' I say. 'But I don't somehow see him as the love of my life.'

'Mr Makepeace?' says Mrs Carson, bewildered. 'He's married with five young children.'

'I believe Will is thinking of a different blacksmith,' I say. 'And I can rule him out. That leaves two more men. There was the man in the beer tent. I don't remember much about him, but he served me some of the finest mead in all the land. I'll keep him on the list.'

'Which leaves only one more,' says Will. 'Think hard, Olivia. Didn't you notice anyone jousting or wrestling who filled your girlish heart with unnamed hopes and dreams?'

'The only man I remember was tilting at the quintain,' I say. 'He started off well, but he ended in an undignified heap on the grass.'

'But he won you a ribbon,' he reminds me.

'True.' I hold up my wrist to show him.

He looks pleased. 'You're still wearing it.'

I shrug. 'I couldn't find any scissors.'

Mrs Ogilvie lays down her cup. 'Are we still talking about computers?'

'I'm sorry,' I apologise. 'Will and I visited the mediaeval fair the other day. We were talking about that.'

'Were we?' says Mrs Carson. 'No wonder I'm confused. I was talking about romantic comedies. Did you have a lovely time?'

'We did,' I say. 'At least, I did. We didn't mean to go there. We were looking for Harfield Mill, but we took a wrong turning and ended up at the fair.'

'It sounds as though you took the right turning,' she says. 'I'm always telling Martin we should visit that fair. They're holding it again at Christmas. Perhaps we should go this year. I'm sure they have some lovely mulled wine.'

'What do you say, Olivia?' says Will. 'Shall we try it again at Christmas?'

'There's no point,' I say. 'It's the sort of place you only find when you aren't looking for it. If you try to make arrangements in advance, it disappears. Besides, neither of us will be here by then. I'm leaving as soon as Lily comes back to work, and you'll have taken all your pictures by the autumn. After that, you'll be off to who knows where?'

'That's such a shame,' says Mrs Carson. 'I was hoping you'd stay with us much longer, Olivia. We've only just got to know you.'

'It is a pity,' agrees Mrs Ogilvie. 'Honeywell seems to suit you.'

'It does?' I say.

She nods. 'You look far more relaxed than when you first arrived. Besides, I enjoy chatting with you when I come to the bakery. So does Bernie.'

I smile at Bernie, lying on his side with his legs twitching. He's chasing something in his sleep, but I'm not sure what. I wonder whether Isabella does this in her sleep too. Maybe she dreams of racing to the Red Lion before they run out of game pie.

'It's a beautiful place to live,' I say. 'You're all very lucky.'

'What's stopping you from staying longer?' says Mrs Carson.

'It isn't my home. You can't just rock up to a new place and decide not to leave.'

'Why not?' asks Will.

'Because life doesn't work like that. You know it doesn't.'

'Not usually,' he agrees. 'But there's no reason you shouldn't stay here if you want to.'

'You're so full of suggestions about what other people should do,' I say. 'Why don't you follow your own advice?'

I expect him to look annoyed, but he doesn't. 'My home is somewhere else.'

'So is mine!' I counter.

'Where's that?'

I start to speak, then stop. I was about to say London, but that's no longer true. I could move back there if I chose. But I wouldn't be going home. I'd be going there to start a whole new life.

Mrs Carson gives me an encouraging smile. 'Where do you call home, Olivia?'

I'm aware of Will's eyes on me as I answer. 'I don't call anywhere home at present.'

'Where does your family live?' asks Mrs Ogilvie.

I stare down at my lap. 'I don't have much family. As you know, my parents died when I was eighteen. I'm an only child, and so were they. My last remaining grandparent died when I was twenty-one.'

Mrs Carson looks horrified. 'You poor child! I had no idea. So, you've been living all by yourself for the past goodness knows how long?'

I feel my face turn red. 'Not exactly. I'd just started university when my parents died, and I spent the next four years there. First, I was in halls, and then I shared with friends for a couple of years. After I graduated, I got a job as a veterinary nurse. I lived in a share house for a few years, then I moved in with my boyfriend.'

She looks relieved. 'So, you do have someone?'

'Not really. He and I recently broke up. That's why I left London. I decided to take a trip for a week or two. I hadn't had a holiday for years. Charlie – my boyfriend – didn't like them, so we hardly ever went away.'

'That's a shame,' she says. 'I love Honeywell, but I love seeing new places too.'

'I was planning to explore the Purbecks,' I say. 'It seems a beautiful part of the world. Still, I can do that some other time.'

'Are you looking for a new job?' she asks. 'Or will you be going back to your job in London?'

'I gave in my notice before I left. And I don't want to go back to that area. There's too much chance of running into Charlie.'

'There are plenty of veterinary nurses around here,' says Mrs Ogilvie unexpectedly. 'There are two working at the practice Bernie and I attend.'

'I expect there are,' I say. 'But I'm not sure whether I want to keep doing that.'

'I thought you loved working with animals,' says Will.

'I do. But I really wanted to specialise in surgical nursing.'

'I didn't know that,' he says. 'What stopped you?'

I open my mouth to say that Charlie did, but I close it again. It's only half true. He was strongly against the idea, but he couldn't have prevented me if I'd been determined to do it.

'I was put off by the length of the course,' I say. 'I have a biology degree, which is a start. But I'd still need to undertake another couple of years' training, which is a huge commitment at my age.'

'Your age!' says Mrs Carson. 'You're still a baby.'

'I'll be thirty next year.'

'That's what I mean. You're far too young to be worried about things like that. If I can learn how to export files at my age, you can think about retraining for a different career.'

'It wouldn't even be a different career,' says Will. 'You're already working in that field.'

'I know!' I say impatiently. 'Do you think I haven't thought about all that?'

'What's stopping you?' he says more gently.

I swallow hard. 'Me! I'm stopping myself. I've spent four years living with a man who thought he knew what was best for me. Not just the small things like how to decorate the flat or which car to drive. The big things too. He spent all his time telling me I was less competent than he was, and I should allow him to make all the decisions about how I spent my money and my spare time. In the end, I came to believe he was right. I believed I was lucky to have him. He had such a clear sense of purpose for our lives, and I had none.'

'That's hardly surprising after what happened to you at eighteen,' says Will in a low voice.

'Maybe,' I say. 'But that's more than ten years ago. I ought to have got over it by now and found my way. About a year ago, I began to think I was ready to do that. But by then, it was too late. Charlie had our future all planned out for us, and it felt unfair for

me to change everything on a whim. I persuaded myself I was
being ridiculous and having an early midlife crisis.'

'What happened?' says Will, his eyes fixed intently on my
face.

'I have absolutely no idea. I thought I'd got it all under
control and was happy with the plans we were making. I really
believed that was true. But I woke up one morning, and
everything had changed. I can't say exactly how, but it had. You
know how you go on holiday somewhere, and you're exhausted
by the journey, so you fall into bed as soon as you arrive and go
to sleep? When you wake the following morning, there's a minute
when you don't know where you are. Everything's changed, and
you don't recognise anything around you. It was a bit like that for
me. It was as though I'd woken up in a strange place, not knowing
where I was or how I'd got there. The only thing I recognised
was me. And it wasn't the me of the past ten years. It was the me
from when I was eighteen, before my parents died. It felt as
though no time had passed since I was that girl – that the
intervening years had been a dream. An extremely vivid one, but
still a dream.'

I stop, unable to go on. Mrs Ogilvie breaks the silence. 'That
was the real you. It was the other person who was a dream.'

I looked her in surprise, and she flushes. 'It was the same
when Edward died. The person I was until then was entirely
different to the person I am now. Sometimes, I look at myself,
and I hardly recognise myself and what I've become. It's like you
say – it's all a vivid dream. It's one of the reasons I love Bernie
so much. He knew me before Edward died. He loved the person
I was then, and he hasn't stopped loving me.'

As if he hears his name, Bernie twitches an ear and half opens
his eye to look at her.

She smiles down at him. 'You're a silly old boy, but I don't
know what I'd do without you.'

I surreptitiously wipe my eyes. I had no idea anyone would
understand. I should have said something sooner. It might have

helped us both. It's strange to think there's another person in the world feeling exactly the same as I do, and that I should have bumped into them like this.

Maybe it isn't so strange, after all. Maybe I'm less alone than I feel. I've resisted talking to anyone in Honeywell about my previous life. I didn't think they'd understand. Yet, here I am, blurting out my deepest secrets to a group of strangers. Not only are they listening with sympathy, but one of them is telling me they feel the same as I do.

I've spent the past ten years feeling horribly alone. Is it possible that all I needed to do was to reach out and tell someone how I felt? If I'd found the courage to do that, would everything have been different?

I'll never know the answer to that, but it doesn't matter. No one can change the past. All they can do is plan the future. I've delegated that responsibility to someone else for far too long. Not so much delegated as allowed him to snatch the reins of my life from my own hands. But that's finally over, and I'm free. The person I was before this all happened is still there somewhere, hoping I'll ask her what she wants. I resolve to do everything in my power not to let her down.

Chapter Twenty-Four

Will disappears after tea, saying he needs to pick up his lens so he can take some nice shots of Mrs Carson's herbaceous border. I offer to help Mrs Carson with the washing up, but she refuses.

'You and Mrs Ogilvie enjoy the sunshine and have a pleasant talk. Martin is somewhere in the house. He can dry the plates for me.'

'Don't you have a dishwasher?' I say. 'I must help you.'

She flaps her hands at me to sit down. 'I have a lovely dishwasher. But I enjoy doing things like this by hand. It's an opportunity to chat with Martin.'

She disappears into the house with the tray, leaving me with Mrs Ogilvie. I wonder whether I should bring up the subject of our earlier conversation, but I'm not sure how. For all I know, she may be embarrassed at having shared something so personal about herself. I know I am. But I also feel strangely light. I've been carrying around this huge, shameful secret for weeks. When I finally found the courage to unburden myself, I discovered it was neither huge nor shameful. I've made some poor decisions over the past few years, but so have millions of other people. They recognise them and find a way to fix them.

I met someone who wasn't right for me, and I stayed with him far too long and allowed him to dictate the terms of my life to me. I didn't realise that was what I was doing. Now that I do, it's up to me to change course. It's no big deal. Lots of people find a new path even in their sixties and seventies.

Mrs Carson is right. I'm young. I have plenty of time. I can stop lying awake at night, worrying myself sick about the terrible decisions I've made and all the doors I've closed to myself. That's the great thing about doors. They close, but they can also open. Even if they're locked, you can find the key if you look hard enough. If the worst comes to the worst, you can break them down.

I've almost forgotten where I am, and it's a shock when Mrs Ogilvie speaks. 'Do you think I could learn to use a computer?'

I take a moment to remember where I am. 'Definitely. Anyone can use one. They aren't half as complicated as you'd expect.'

'So everyone says, but I'm not sure I'd cope. It's difficult to learn new things at my age.'

'You aren't eighty yet!' I tease her. 'It wouldn't take you long. Do you have any special reason for wanting to learn?'

She hesitates. 'Angela has been talking to me about those email things.'

'You'd like to send an email? Good for you! I can help you with that if you don't want to go to those classes. Although they sound like fun. You might enjoy them.'

'Angela says they hold them in the evenings,' she says. 'I couldn't leave Bernie by himself. He wouldn't like it. And I don't suppose they'd allow him into the classes.'

'It would be terribly boring for him,' I say. 'He wouldn't know what was going on or why no one was paying any attention to him. But that isn't a problem. I'd love to come and babysit him. I mean doggy sit. Or I could take him for a walk. It would only be for an hour or two.'

'No one but me has ever looked after him,' she says doubtfully. 'Still, you aren't the same as everybody. You're trained.'

'That's right,' I say. 'I can't perform operations, but I can do most other things. And you can give me the vet's number, in case.'

'It's an idea,' she says.

'It's a great idea,' I urge. 'We should get you enrolled at once. The quicker you start, the sooner you'll be able to send an email. Do you have any one particular in mind?'

'My sister in Australia,' she says.

'How do you contact her at the moment? Do you call her?'

Her face closes. 'We haven't spoken for a while. If we need to pass on any information, we write a letter.'

Obviously, this is a touchy subject, and it's none of my business. But she's the one who brought it up, so I risk a further question. 'How long is it since you saw her?'

'About six years.'

'Have you never been over to visit her?'

'I can't,' she says. 'I have Bernie. My sister lived in Winchester until she left England, so we saw each other quite often. She moved to Australia just before Edward died. We were supposed to join her. We were all planning to buy a house together in Melbourne. Mabel went on ahead, while we got ready to sell the house here and pack up our things. Then Edward had his heart attack, and everything changed.'

'Of course, it did. Did you think about joining her later?'

She shakes her head. 'Edward and I had planned to take to take Bernie over there with us, but he wasn't well enough. Mabel and I had a bit of a falling out over it. She said I should have waited and got myself a dog in Australia. Then she said I should bring Bernie with me. Animals fly all over the world nowadays, and she was sure he would be fine. But the vet wasn't too happy about it. Bernie had respiratory problems when he was a puppy, and I didn't know how he would manage on an airplane. I couldn't take any unnecessary risks with him. He was all I had left. I'm sure Edward wouldn't have wanted me to risk Bernie's safety.'

'Does Bernie still have respiratory problems?' I say.

'No, he grew out of that, thank goodness. But by then it was too late. Even if I'd wanted to move over there, I don't think Mabel would have wanted me.'

'I'm sure that's not true. Your sister was disappointed. People say things they don't mean when they're upset.'

She purses her lips. 'I wrote to her a couple of years later and suggested she came back home to live with me. I have a second bedroom in the cottage. But she said she was happy where she was, and she wasn't the one who had changed the arrangements.'

I'm not sure what to say. It seems Mrs Ogilvie's sister is as stubborn as she is. I can imagine the situation, with neither of them being prepared to make the first move to apologise and climb down. It's a pity, at least for Mrs Ogilvie. I don't know what kind of social life her sister has in Melbourne, but it's obvious Mrs Ogilvie is lonely and isolated.

'It's lovely you want to learn how to send her an email,' I say at last. 'Do you know whether Mabel has a computer?'

'I expect she does,' says Mrs Ogilvie. 'She was always one to move with the times.'

'Is she your older or your younger sister?'

'I'm the eldest daughter,' she says, looking so forbidding I don't dare ask for any further details.

Mrs Carson appears at the French windows, and I wave to her. 'It looks as though Mavis Sotherby has one more recruit for the Silver Surfers.'

She looks delighted. 'How exciting! Who's that?'

'Mrs Ogilvie. Do you think there will be room for one extra?'

'Of course, there will. What a marvellous idea. I'm afraid she won't be able to bring Bernie.'

'Not a problem,' I say. 'I've persuaded Mrs Ogilvie to allow me the honour of taking care of him that evening. I can't wait.'

She looks relieved. 'How kind of you. I'll give Mavis a call this evening. The classes are on Friday from six o'clock until eight o'clock.'

I half expect Mrs Ogilvie to veto the entire plan, but she doesn't. Maybe she's so carried away by the whole thing that she'll go home this afternoon and book herself a last-minute ticket to Australia. I'll arrive to collect Bernie on Friday, only to find a for sale sign on the lawn and the front door swinging open.

Will appears around the side of the house, holding a small bag. 'I have the lens. I'll start by taking a few pictures of the flowers in the rockery to assess the light.'

He wanders around the garden, bending down and photographing individual blooms. He straightens up and beckons to me. 'Olivia, can you give me a hand?'

'What a wonderful idea!' says Mrs Carson. 'It's getting rather hot out here, Edith. Shall we sit in the house?'

Mrs Ogilvie gets to her feet, and Bernie wakes up. I click my fingers at him. 'Come and have a run around with me while Will photographs the flowers.'

Bernie races over and jumps up at Will, who takes a hasty step back. 'You can wash Olivia's face, not mine. At least, not when I'm holding this.'

Mrs Carson and Mrs Ogilvie disappear into the house.

'Where do you want him to pose?' I say.

'I don't know,' says Will. 'Could you play with him a bit while I try to get some natural shots?'

'Only if you promise not to take any pictures of me.'

'I'll do my best,' he says. 'I can crop you out later, anyway. Unlike you, I have access to one of those newfangled computer things.'

I give him a pitying look. 'I edit all my photos on my phone.'

'Aren't you the technophile?' he says. 'I should have come to you instead of taking a photography course.'

'Did you study photography for your degree?'

'Not a degree, as such, but I took a certification,' he says. 'I printed it out, and everything. Remind me to show you some time.'

'What sort of certification?' I ask, moving Bernie away from the geraniums, where he's busily engaged in checking for bones Mrs Carson may have buried there for a rainy day.

'It was an online course,' he says. 'The company was based somewhere in the Caymans, if I remember correctly. I can't go back and check because they went bust soon afterwards.'

'How long was the course?'

'Two days. But it was fairly intensive. We weren't allowed to miss any of the modules. We covered the whole subject pretty thoroughly. It was two thousand pounds well spent.'

'Really?' I ask incredulously.

'No, not really,' he says. 'Sorry, Olivia. I couldn't resist. You seem to have such a low opinion of what I do.'

'That isn't true! I don't know much about it.'

'That's easily remedied,' he says. 'What would you like me to tell you?'

'Where did you really train?'

'I did a fine arts degree at Goldsmiths. I planned to go into textile design, but I got involved in a black-and-white photography project during my second year, and I was hooked.'

'Is that what you like best? Black-and-white photography?'

'Not necessarily. I choose the most appropriate medium for whatever I'm doing. Bernie, for instance' – he nudges Bernie with his toe to stop him from beginning a second excavation in the begonia bed – 'will look better in colour. It will catch his lively personality. He doesn't strike me as a candidate for a moody, atmospheric shot.'

As if to prove us wrong, Bernie sits down in front of the flowers and gives me a soulful look. It's the look of a dog who is often misunderstood but who takes all the buffets and blows of life with saintlike patience.

'That's the one!' whispers Will, reaching for his camera. 'Don't distract him, Olivia. In fact, don't breathe for the next five minutes if you can manage it.'

He bends down until he's almost on a level with Bernie. For a wonder, Bernie doesn't move. His attention has been caught by a butterfly above his head. He watches it, entranced.

Will straightens up. 'That should do it. We couldn't have planned it more perfectly if we'd tried.'

He shows me the screen on his camera.

'That's incredible!' I say. 'Mrs Ogilvie will love this. I can't wait to see it printed out full size.'

Even seen in miniature, it's an impressive picture. Bernie is sitting in a patch of sunlight, surrounded by flowers. The sun catches the golden fur around his head, turning it to gold. The butterfly hovers tantalisingly near his face. Bernie is looking up at it as though he's Saint Francis of Assisi and has spent his entire life talking to all other living creatures and administering to the poor.

'How did you get the butterfly in focus as well as Bernie's face?' I ask. 'When I take pictures of two different things, one of them is always slightly out of focus.'

Will gives me a smug look. 'That's the beauty of a course like the one I took. On day two, they taught us about the twiddly bit you turn on the lens that does something or other with the focus. Like I say, it was two thousand pounds well spent.'

'Fine,' I say. 'Don't tell me. I wouldn't understand, anyway. Are you taking any more pictures?'

'Not unless Bernie does something exceptional like dancing on his hind legs while reciting The Wreck of the Hesperus. Or he gets another thorn in his paw.'

'How would that help?' I say.

'You could bend down and administer to him. It would make a wonderful picture. You in your nurse's uniform, tenderly caring for a helpless creature. I could show it at the Royal Exhibition. It would be bound to get us at least a highly commended.'

'I have a better idea,' I say. 'I'll jab a sharp stick into your hand and take pictures of Bernie removing it. That should win us more than a highly commended.'

He shakes his head as he zips his camera back into its bag. 'Sometimes, I don't think you take either my career or me seriously.'

'I don't. In fact –'

I break off as a squirrel appears from somewhere behind the flower bed. It streaks across the lawn at top speed. Bernie, all traces of his former angelic pose disappearing, pelts after it as fast as his legs will carry him.

Will makes a grab for his camera bag and fumbles with the zip, while I dart after Bernie, shouting at him to leave the poor squirrel alone. He takes no notice, and I speed up, still shouting.

I round the corner just as the squirrel makes a dash for the nearest tree and launches itself towards the trunk. Without thinking, I pull out my phone and point it at the tree. I click several times as Bernie makes an ineffectual leap for the lower branches. He lands on his back and rolls over. With a quick look around to make sure no one has noticed his humiliation, he trots into the house.

Will appears behind me. 'Why did I put my camera away? That would have made the most amazing sequence.'

I look down at my phone screen and smother a laugh.

'What?' says Will, and I wordlessly hold out my phone.

His eyes widen. 'That's not possible.'

I give a nonchalant shrug. 'It's nothing. They taught us how to take pictures on day one of the course on how to use a mobile phone. Step one – switch on your phone. Step two – point and shoot.'

He bursts out laughing. 'Touché! That's an amazing photo. Well done.'

I look at the picture again and have to agree. It may be an absolute fluke, but that doesn't detract from the beauty of the shot. It's a moment of sheer, unadulterated canine joy. Bernie, with the joyful light of determination in his eyes, is leaping towards the squirrel like an acrobat defying gravity. His fur is practically sparking with electricity.

The squirrel is a few feet above his head, looking back over its shoulder with what seems like a look of derision. It's a shot in a million – the sort of picture you could never in a hundred years expect to achieve unless you weren't trying to. A concatenation of chances no one could plan, but which come together in the most perfect way imaginable. Much like my time in Honeywell.

I beam up at Will, all thoughts of teasing him forgotten in the joy of the moment. 'I can't believe I did it!'

'You're amazing, Olivia. Has anyone ever told you that?'

And, without waiting for me to answer, he pulls me into his arms and kisses me.

Chapter Twenty-Five

For a second, I'm too surprised to react. I almost respond to the kiss. It feels the polite thing to do. But my brain kicks into gear before I can do anything to make this whole situation more confusing than it already is.

I step back, and he releases me at once. 'Olivia?' he says, his voice shaky.

I'm not sure what to do next. Romantic conventions would seem to dictate that I slap his face, but that seems extreme for one quick kiss. It must have been the surge of adrenaline after the mad dash across the lawn and subsequent successful photograph that made Will lose his head. I can understand that. I almost kissed Bernie myself when I saw the picture.

'My picture isn't that good!' I say, trying for a light tone.

He looks dazed. 'What picture?'

I wave my phone at him. 'This one!'

He hardly seems to hear me. 'I've wanted to do that for a long time.'

'Do what? You mean kiss me? That's ridiculous.'

'No, it isn't. When I saw you stomping off down the road that day, I knew it was the start of something special.'

'I didn't stomp,' I say defensively. 'I set off in a purposeful manner.'

'When you turned around and walked back towards me, I felt as though I'd won the lottery.'

This isn't the point. All he needs to do is to acknowledge he got carried away with the emotion of the past ten minutes and did something stupid. Then we can put it behind us.

'Never mind about all that,' I say. 'It has nothing to do with what just happened.'

'It has everything to do with it,' he says. 'I'm trying to tell you how I feel about you, but you aren't making it easy.'

'Because that isn't how you really feel. Don't make this something it isn't. You kissed me. It wasn't the best idea, but I can see why you did it. Can't we forget it and carry on as we are?'

'Is that what you want?' he asks in a low tone.

'We're both leaving this place soon, and we won't see each other again. Even if we … if you wanted something else, it couldn't happen. You going back to London, and I'm not. It isn't a recipe for a happily ever after.'

He starts to speak, but I stop him. 'Besides, I'm not interested in another relationship. Not now. Possibly not ever. I'm not good at them.'

'That's nonsense!' he says. 'Everyone has a few relationship disasters. You learn from them and move on. The human race would have died out by now if everyone who had a break up stayed single for the rest of their lives.'

'That isn't my problem. I don't owe it to humanity to repopulate the earth. It's overcrowded, anyway.'

He smiles. 'I didn't put that too well, did I? Are you telling me you plan to stay single because of one bad relationship?'

'A disastrous one,' I correct him. 'And I don't know. I haven't given it much thought.'

He reaches for my hand. 'Do you think you could consider it now?'

I pull my hand away. 'Why should I? Why can't you listen to what I say and respect it? Why does every single person in my life think they know better than me what I want and what's good for me?'

'They don't,' he says. 'At least, I don't. I know you've been living with a complete loser, but please don't judge all of us by one man.'

'Not all men? How many times have I heard that?'

'That isn't what I meant!' he says. 'But I'm not Charlie. I'm nothing like him. Why refuse to give me a chance because he was a controlling jerk?'

It's possible that he's right. But how can I know? Charlie didn't start off by controlling my every movement. I wouldn't have stayed with him if he had. It all happened imperceptibly, without me noticing. By the time I did, I was trapped, and I couldn't tell what was real and what wasn't.

'Perhaps that wasn't fair,' I say. 'You may be nothing like Charlie. You don't seem to be. But I no longer trust my own judgement.'

'I could give you references,' he says with a half-smile. 'I'm sure I could find people to vouch for me.'

'You mean old girlfriends?'

He recoils. 'I do not! That would be weird. I meant professional references. A tutor from college, my bank manager, the local vicar, that sort of thing.'

'Do you know your local vicar?'

'I do. I took the pictures for his church's five-hundredth anniversary. He was delighted with them.'

I can't help smiling. 'I'm sure he was. But that doesn't mean he has the faintest idea who you are as a person.'

'He knows I'm punctual, and my prices are very reasonable.'

'Punctuality is important when you're dating,' I agree. 'But unless you charge people to date you, the other part isn't relevant.'

'I don't,' he says. 'To prove it to you, I'd like to buy you dinner tonight. And I promise to turn up on time.'

I almost agree, but something stops me long enough for common sense to kick in. 'It's very kind of you, but the answer is no.'

'No for tonight, or no forever?' he says.

'No forever. I'm sorry, Will. You seem like a nice guy, but so did Charlie.'

'Do you plan to judge everyone by how he behaved?'

'Perhaps, but that's my prerogative.'

He shrugs. 'True enough. What do you plan to do when you leave here? Where will you go?'

'I'm not sure. I'm finding it difficult to make any plans. Whenever I try, my brain spins off the subject and ends up somewhere different.'

'That's very natural,' he says. 'Maybe you should allow someone else to help.'

'Who?' I say, not catching his meaning.

'Me,' he says. 'I'm going back to London soon. You'd be welcome to stay with me until you're back on your feet. I have a two-bedroom flat, so you'd have a space of your own ...'

'No!' I burst out before he can finish. 'You don't get it, do you? You're the same as everyone else. You think you know what I want and what I need. All you have to do is tell me what you have planned for my life, and I'll fall into line. I thought better of you, which shows I'm right to doubt my judgement.'

'I didn't mean it like that,' he says.

'No one ever does. There's no point in continuing this discussion. You and I are not happening, Will, and the sooner you accept that, the better. I have to go.'

I turn abruptly and follow Bernie into the house. I find him sitting on the sofa next to Mrs Ogilvie, who's looking at a photo album.

Mrs Carson jumps up when I come in. 'Have you and Will got what you want?'

'Not exactly,' I say in a low voice.

'What a shame,' she says. 'Perhaps the pair of you can try again another time?'

I ruffle Bernie's head, and he licks my hand. 'I'm afraid I have to go. I promised my landlady I'd be home in time to help her with something.'

I hope to goodness she doesn't ask me what. I can't imagine what tenants help their landladies with. Re-tiling the roof, perhaps, or sharpening the lawn mower blades?

'Is Will going with you?' she says.

'He's in the garden. He's still taking pictures of the flowers. I've said goodbye to him. I really must go now. Thank you so much for inviting me. Goodbye, Mrs Ogilvie. Bye, Bernie.'

I leave the room before she can answer. I walk down the drive, my head spinning with the events of the afternoon. What was Will thinking? He had no right to kiss me like that without asking. He must have assumed I felt the same as him, but he had no business doing so. He could have had the decency to ask first. And what was all that about me going to stay with him in London? Clearly, he's put some thought into these plans. I wonder how long he's been thinking about them and why he hasn't mentioned them to me.

I'm so tired of people planning my future without even the basic courtesy of consulting me. Isabella was the first. She decided when she met me that I ought to live in Honeywell, and she tricked me into it. Now Will thinks I ought to go back to London and the life he's planned out for me. And he hasn't even tried to trick me into it. He assumes I'll be fine with it, which is worse.

Is this my fault? Do I give out vibes of complete incompetence? In which case, was Charlie justified in taking over my life once it became clear I would never do so myself? He may have waited for years, hoping I'd step up and take responsibility for myself and only picked up the reins when he saw I wouldn't.

It's a depressing thought, but I hope it isn't true. I coped fine until I met him. I got a good degree and had great plans for the future until he persuaded me I was being selfish in refusing to think what was best for us as a couple.

I pick up the pace as I walk home. The faster I walk, the more difficult it is to think about my life and what a mess it is. I'm almost running by the time I reach Cherry Street. I slow to a jog and wait until my breathing has returned to normal before walking sedately up the garden path. I don't want Eleanor to catch sight of me and ask questions.

The way my afternoon has been going, she'll probably tell me she's been giving my future a lot of thought, and she's decided the best thing for me is to stay in Honeywell and join her in a property investment business.

Chapter Twenty-Six

'How did it go?' says Isabella the moment I walk into the bakery the following morning.

'How did what go? Oh, you mean the thing with Bernie? We got some photos of him.' I hang my bag on the hook and reach for my overall.

'That's good,' she says. 'But I meant how was the afternoon overall? Did you and Will have a nice time?'

'I wish everyone would stop going on and on about Will!' I snap.

She looks surprised. 'I wasn't going on about him. I was asking how your afternoon went.'

'Well, don't!'

She doesn't say anything more, which surprises me. She's usually such a chatterbox.

I switch on the coffee machine and stare out of the window while it warms up. Why did Will have to spoil things like this? First by kissing me, although I did my best to give him a way to back down from that. Then by pursuing the subject and telling me what I ought to be doing with my life. Why couldn't he have followed my lead and made a joke of the whole thing?

'Abby's been making custard slices,' says Isabella.

'And?' I say.

'I thought you might like one.'

'I'm not hungry. I'll make myself a cup of coffee, then check the orders.'

'I've already done that,' she says. 'I checked them while you were staring into space, muttering about men.'

I blink. 'I did no such thing. I haven't said a word since I got here.'

'You said it with your eyes. If ever a woman had a face that was easy to read, it's you, Olivia. What has he done?'

'What has who done?' I counter, but it's no good. She's like Bernie with a bone.

'Will, of course. You left here all excited about having tea with him. Now you're like a bear with a sore head. I doubt Mrs Carson said anything to upset you. That woman's a living saint. And for some inexplicable reason, you seem to get on well with Mrs Ogilvie. Which only leaves one person.'

I drop into the nearest chair and sigh. 'If I said I'd prefer you to leave it for now, would you take the slightest bit of notice?'

She steams the milk. 'That's hard to say. Possibly, if you were very stern with me. But I know you'd like to talk about it, and there's no one else here at the moment, so why don't you?'

'Perhaps because I'm sick and tired of people telling me what to do. It seems everyone around here knows what I want, and how I feel. Is that a Honeywell thing, or are you all bored?'

The smile disappears from her face. 'Is that how you really see us?'

I want to back down, but I'm not sure how. 'You must admit you've taken control of my life and told me what to do.'

She hands me a mug. 'I don't think so. I gave you a way out when it seemed as though you needed one. That's all. It was your choice to take it. You could have said, "No, thank you," and kept on driving.'

'And you wouldn't have been disappointed and tried to change my mind? Come on, Isabella. You did everything you could to trick me into staying here. First, you told me the mechanic couldn't fix my car. Then you talked me into working here.'

'I wanted you to stay,' she says, sitting down opposite me. 'Is that a crime? You looked as though you needed time out, and I needed some help. Why not do something that was in both our best interests?'

'Maybe. But I'm still here weeks later.'

'You're free to leave at any time,' she says. 'Why haven't you?'

'I don't know. Maybe I should.'

She takes a sip of her drink. 'What happened yesterday?'

'Nothing! At least, nothing much. We were having such a lovely afternoon together. Then Will went and spoiled it all by kissing me.'

I half expect her to give one of her trademark whoops and throw her arms around me. She doesn't.

'Did you mind?' she says.

'Of course, I minded! I told him not to do it again.'

'I thought you liked him,' she says mildly.

'I do like him. I imagine most people do. What does that have to do with it?'

She bites into a gooseberry slice. 'You must have known how he felt about you.'

'I didn't. I still don't. He got carried away when we took a great shot of Bernie yesterday, that's all. It doesn't mean anything more than that.'

'If you say so.'

I eye her resentfully. 'Why don't you believe me? I only met Will a few weeks ago. And you both know I've just got out of a bad relationship.'

'True,' she says. 'But there's no reason why you shouldn't meet someone else and move on. Most people do.'

'Not me. I'm not good at relationships.'

She snorts. 'Don't give me that! You must have had other relationships before this Charlie. What happened with those?'

'I dated a few people during university,' I say, 'but I wasn't ready for anything serious. Charlie was the first man I stayed with for long enough to move in with and think about spending the rest of my life with. And look how that turned out.'

She props her chin on her hands. 'He sounds awful. I can see how he might have ground you down. But that's all over now. You have to move on with your life.'

'I don't want to move on with my life,' I say. 'At least, not until I've worked out why I made such a poor decision.'

'What's the answer?' she says.

'I'm terrible at relationships?' I hazard.

'No one is terrible at relationships,' she says. 'There's nothing to them. Be yourself and find someone who likes who you are.'

'That's nonsense. It's far more complicated than that.'

She picks up a white chocolate cookie and bites into it. 'Only if you make it complicated.'

'That's not true,' I say. 'You can like someone a lot but discover you're completely incompatible.'

'Is that what happened with Charlie?'

'I'm not sure. All I know is that I couldn't stay there another minute.'

'Were you in love with him?' she says.

'I don't know.'

'Which means no. If you're in love with someone, you know about it.'

'I thought I was at first,' I say. 'But things started to go wrong after we moved in together. That was my fault, not Charlie's. I'm not terribly tidy, and I wasn't good at prioritising our relationship in the way I should have done.'

'That's rubbish,' she says. 'Who cares how tidy you are? Anyway, I've seen your room at Eleanor's house, and it's fine. And what does that mean – prioritising your relationship?'

'I kept thinking of myself as single,' I explain. 'I can see why that hurt Charlie. Whenever an opportunity to do something came up, I only thought about whether I wanted to do it, not whether we wanted to do it.'

She looks bemused. 'What's wrong with that? You don't become one half of yourself just because you're in a relationship.'

'But you ought to think about the other person and be prepared to compromise.'

'From what you've told me, you did an awful lot of compromising,' she says. 'Did he do any at all?'

'He was always thinking of me and what was best for me. All his plans were for us as a couple.'

'Did those plans include things you wanted too?'

'That's the problem,' I say. 'I've never been good at thinking about the future. But one of us had to.'

'Why do you think that is? I mean, why haven't you thought about your future?'

'I'm too unfocussed,' I say. 'I've never known what I wanted, and I don't make proper plans.'

'Neither do I,' she says. 'I like to live for the day. So, you allowed other people to make plans for you?'

'Only because I didn't know what I wanted. I couldn't even decide what to study at university.'

She looks amused. 'You stuck a pin in a list of subjects?'

'Not exactly. But my tutors all agreed I was better at science than any other subject. It made sense.'

'And what happened after you graduated?' she says. 'Did your lecturers tell you which jobs to apply for?'

'No, I decided that for myself. Charlie was happy enough with my choice. He's a high earner, so he wasn't too bothered by what I did.'

'That's big of him,' she comments.

'You're taking everything I say the wrong way!'

She considers me carefully. 'Do you know what I think?'

'I don't, but I imagine you're about to tell me.'

'I think you've spent so long being told what to do by other people that you've never got to know yourself. The first day I met you, you seemed almost relieved when I told you what to order because you didn't have to decide for yourself.'

'Or because I genuinely didn't care,' I say. 'Not everyone sees food in the same way you do.'

'I know!' she says. 'I can never understand it. But it wasn't a one off. I've noticed since then that you have great trouble in deciding about the smallest thing. I don't think you were born an indecisive person. I think you became one because the people around you thought they knew what was best for you. Maybe it came from good motives. Maybe they thought they were protecting you. But here you are, with no idea of what you want from life because you've never been allowed to think what that might be.'

Her expression softens. 'I'm sorry, Olivia. I know I'm interfering, just like everyone else in your life. But I hate to see you thinking of yourself as someone who has to do what others want her to do because she's never learned what she herself wants.'

'I get that,' I say. 'But that's all the more reason not to jump into a new relationship.'

'I suppose so,' she admits. 'But I'd hate for you to let something good slip through your fingers because you think you're terrible at relationships.'

I pick up my hairnet. 'I'll bear that in mind. I've promised to give Abby a hand planning the party food, so I'd better go.'

'And those books won't cook themselves,' she says. 'Off you go. But think about it, ok?'

'I will,' I promise, although I'm not entirely sure what I'm supposed to be thinking about. In the meantime, I have a party to plan, and I'm determined to make sure it's perfect in every way. Philosophical reflections will have to wait.

Chapter Twenty-Seven

I don't expect Will to come into the bakery again for a few days, if ever. He must be upset things didn't go the way he wanted on Wednesday. Hopefully, I won't see him before the party next Saturday. It will be easier to meet him when there are plenty of other people around.

So, I'm surprised when he wanders in after lunch and greets me as though nothing has happened. 'Hi, Olivia. How's it going?'

'I'm fine, thanks,' I say cautiously, aware of Isabella's eyes on me.

'Great,' he says. 'I'm after half a dozen currant buns for my landlady, if Abby's made any?'

'You're in luck,' says Isabella. 'She made a fresh batch this morning. Can I make you a coffee while you're here?'

I shoot her an annoyed glance. It's one thing being polite to a customer. It's quite another to invite them to stay for a second longer than they have to.

'Sounds good,' says Will, dropping into a chair.

'It's time for your break, Olivia,' says Isabella. 'I'll make you a coffee too. You can sit and chat with Will while you drink it.'

'Great idea,' says Will easily. 'I need to talk to you about the photographs you want for the party.'

'Are you still doing that?' I say.

'Why not? Were you planning to do them yourself after yesterday's triumph?'

'What triumph?' says Isabella.

'Olivia has discovered a promising new career taking action photos of badly behaved dogs,' says Will.

I open my phone and show Isabella the shot of Bernie leaping for the squirrel.

'That's incredible!' she says. 'Will's right. You should think about becoming a professional photographer.'

'I'm perfectly happy looking after animals,' I say. 'I'll leave the artistic stuff to Will.'

'Why did you think I might not take the photographs?' he asks me.

Isabella looks from me to Will. 'I'll take my coffee to the office. I can drink it when I'm doing the accounts. Keep an eye on the customers for me, Olivia.'

'I'm glad you're still doing the photographs,' I tell Will. 'I thought you might find it a little awkward, that's all.'

'Because I kissed you?'

I flush. 'I suppose so.'

'Does that make things awkward for you?'

'Not at all!' I say with forced breeziness. 'Forget it.'

'I won't do that,' he says in an unusually serious tone. 'But it has nothing to do with whether or not I take photos at the party.'

I fix my gaze on my mug. 'Thanks.'

Neither of us speaks for a moment. The tension is broken when the doorbell jangles. I jump to my feet in relief. Any customer is better than this awkward silence.

The door opens wider, and Bernie rushes in. He gives an excited bark when he sees me, then sits by the counter and looks hopefully at the basket of biscuits.

'Good morning, Mrs Ogilvie,' says Will, pushing back his chair. 'I'm afraid I've taken your table. I'll move our drinks to another one.'

'Not at all,' she says. 'There's plenty of room for the three of us. I'm pleased to have found you here. Bernie and I have had such exciting news. We had to come to the bakery at once to tell you.'

Bernie gives another excited bark.

'He's trying to tell us your news before you can,' I say.

'Is it something about a cat having fallen down a well?' suggests Will.

I catch his eye and grin. The tension between snaps, and I feel as though everything has returned to normal. Perhaps not exactly the same as it was, but something I can live with.

'Can I get you a pot of tea?' I suggest to Mrs Ogilvie. 'If Bernie can keep his news to himself for two more minutes.'

'A cup of tea would be very welcome,' she says. 'It's a warm day, and we were in a hurry to get here. Would you mind finding a biscuit for Bernie too? He likes the ones with the green speckles.'

She waits until I return with the tray of tea things. Bernie has given up trying to tell us the news and is lying by the counter, pretending his biscuit is a rat he's determined to corner.

Mrs Ogilvie beams at us. 'When I went to the Silver Surfers last week, Mavis showed me how to send an email. She helped me to create my own account.'

Will gives a low whistle. 'I'm impressed. It took me weeks to teach my mother how to email.'

'Mrs Carson told me you're a quick learner,' I tell Mrs Ogilvie, who looks pleased.

'I wrote down everything Mavis said, so I wouldn't forget it once I got home. It was far less complicated than I thought.'

'You'll have to give us your email address,' says Will. 'Then we can send you messages.'

Mrs Ogilvie reaches into her bag and pulls out a piece of paper. She peers at it. 'Mavis says it's important to choose one you can remember. Mine is BernieAtTheSugarloaf@gmail.com.'

Will gives a shout of laughter. 'That's wonderful. I'll write to him tonight and send him a picture of a bone!'

'Is that what you came in to tell us today?' I ask.

'Not exactly,' she says. 'I sent an email to my sister!'

'How did you know her email address?'

She looks even more pleased with herself. 'Mavis helped me to look her up online. We did a search!'

'You searched her name and location?' says Will.

She nods. 'I typed her name and the suburb she lives in. The people who do the internet searches told me all about her. They said she runs a yoga class each week, and they told me her email address if I wanted to join it.'

'It's a heck of a way to travel for a yoga class,' says Will.

I give him a reproving look. 'It's a wonderful idea. So, you contacted her?'

'I did,' says Mrs Ogilvie proudly. 'I told her I was now on the line, and I told her my email address.'

'In case the people who do the internet searches forgot to mention it,' Will murmurs in my ear.

I ignore him. 'How long did she take to answer?'

'I got a reply today,' she says. 'I came straight up here to tell you all about it. Mabel didn't want to write to me until she'd made all the arrangements.'

She sounds so delighted I can't help smiling. 'Arrangements?'

'That's what I came to tell you,' she says. 'Mabel is coming over to England! Isn't it exciting?'

Will is the first to speak. 'That is exciting. When is she arriving?'

'Friday,' she says. 'She says she'll take the weekend to get over the jetlag, and then she'll come to see me.'

I almost mention her birthday, but I stop myself in time. I don't want to let Mrs Ogilvie know I've remembered the date. It could lead to a complicated discussion and even, heaven forbid, her realising something is up.

'I'm so pleased for you,' I say. 'You'll both have a lot of catching up to do.'

'We will,' she says. 'She hasn't met Bernie yet.'

It's typical of Mrs Ogilvie that when she receives this news, the first thing that comes to mind is Bernie.

'I'm not sure exactly when she's coming down to Honeywell,' she says. 'But I expect she'll call me sometime over the weekend.'

Will and I exchange glances, but neither of us speaks. Mrs Ogilvie doesn't notice. She's too busy fussing over Bernie and making sure his bowl of water has been freshly filled.

She stays for about an hour. I have to work, but Will sits and chats with Mrs Ogilvie until she leaves. He's such a nice man. Not everyone would have the patience to spend an afternoon talking about the history of a village they barely know and the imaginary ailments of a spoiled dog.

As soon as she and Bernie have left, I join Will again. 'What do you think of this news?'

'I think it's great,' he says. 'It's a pity her sister isn't arriving a day or two earlier or she could have come to the party.'

'That occurred to me too. It's bad timing. But she may not even have remembered it's her sister's birthday. Mrs Ogilvie doesn't seem to think much about birthdays. Perhaps this Mabel is the same.'

Isabella appears from the kitchen, and we fill her in with the news.

'That's wonderful!' she says when we've finished. 'We have to get hold of her and persuade her to come down for the party.'

'I thought about that,' I say. 'But it's no good. We won't be able to find her without letting Mrs Ogilvie know something's up.'

'Don't be so defeatist,' she says. 'Of course, she's coming to the party. It's perfect! I'll find out which hotel she's staying at and call her there.'

'It would be wonderful if you could,' I say. 'Mrs Ogilvie would love it. She was so excited when she came in to tell us.'

Will says goodbye, and I spend the rest of the afternoon filling out the orders for our suppliers. Isabella trusts me to do some of the paperwork now, and it makes a nice change from making tea and coffee.

I leave at five thirty and walk home. It's a beautiful afternoon, and I decide to walk down to the water meadow after dinner. It's become one of my favourite Honeywell walks. It's so calm and peaceful, and I always return from it feeling less stressed.

My phone rings, and I look at the screen. To my surprise, I see it's Allie, the other nurse from my veterinary practice. Is she calling to tell me the place is falling apart without me and begging me to come back?

'Hello,' I say cautiously.

'Olivia? I didn't think you'd answer.'

'Did you think I'd changed my number?'

'I thought it was possible,' she says. 'Charlie says he hasn't been able to reach you.'

My heart gives a sickening swoop. 'You've seen Charlie?'

'He came in this morning,' she says. 'He said you left London a while ago, and he hasn't been able to get in touch with you. Are you all right? Is something going on?'

'I'm fine,' I say. 'I needed a break. I didn't expect Charlie to contact you.'

'He seemed really worried,' she says. 'I didn't realise you'd left London. I've been meaning to call you, but you know how it is. Where are you?'

'I'm staying with friends,' I say. I'm not sure what makes me say that, but I don't want to get into a long explanation with Allie. We were friendly enough as co-workers, but I never saw her outside the office.

There's a long pause before she speaks again. 'Look, Olivia, this is none of my business, but I told Charlie I'd try to get in touch with you. And now I have.'

'And now you have,' I agree.

She sounds confused. 'Should I give him a message?'

I relent. This is nothing to do with her. It's my problem, not hers.

'There's no need,' I say. 'I'll give him a call myself. I appreciate you taking the trouble to call and let me know what's going on.'

'No trouble,' she says. 'Are you sure you're ok? Is there anything I can do for you?'

I force myself to speak in a light tone. 'I'm absolutely fine. Thanks for calling. Perhaps I'll see you the next time I'm in London.'

We say goodbye and ring off. I look at my phone, not sure what to do next. I'll have to unblock Charlie. I can't have him going around all my friends, telling them goodness knows what about why I left. It's time I dealt with this myself.

I look at my screen, my finger hovering over the button. Charlie has every right to be upset that I've blocked him. It wasn't the most mature thing to do. But it's given me the break I needed. He's still been there on my phone, waiting, but I've been able to put him on hold for a few weeks.

Hearing Allie's voice has jerked me back to reality. I've been living in a bubble in Honeywell for the past several weeks. I haven't had to think about real life and what I'm going to do next. That's over now. I could keep Charlie blocked for a while longer, but the bubble has burst. My London life has discovered my Honeywell life, and my two worlds have collided. It's time I stopped running away. I have to speak to him some time, and the longer I leave it, the worse it will be when I finally do.

I scroll through my contacts and unblock him. I look at his name on the screen. This isn't a lifelong enemy. This is the man with whom I've spent several years of my life. It's ridiculous to feel scared of talking to him. Without allowing myself to think further, I click on his name and wait. The phone rings several times. If it goes to answerphone, I'm hanging up. This isn't a conversation I can have with the machine. I almost hope it does. It would give me an excuse not to talk to him tonight. But I don't want the prospect of an unpleasant phone call hanging over me all evening.

The ringing stops, and his voice makes me jump. 'Hello?'

I take a deep breath. 'Hi, Charlie. It's Olivia.'

Chapter Twenty-Eight

Thankfully, the train is waiting when I arrive at the station on Friday. I find my seat and stare of the window, wondering what the day will bring. Will it end with things smoothed over with Charlie or with me more confused than ever? Not for the first time, I wonder what's wrong with me. Everyone else seems to navigate their lives with perfect ease, whereas I stumble from disaster to disaster, hurting people as I go, without even the satisfaction of seeing my life move forward.

The problem is that I don't know in which direction I want to go. I never have. I'm so busy thinking about this that I barely notice the train moving away from the station.

'Olivia?'

I jump before realising it's Will. 'What are you doing here?'

He sits in the seat facing me. 'The same as you, I assume. I'm going to London.'

'Oh.'

I don't know what else to say. Why is he going back to London? For work, or for something else? Maybe he's doing what I'm doing. I may not be the only one with unfinished relationship business. He hasn't told me much about the girlfriend who left him for someone else. He didn't speak about her bitterly when he told me how their relationship ended. That may mean he still holds out hope for the future. Good luck to him, if so. It's better to make very sure the past is dealt with before moving on. If it becomes apparent you've made a mistake and you wish you'd done things differently, all well and good.

'Isabella tells me you have urgent business in London,' he says when I don't speak.

'That's right. I'm meeting someone. Why are you going to London?'

'I have to pick up a few things from the office and give my boss an update. Does Isabella know where you're going?'

'Yes. I had to ask for the day off. She was very nice about it. She told me this was the best train.'

'She told me the same thing when I said I was going up to London,' he says. 'She didn't mention you were going too. I could have given you a ride to the station.'

'She didn't mention you'd be on the train,' I say. 'Which train will you be coming back on?'

'The six o'clock,' he says. 'I means killing time in London, but she mentioned the earlier trains involve several changes. Which one are you taking?'

'The same one. She told me the same thing.'

'Perhaps we could get together this afternoon?' he says. 'How long will your meeting take?'

'I have no idea.'

'Can you give me a ballpark figure?'

'No.'

He sees my expression and shrugs. 'Fine. Why don't you call me when you're finished with whatever you're doing, and maybe we can meet up.'

'I didn't mean to bite your head off,' I say. 'But I didn't know how to mention it.'

'Mention what?'

I pleat my fingers in my lap. 'I'm meeting Charlie.'

'Oh.'

He doesn't say anything more. It's better if I leave it there, but for some reason I don't want to.

'I called him a couple of days ago, and we talked,' I say. 'He wants to meet me and see whether we can work this thing out.'

'I see.'

'We were together for nearly six years,' I say. 'That's a long time. I owe it to him to talk about it. I walked out on him without warning. That's an awful thing to do to anyone.'

'Maybe,' he says.

'There's no maybe about it. Imagine if Melissa had done that to you – just disappeared one day without making the slightest attempt to explain what was going on in her head. How would you feel about that?'

'It depends,' he says. 'I agree it was a pretty drastic thing to do. But you had your reasons, or you wouldn't have done it.'

'That's the point. I didn't have a reason. It would have been much easier if I'd decided there was something specific that wasn't working for me. But I didn't. I ran away on an impulse. That's a fairly immature thing to do.'

'Or a desperate one,' he says.

'I wasn't desperate. You may have got the wrong idea about Charlie. He didn't hit me or anything like that.'

'I should hope not!' he says. 'That's a pretty low bar for a relationship – he didn't hit me!'

I give an impatient sigh. 'That's not how I mean it. I'm saying I had no particular reason to leave.'

He raises an eyebrow. 'Do you need a particular reason to leave a relationship?'

'Of course, you do. Otherwise, no one would ever stay with anyone long term. Anyway, I didn't have a reason.'

'Except that you didn't want to be there.'

'But that wasn't Charlie's fault. That was mine. He didn't change. I did.'

He shrugs. 'You're entitled to change.'

'But I ran away. I shouldn't have done that. No wonder Charlie was hurt. And now I need to do the adult thing and deal with it properly.'

'I see,' he says. 'And what does that involve? Do you plan to get back together with him?'

His tone is neutral, but his eyes are anxious. I feel a pang of guilt. I didn't set out to hurt people, but I've done it anyway. When will I learn to behave like an adult and think through the consequences of my decisions?

'I don't know what I'm going to do,' I say in a low tone. 'Our time together wasn't all bad. In fact, most of it was good. I don't want to wake up one morning and realise I've thrown away something valuable. I've been with him for most of my adult life.'

'The fallacy of sunk costs,' he says. 'It isn't a good yardstick by which to live your life.'

'Neither is throwing away something which may be as good as it gets,' I say.

He gives me a half smile. 'We're all encouraged to recycle these days. But we can take it too far.'

'I'm talking about a relationship, not an empty baked bean tin!' I snap.

'I was only teasing.'

There's nothing I can say to this. He may find the whole thing amusing, but I don't.

He seems to read my thoughts. 'I'm sorry, Olivia. I was trying to lighten the mood. Where are you meeting him? At your flat?'

'No. He wanted to, but I didn't.'

When Charlie mentioned meeting at the flat, I felt the same impulse to flee I felt on that fateful morning I left London. Can it only be a couple of months? It seems like years ago.

'He suggested meeting at an ice cream bar I like,' I say. 'It was nice of him. I didn't realise he knew about it.'

'Haven't you been there together?' he says.

'Not very often. Charlie isn't keen on ice cream, which makes it even more thoughtful that he wants to meet me there today. And it shows he isn't angry with me, which is a relief.'

'It would be strange if he was,' says Will. 'No one does what you did without an excellent reason. He wouldn't be much of a partner if his first reaction was to feel angry.'

'I've already told you he wasn't. But he sounded upset on the phone. It made me realise how badly I've treated him.'

He doesn't look convinced. 'Be careful, Olivia. You aren't responsible for anyone else's emotions.'

'I never said I was.'

He looks as though he'd like to say more, but he refrains. 'We'll be in London by eleven o'clock. When are you meeting him?'

'Half past eleven. I'll take a taxi. As long as the train arrives on time, I'll be fine.'

I don't add that Charlie hates it when I'm late. There's no point in giving Will any more ammunition. He seems eager to criticise Charlie. Possibly it's hurt pride on his part or male insecurity. Whatever it is, there's nothing I can do about it, and it won't help us to discuss it further.

The rest of the journey passes uncomfortably. We seem to have lost the easy camaraderie that's characterised the past few weeks. I don't want to be standoffish and cold, but I can't think of anything to say that won't lead to the increasingly long list of forbidden subjects between us.

The train starts to slow, and he reaches into the overhead locker for his backpack. 'We'll arrive in a few minutes. Do you have everything?'

I indicate my handbag. 'I didn't bring much with me. I thought I might pick up a few things from the flat before I leave, depending on how things go.'

'Will Charlie be coming back to Honeywell with you?'

'What?'

'I thought you might invite him to the party,' he says. 'You've worked so hard to arrange it. He'll be pleased to see how well you've done. He'll be proud of you.'

I don't know why the thought of inviting Charlie is such a shock. If Charlie and I get back together, it would be only natural for him to come to Honeywell and see where I've spent the past couple of months and what I've been doing.

I'm not so sure he'll be proud of me. Charlie isn't one for surprise parties, which is fine. Lots of people aren't. And he isn't good with strangers. He lacks Will's easy touch with people. It's not that he doesn't get along with people. He does. But he prefers people with whom he shares common interests.

I can't imagine him talking to Isabella about the bakery business or chatting about the history of Honeywell with Mrs Ogilvie. Why should he? They're only interesting to me because I've ended up living there. If I'd read about them in a book, I might not bother to finish it.

'I expect he'll be busy,' I say. 'He works most weekends.'

'Too bad. Well, here we are.'

We walk across the concourse to the taxi rank.

'Would you like to share a taxi?' I ask, not sure whether I want him to say yes or no. Now that the time has come to face Charlie, my confidence is evaporating. It's a good thing Will is here. If not, I might be tempted to jump back on the train and return to Honeywell. But I can't do that with him watching me. There's nothing for it but to go through with it.

'My office is in Canary Wharf,' he says. 'Where are you headed?'

'The Meltdown is in Wimbledon,' I say. 'So, that won't work.'

I climb into the nearest taxi and open the window. 'I'll call you and let you know what I'm doing this afternoon if you like.

'Sounds good,' he says. 'Good luck, Olivia.'

He waves and climbs into the taxi behind me.

'Where to?' says my driver.

I'm so busy watching Will's taxi disappear down the street that it takes me a moment to remember where I'm meeting Charlie. I resist the urge to command the driver to 'follow that taxi' and focus on reality.

'The Meltdown, please,' I say. 'It's in Mayfield Street.'

'You've got it.' He noses away from the kerb.

He pulls up outside The Meltdown far too quickly. I've barely got my thoughts in order and prepared myself for this meeting. Perhaps it's better this way. No good comes of overthinking this sort of thing. And I'm not meeting a stranger for a job interview. I'm meeting Charlie, the man with whom I've been in a relationship for six years, and with whom I was living until very recently. I don't know why I've allowed myself to get so wound up.

I straighten my skirt and smooth down my hair before pushing open the shop door. The jangle of the bell is alien, although I've been here a hundred times over the years. I've become accustomed to the Sugarloaf doorbell, that's all. But it makes me feel like a stranger, and I don't like it.

I spot Charlie at once, sitting at a table in the far corner, studying a menu. He hasn't noticed my arrival. His dark hair is brushed smoothly back from his forehead, and his expression is serious. He looks exactly the same as the first day we met. He's even wearing a similar pale blue sweater.

He looks up and sees me and lifts a hand in greeting.

I take a deep breath and walk over to meet him, pleased to find my legs have stopped shaking. 'Hi Charlie!'

Chapter Twenty-Nine

He stands and kisses my cheek. 'You came! I wasn't sure you would.'

I can't help glancing at my watch to make sure I'm not late, although I know I'm not.

He pulls out a chair for me, but I point to my usual booth. 'Do you mind if we sit there? I prefer it.'

He doesn't comment as he sits down. I pick up a menu and study it. I have no idea why. I always have the same thing when I come here.

I lay it down again when the silence threatens to become awkward. 'How are you?'

'How do you think?' he says.

I resume the study of my menu. Thankfully, we're interrupted by the server.

'Hi, I'm Gavin,' he says. 'Welcome to The Meltdown! What can I get you today?'

'Just a coffee,' says Charlie.

'Don't you want an ice cream?' I ask him.

'I'm fine with a coffee. Double espresso, no milk.'

Is it my imagination, or does Gavin look disappointed? I resolve to tip him as though we've both had an ice cream. It's a reasonable expectation that people coming to a place called The Meltdown are here to eat some of the product.

'I'll have a Frostbite Delight,' I say.

'Great choice!' says Gavin. 'That's my favourite too.'

'Do you know him?' says Charlie when Gavin has left.

'I don't think so. Do you?'

He gives an impatient shrug. 'Of course not. But the pair of you seem extremely friendly. And I know you come in here often. I wondered, that's all.'

'I'm not good with faces,' I say. 'But I don't think so.'

Gavin returns with Charlie's coffee.

'The chef's making your Frostbite Delight,' he tells me. 'I told him to put extra crushed candy canes on top.'

'They're my favourite bit!' I say.

'They're everyone's favourite bit.' He looks at Charlie. 'Are you sure you won't change your mind?'

Charlie shakes his head. 'Can you bring me a clean saucer? You've splashed coffee in this one.'

'It's only a drop,' I say. 'Use one of these napkins.'

'I'd rather have a clean saucer,' he says.

I wait until Gavin returns to the kitchen. 'You weren't very nice to him. He's probably working for minimum wage.'

'Lots of people work for minimum wage,' says Charlie. 'It's no reason for poor service. But I didn't come here to talk about coffee.'

'I don't suppose you did. Why don't you go first? I'm feeling a little awkward.'

'Which is hardly surprising,' he says. 'This entire situation is awkward.'

'I know. I'm sorry, Charlie. I'm not sure why I left the way I did.'

'Neither am I,' he says. 'But I'd like to hear what you have to say.'

'I've already said I'm sorry.'

'But you haven't told me what made you do it.' He takes my hand. 'If you could give some more explanation, help me understand.'

I don't pull my hand away, but neither do I return his pressure. This isn't going how I expected. I thought he wanted to see me so he could explain what I did wrong. That's how it usually goes. I upset him, and he tells me how he feels about it. I'm not used to him asking me for an explanation.

'You owe me that,' he says. 'I left for work a couple of months ago, thinking everything was good, thinking we were planning a future together. I arrived home to find you'd left without an explanation. All I got was a scribbled note saying you were fine and not to worry about you. How do you think that made me feel?'

'It wasn't ideal,' I say.

'Ideal? Is that really how you want to play this?'

I try again. 'It must have been upsetting for you.'

He rolls his eyes. 'That's rather an understatement. But let's go with that and say yes, it was upsetting for me. As far as I was aware, I hadn't done anything to justify being treated like that. I couldn't understand it. I tried to call you, but your phone was turned off.'

'I didn't have any phone connection for most of that day,' I say. 'It was terrible timing. My car broke down, and –'

He stops me. 'Eventually, I stopped trying to call you. I thought you might need some space, so I decided to call again the next day. You still didn't answer, so I texted you. That's when I found you'd blocked me.'

'One Frostbite, with extra peppermint candy,' says Gavin, plonking a large glass plate in front of me.

Charlie looks at my ice cream in disbelief. 'Is that what you usually order?'

I dig my spoon into the fudge sauce. 'Long experience has taught me it's the best thing on the menu. Would you like to try some? There's plenty here for both of us.'

'I'm fine with my coffee.'

'All the more for me.' I take a bite of the peppermint ice cream.

'What's happened to you, Olivia?' he says.

'What do you mean?'

He considers. 'You've changed. I can't put my finger on what it is, but something's different. Are you planning to tell me what it is?'

I stir the cookie crumbs into the fudge sauce. 'It's only been a few weeks. How much can I have changed?'

'Where have you been?' he asks abruptly.

'In the countryside.'

'Is that it? Aren't you going to give me any details?'

'Not right now. It isn't relevant.'

'What have you been doing?'

'Also not relevant,' I say.

His face darkens. 'I think it is. But that isn't the most important question.'

'What's that?' I say, my mouth full of ice cream.

'Don't play games, Olivia. You know I hate that. Who were you with?'

'No one!' I say, startled. 'Who would I have been with?'

'You tell me! I was left to imagine all sorts.'

I feel a surge of contrition. 'You thought something terrible had happened to me? Like an accident?'

'I'd have heard from the hospital or the police if you'd had an accident,' he says. 'I assume I'm still listed as your next of kin?'

He's right. It hasn't occurred to me to change that. I don't know who else I'd put. Mrs Ogilvie? Bernie? I stifle a grin at this thought.

'Is something amusing?' he says.

'Not at all. So, what terrible thing did you imagine happening to me?'

'I assumed you'd met someone,' he says curtly.

'I've met lots of people,' I say, not taking his meaning.

'You know perfectly well that's not what I mean.'

Light dawns. 'You mean a man?'

'It's the obvious conclusion to draw.'

I lay down my spoon. 'Do you think I met someone while I was away, or that I ran off with someone?'

'How should I know? All I know is that you disappeared one day without warning and didn't come back. What was I supposed to think?'

'Plenty of things,' I say. 'You could have thought that maybe I wasn't happy with my life, and I didn't know how to talk to you about it. You could have thought things had got too much for me, and I'd snapped. You could have thought I was so overwhelmed by everything that I wasn't thinking straight, but I couldn't keep living a life I hadn't chosen.'

'Are you saying it wasn't a man?' he says, looking confused.

I sigh. 'I don't want to dignify that question with an answer. But if I don't, I know you'll assume the worst. So, no, I didn't run away with a man.'

For the first time since we met, he looks unsure of himself. 'I don't understand. Are saying you left for all those other reasons?'

'All I know is that I couldn't do it anymore. I couldn't keep living the life I'd been living. I had to get away.'

'Why didn't you talk to me about any of this?' he says.

'You wouldn't have listened.'

'Yes, I would.'

'Not properly. You'd have told me I was being ridiculous. You'd have said we'd made plans together, and I was ditching them because of some silly emotional reason. You'd have told me why I was wrong to have felt the way I did, and I'd have ended up agreeing with you.'

'That's not true,' he says.

'Yes, it is, Charlie. It's my fault. I should have realised a long time ago we weren't right for each other.'

He reaches over and takes my hand again. 'But we are! I had no idea you felt like that. Now that I do, things can change. I can change.'

I stare at him, confused. Is this really all I needed to do – to be honest with him about my feelings and my dreams? Could all of this have been avoided if I'd been different? More importantly, could we make it work better this time around? He seems to think so. He hasn't told me I'm wrong to feel the way I do. He hasn't argued with me.

Charlie leans forward, his tone urgent. 'Come home, Olivia. We can work this out. You left without giving me a chance to change.'

I hesitate. He's quite right. I didn't try to talk to him. I told myself there was no point. But maybe I was wrong. I've spent this entire time thinking about myself and how unhappy I was. I haven't given a single thought to how Charlie has been feeling. I feel a huge wave of guilt.

'Charlie –' I begin.

But he isn't listening. He's staring over my shoulder, and his lips have tightened.

'What's wrong now?' I say.

'There's a man over there trying to attract your attention.'

'Don't be ridiculous. You always think –'

I turn my head and break off. Will is standing in the doorway, pointing me out to Gavin and handing him a slip of paper.

He grins when he sees me looking at him. 'Sorry to disturb you, but you aren't answering your phone.'

I looked down at my screen and realise there are several messages. I turned my phone to silent when I got out of the taxi. Charlie hates me taking calls or looking at texts when I'm with him. He says it's only basic politeness to focus on the person you're with.

'Why were you messaging me?' I say, and Will grins again.
'To let you know we need to go to the zoo!'

Chapter Thirty

I stare at him in confusion. 'Did you just say the zoo?'

'That's right,' he says. 'London Zoo, to be exact.'

'Olivia?' says Charlie. 'What's going on?'

I remember his presence for the first time. 'Will, this is Charlie. Charlie, this is Will. He's a friend of mine from Hon … from the place where I've been staying.'

'Nice to meet you,' says Will.

Charlie's face darkens as he looks from me to Will. 'So, that's what's been going on!'

'No, it isn't!' I say. 'Will is just a friend, aren't you, Will?'

Will doesn't answer, and Charlie's face grows grimmer. 'Don't lie to me, Olivia. I can always tell.'

'I'm not lying!' I burst out.

'It all makes sense now,' he says, hardly seeming to hear me. 'All that nonsense you've been giving me about not knowing who you are and not feeling listened to. That was all just a pretence, wasn't it?'

He points to Will. 'He's the reason you left me!'

'No, he isn't,' I insist. 'I didn't meet Will until after I'd left London.'

'How long after? Don't lie to me.'

'I'm not lying!' I almost shout. 'I *did* leave you for all the reasons I said. And I didn't meet Will until after I'd left you.'

'How long after?' he repeats.

'About five hours, wasn't it?' says Will.

Why does he think that was a good thing to say? Can't he see how upset Charlie is? This is a time for pouring oil on troubled waters, not for throwing a lighted match at the oil can.

Will takes a couple of steps towards us, and Charlie jumps up to face him. 'Do you think this is funny?'

'Not in the sense of being amusing,' says Will. 'Funny weird, maybe.'

I touch his arm. 'Don't, Will.'

Charlie glares at me, and I drop my hand.

'Olivia?' he says again. 'I want the truth. I think I deserve it, don't you?'

'You do. And I've told you what happened. I left you because I felt as though I'd lost myself. I took a train out of London, picked up a car, and it broke down. Will happened to come along and rescue me. That's all. It was a complete coincidence that he and I met.'

I turned to Will despairingly. 'Can't you see this isn't a time for jokes?'

He looks at Charlie. 'I imagine there's never a good time for jokes with this one.'

Charlie takes a step towards him. I expect Will to take a step back, but he doesn't. He doesn't seem remotely bothered by Charlie's aggressive demeanour.

'What Olivia says is quite true,' he adds calmly. 'She left London for reasons of her own, and she and I happened to meet later that day. I'm not sure why you need me to tell you that. Isn't Olivia's word good enough for you?'

I'm surprised to see Charlie flush. 'Of course, it is,' he says stiffly. 'This whole thing is rather odd, that's all.'

'It *is* odd,' I break in hastily. 'I can see why you might have thought so.'

'I can't,' says Will.

Charlie almost audibly grinds his teeth. 'You stay out of this! If what you say is true, you've only known Olivia for a few weeks. She and I have been together for more than six years.'

'So she tells me,' says Will. 'You'd think you might know her a little better after all this time.'

'Will –' I begin, but Charlie interrupts me.

'I know her a lot better than you do. You've known her for a few weeks, and you have the audacity to think you know all about her. You don't. I'm the one who's looked after her and protected her all these years, not you.'

'Very commendable,' says Will. 'Did you ever stop to ask yourself whether that was what she wanted?'

'Of course, it was!' snaps Charlie. 'She was a mess when I met her. She had no idea what she wanted to do with her life. She still doesn't. She's impulsive and a dreamer, and she needs someone in her life to keep her on track.'

'No, I don't!' I break in. 'I may be impulsive and unfocused and all those things you say. But what's so wrong with that?'

'Nothing,' says Will.

'You were perfectly happy with me before you met this idiot,' says Charlie. 'I don't know what nonsense he's been filling your head with, but you're a fool if you listen to him. Look at everything you've thrown away – a good job, a nice flat, a great relationship. And for what? Some idiot you meet on the side of the road who happens to have a towbar?'

'Not even that,' says Will, his eyes alight with laughter. 'Sports cars don't usually come with a towbar.'

'Sports cars!' says Charlie contemptuously.

'Can you both stop this?' I say. 'Charlie, for the last time, I didn't leave you for Will. I left because you don't want to be with me. You want to be with the version of me you've created in your head. I thought I wanted to be that person, but I don't. You want someone who's content to stay at home and clean your house and look after you and never have an opinion of their own. That's not me, and it never will be. I left you because I almost disappeared when I was with you. I didn't realise it at the time, but I do now. I needed some time alone to think about who I want to be and what I want to do.'

'Suit yourself,' he says resentfully. 'But don't expect me to be waiting around for you when you come to your senses.'

'I've never expected you to wait around for me,' I say.

'Whatever. See you, Olivia. Good luck with your new man!'

He pushes past Will and strides out of the ice cream parlour without even looking at me.

I sit down abruptly, and Will slides into the booth opposite me. 'I'm sorry, Olivia. Are you ok?'

'I'm not sure. What just happened?'

He picks up Charlie's discarded menu. 'Don't hold me to this, but my impression is that you two just broke up.'

'I'm not talking about that,' I say. 'I came here today trying to get some closure. And now he's stormed out without even listening to me.'

He considers me carefully. 'Do you mind?'

I think about this. I ought to mind. I've just thrown away six years of my life. But somehow, I don't.

'No,' I say. 'In fact, I'm relieved.'

He waves to Gavin. 'I'm not surprised. The guy's a jerk.'

'You don't know him,' I say out of a sense of fairness to Charlie.

'I don't have to. Two minutes was more than enough.'

He looks at Gavin. 'What do you recommend?'

'You're ordering ice cream?' I say, surprised.

'Isn't that what you're supposed to do in a place like this?'

Gavin looks pleased. 'It is, indeed. I can recommend the Tropical Bite and the Frostbite Delight.'

'Is that the Frostbite?' Will asks me.

I survey my plate ruefully. 'It was, but it seems to have melted. Never mind. It will taste almost as good.'

'Can you bring her another of those?' he asks Gavin. 'And I'll try that Tropical thing.'

'That isn't necessary,' I say, but Gavin has already picked up our menus and left.

'Don't worry,' says Will. 'I'm paying.'

Gavin returns a few minutes later with the two plates. 'Enjoy!'

Will picks up his spoon. 'How can we not? This looks amazing. Do you want to try mine, Olivia?'

'No, thanks. I won't have room for mine if I do.'

He takes an enormous mouthful of coconut ice cream and mango sauce.

'Was I hallucinating earlier, or did you say something about the zoo?' I say.

He swallows his mouthful. 'I'd almost forgotten that in all the excit ... I mean the upset.'

I can't help smiling. 'Really? Is that what you meant?'

'I don't remember. Anyway, we need to go to the zoo as soon as we finish our ice cream.'

I lay down my spoon. 'Have you been seized with a sudden overwhelming urge to feed some tigers?'

'Penguins are more my style,' he says. 'They're less bitey.'

'Unless you're a fish.'

'Which I'm not. Perhaps I should start at the beginning.'

'It isn't your usual style,' I say, 'but it might be best.'

He considers. 'To cut a long story short, I set off for my office when I left you. I was halfway there when Isabella called and told me she'd managed to track down Mabel. She's been calling the hotel all morning. When she finally got through, the receptionist told her Mabel had just checked out.'

'How annoying!' I say. 'So, we've missed her?'

'We would have missed her,' he says. 'But Mabel mentioned to the woman on reception she was going to the zoo after lunch.

That's where she's headed now. Apparently, she's wearing a bright pink jacket. Isabella is certain we'll find her there.'

'That's rather vague,' I say. 'What are we supposed to do – run around all afternoon, shouting her name?'

'I'm not sure. Isabella couldn't talk for long. She said she knew she could trust to our ingenuity.'

I push away my plate. 'That's all very well, but London Zoo is massive. Have you been there?'

'Not since I was a child. But Isabella seems to think it's our last chance. Who knows where Mabel is staying tonight?'

I pick up my bag. 'Have you finished?'

'Almost.' He shovels in the last couple of mouthfuls. 'I'll pay the bill while you call a taxi.'

'We can take the underground,' I say.

'No time,' he says. 'It's nearly one o'clock. That counts as after lunch. She may be there already, wandering around the kangaroo enclosure, marvelling at how similar everything is to back home.'

I put a large tip underneath my plate. 'Fine. I'll get us a taxi.'

Five minutes later, we're driving towards the zoo. Will looks at his watch. 'We'll be there in about twenty minutes. We should make a plan.'

'You mean Isabella hasn't already made one for us?'

'Not that I'm aware of,' he says. 'Here's what I think we should do. As soon as we arrive, we'll get ourselves a couple of maps and mark them into sectors. That way, we can cover twice as much ground.'

'But we don't know what she looks like,' I object. 'We can't walk up to every woman wearing a pink jacket and ask her whether she's Mabel.'

'It may come to that,' he says. 'But hopefully not. It's a pity we don't have a photograph of her, but there's bound to be a family resemblance. That should narrow it down a bit. We'll focus on any woman who appears to be in her seventies and looks even vaguely like Mrs Ogilvie.'

'Are you enjoying this?' I say as the taxi pulls up outside the main entrance of the zoo.

He leans over and opens my door for me. 'Immensely! Aren't you?'

'Absolutely not!'

'Your face says differently. Come on, let's find ourselves some maps.'

Chapter Thirty-One

I'd forgotten how large this zoo is. To make it worse, the taxi has pulled up behind a coach marked *Camden Holiday Club*. Children are pouring out of it and running towards the main entrance.

Will grabs my hand. 'If we wait for this lot to go in, we'll be here for hours. Come on, let's make a run for it.'

We dodge around a knot of children standing next to the turnstiles.

'Coming through!' shouts Will, dragging me behind him. 'Two adults, please.'

'Hey, wait your turn!' shouts one of the boys.

Will looks back over his shoulder. 'It's an emergency. One of the giraffes has got itself tangled in … er … I mean, it's escaped from its cage and is …'

'Giraffes don't live in cages!' says a small girl indignantly.

'You're quite right,' I say. 'This gentleman has got confused. He meant to say gorilla. One of the gorillas has escaped, and we have to persuade it to go back inside its cage before any of you are allowed in.'

'Nice one!' says Will. 'Hurry up before we discover all the gorillas have gone on holiday.'

One of the holiday club helpers strides towards the kiosk. 'Is this true? I've just been told one of your leopards has escaped and is roaming around the zoo.'

'It's a gorilla,' the small girl corrects him. 'That man over there is going to catch it.'

She points to Will, who pulls me through the turnstile at top speed. With a wave of his hand to the group of children, he starts running. I run as fast as I can to keep up with him, but his legs are considerably longer than mine, and I'm quickly out of breath.

He notices me lagging behind and stops running. 'Sorry, I was just trying to get away from those children. Let's start with the African animals.'

We walk past the hippos and giraffes until we reach the giraffe enclosure. I'm pleased to see the giraffes seem to be safely inside. Hopefully, the gorillas are all in their enclosure too.

'How do you want to do this?' I ask Will. 'Should we split up so we can cover more ground?'

'Why don't we spend an hour or two looking for her together?' he says. 'We can split up later if we get desperate.'

I look at my map. 'Time to search the rainforest.'

'They have rainforests in Australia,' says Will. 'We're quite likely to find her there.'

The moment we enter the building, Will gives a grasp and grabs my arm.

'What is it?' I say. 'Have you found her already?'

He pulls his camera out of his bag. 'No, but I've found something even better. Look at that sloth on the branch!'

'It's very nice,' I say. 'I heard the zoo had a baby sloth recently.'

He screws a lens onto his camera. 'You don't understand. I'm talking about the soft drink commercial our company is bidding for. This would be absolutely perfect!'

'What would?'

He points. 'The sloth! It would be a great concept for this new line of drinks. It's a range of sparkling fruit juices called Slo-

Mo. The producers have decided the market is saturated with energy drinks filled with caffeine and sugar and goodness knows what, designed to give people a boost. This product line is all about slowing down, appreciating life, that sort of thing. As soon as I saw that sloth hanging on the tree, watching the world go by, I knew we had it! I have to get some shots of him to show my boss what I'm talking about.'

'It's a great idea,' I say. 'But won't you need permission from the zoo if you want to do something like this?'

'This is just to give my company a rough idea of what we have in mind. You'll have to be in it too.'

'Oh no!' I take a step backwards and raise my hand to cover my face.

'Please, Olivia. It's no good unless you do.'

'Yes, it is. Show them a really good picture of the sloth, and they'll get the idea.'

'That's not how it works,' he says. 'The bidding closes tonight. This is a surefire winner.'

'If I agree to do this, can you blur out my face?' I say.

'I suppose I could. It would be rather unusual. Most people are dying to get their faces into ads.'

'Not me,' I say. 'But that's a good idea. There must be plenty of people here today who would love to help you out.'

I point to a group of teenagers looking at the flying foxes. 'Why don't you ask one of them?'

'Because I know you,' he says. 'I'll get a much better picture if I use you. It will only take five minutes.'

'We're supposed to be searching for Mabel, not making me the star of Britain's funniest home videos.'

'I just need a few still shots,' he says. 'It's lucky you're wearing that coral dress. It will show up beautifully against the greenery. If you stand over there, the light will be perfect. And you need something to drink.'

'I'm fine,' I say. 'We can stop at the cafe later if we're thirsty.'

'I don't mean that,' he says. 'I need you to be holding a bottle. We're advertising a drink, remember? Do you have a bottle of water in your bag?'

'I drank it on the train.'

He thinks for a moment. 'Stay here!'

He strides over to the group of teenagers and returns a moment later with a bottle half full of a revolting-looking bright orange drink. He hands it to me. 'It only cost me ten pounds!'

'I don't care how much it cost you,' I say. 'I'm not drinking this.'

He adjusts my arm. 'You'd better not. We need it for the photo. That's perfect. Can you turn your head and look at the sloth? Keep your arm exactly in that position.'

He moves slowly around me, snapping away, while I stand there, increasingly embarrassed. The teenagers have walked over to join us and are watching me with frank interest, which makes me even more embarrassed.

'Just a couple more,' says Will. 'I need you to pretend to drink whatever that is.'

'I want a huge bonus for this,' I grumble.

'I'll have you on the front page of every magazine in the country,' he promises, taking several more photographs.

He puts his camera back into his bag. 'We have to get going.'

'Thanks for the drink,' I say to the teenagers. 'Do you want it back?'

One of the boys takes the bottle. 'I'm not giving you the money back. He said I could keep it.'

'No one's asking for the money,' says Will. 'You can use it buy yourself a few more disgustingly flavoured drinks.'

He looks intensely pleased with himself as we leave the building. 'I'll send these pictures to Marcus, and he can include them in the pitch. I'd be willing to bet we win the contract. And it's all thanks to you, Olivia.'

'I let the drink do most of the work,' I say. 'The sloth did the rest of it.'

His face lights up. 'Look over there!'

'The outback?' I say. 'Do you think Mabel is homesick already?'

'Very possibly,' says Will. 'Look at all those kangaroos and wallabies and other bouncy creatures. We'll probably discover Mabel leaning over the fence, feeding them whatever it is they eat. Chocolate raisins, or cheese slices, I expect.'

'She'll be thrown out at the zoo if she tries anything like that,' I say. 'And quite right too.'

I point to the emus. 'There's a woman in a pink jacket over there. Do you think that's her?'

'Could be,' he says. 'Shall we go and talk to her?'

We make our way towards the woman, who is watching the animals with interest.

'Excuse me,' I say. 'Could I have a quick word with you?'

She doesn't seem to hear me. I try again. 'Are you by any chance Mabel?'

She turns and studies me without speaking. It's a simple enough question. She must know whether or not she's Mabel.

'We're looking for Mabel,' says Will slowly and clearly. I can see he's wondering whether the elderly woman is hard of hearing.

'Is there a problem?' says a man, walking towards us.

'No problem,' I say. 'It's just that we're trying to locate a woman called Mabel. We have a message for her.'

I sound as though I might be from a government agency, but I can't help it.

'This is not the woman you are looking for,' says the man.

I suppress an urge to demand the woman's identification papers. We aren't in an Orson Welles film.

'That's a pity,' says Will. 'The woman we're looking for has just arrived from Australia.'

'And the woman you are speaking to is here on holiday from Slovenia,' says the man. 'She does not speak much English.'

Will and I make our escape as quickly as possible.

'So much for the siren call of the kangaroos,' I say.

'It was worth a try,' says Will. 'Where to next?'

I look at my map and laugh. 'You may want to sit this one out. It's the reptile house!'

He gives an involuntary shudder. 'You don't really think she'd be in there?'

'It's as likely as anything. I'll check it out while you go and hunt for Mabel around the tiger enclosure. Unless you're terrified of big cats too? In which case, you can go to the petting zoo.'

'I'm perfectly all right with lions and tigers,' he says with dignity. 'I'll meet you back here in ten minutes.'

I enter the reptile house and walk up and down, squinting into the darkness. There's no sign of Mabel here. As I turn to come back out, I see the group of teenagers who sold us the drink. I give them a friendly wave as I pass.

'Excuse me,' says one of the girls. 'Could you sign my T-shirt for me?'

'And mine!' says another girl eagerly.

'Why do you want me to sign your T-shirt?' I say, confused. Is this some teenage rite of passage – walking up to a complete stranger and persuading them to write all over your clothes? Will they video it and put it on TikTok to embarrass me?

The first girl pulls off her jacket. 'I can't believe you're here at the zoo today, and we bumped into you!'

This is getting weirder by the minute. 'It was very nice to meet you all,' I say. 'But I have to get going.'

The girl looks devastated. 'Please! Everyone will be so jealous. Chantelle Briggs is always saying what a loser I am. This will show her.'

'And it will shut my sister up,' agrees the other girl. She produces a pen from her pocket and hands it to me.

'You really want me to sign your T-shirt?' I say. 'But why?'

All the girls burst out laughing.

'You're funny!' says one of them. 'She's really funny, isn't she?' she asks the others, and they agree I am.

'Can you write your name and a personal message?' says the girl. 'I'm Sophia.'

'I think you have me mixed up with someone else,' I say politely.

'No, we haven't,' she says. 'That man you were with told us who you are.'

Light begins to dawn. 'The man with the camera? What exactly did he tell you?'

She gives me a starstruck look. 'That you're Olivia Sullivan! The famous supermodel and influencer.'

'Is that right?' I say. 'Had you heard of me before?'

She shakes her head. 'I'm sorry. I hadn't. But he says you're really famous.'

'I'm afraid he was teasing you,' I say. 'I'm not famous at all.'

She looks confused. 'But he was taking pictures of you.'

'He does that. He isn't very good, but no one likes to tell him that. He'd be devastated.'

I take the cap off the pen. 'I can still sign your T-shirt for you, if you like.'

She snatches it off me. 'No way! My mum would kill me.'

'I can't believe you pretended you were famous,' says one of the boys in a disgusted tone as they walk off.

I catch up with Will outside the reptile house. 'You'll never believe what just happened to me in there! Those teenagers we met all asked me to sign their T-shirts. It must be some new craze.'

His eyes widen. 'Did you agree?'

'Of course! I thought it was sweet. I signed all their T-shirts, and a few of them asked me to write messages on their jeans too. Luckily, they had a permanent marker with them, so it won't wash out. We'll probably see them again soon. They were just going to show their parents.'

He gives me a horrified look. 'I don't think you should have done that.'

'Why not?' I say airily. 'It's just a bit of fun. They'll probably ask you too if they see you. Not that I left much room, but maybe you could sign their bags or something.'

He looks even more anguished. 'Are you sure the pen was permanent?'

'Absolutely,' I assure him. 'It won't wash out. The only way to remove it would be with specialist dry-cleaning, and that would be extremely expensive. But they won't want to do that.'

I bite the inside of my cheek to keep myself from laughing. That will teach him to tell random groups of teenagers I'm a supermodel. I have no idea why any of them would have believed it. I'm at least six inches too short. Maybe there are no height restrictions for influencers.

I give him my brightest smile. 'Shall we go and check out the gorillas?'

'Olivia –' He breaks off as the group of teenagers emerge from the bird safari and start walking towards us. He studies them closely, then looks at me. I'm unable to hide my grin.

'I suppose I asked for that,' he says.

'You did indeed.'

The teenagers give us a disgusted look as they walk past.

'We knew all along she wasn't a model,' says one of the girls. 'She isn't nearly skinny enough.'

'And your photographs are rubbish!' one of the boys tells Will.

They give us one last contemptuous look and disappear towards the cafe.

'How do they know what my photographs are like?' says Will.

'I may have mentioned your lack of talent,' I say. 'I felt it was the least I could do.'

'It was,' he agrees. 'Shall we agree to call it quits?'

'Maybe that's best. At least they didn't comment on your physique.'

'That had to hurt,' he says. 'Imagine being told by a random teenager you aren't underweight.'

'They can be very harsh,' I say. 'But I'll try to deal with it.'

He looks at his watch. 'I need to call the office and let them know I'll be sending over these pictures as soon as possible. Will you check the next place, and I'll meet you there when I'm done?'

I set off for Penguin Beach. I'm pretty sure they have penguins in Australia. If Will's theory is correct, I may find Mabel hurling chunks of haddock into the water. I suspect I won't. This whole idea is nonsensical. How likely are we to find one woman in all these crowds? She may not even have come to the zoo today. She could have mentioned it as one of several options to fill her afternoon, and the receptionist passed it on to Isabella as fact.

Even if Mabel is here, it's just as likely that Will and I are several steps behind her everywhere we go. We need to split up and go around the zoo in opposite directions. We stand far more chance of finding our quarry that way. If it gets towards closing time and we still haven't found her, Will can try to persuade someone to allow us to use the Tannoy system. I hope it doesn't come to that. The embarrassment would be too much for me.

I suspect we'll have to admit defeat and return to Honeywell without having made contact with Mabel at all. It would be a shame to fail at the very last minute, but I don't know what else we can do.

As I expected, there's no sign of a woman in a pink jacket admiring the penguins. I pull out my phone to text Will and tell him I'm moving on to the butterfly house when it rings.

'Hi Will,' I say, without looking at the screen. 'I'm heading over to the butterflies.'

'It's not Will. It's me!' says Isabella's voice. 'I'm so glad I've got hold of you. It's an emergency.'

'What now?' I say. 'Have the koalas gone on strike for more eucalyptus leaves? Have the elephants escaped?'

'Not that I've heard,' she says. 'But wouldn't that be exciting? It's Will. I called him just now to see how you're getting on, and he told me he's hurt his ankle. He's in the Terrace Restaurant. Do you know where that is?'

'I'm right next to it,' I say. 'Is he badly hurt? What happened?'

'I don't know. His battery was almost out of power. He can tell you when you get there. Let me know what's going on.'

I'm already running down the path towards the terrace restaurant. What can have happened to Will? Did the group of teenagers catch up with him? Even if they did, they would hardly have started a fight with him. Did they insult his photography skills, and he chased after them, spraining his ankle in the process? That's also unlikely. Knowing Will, he would just have laughed.

I burst through the door and look around for him. There's no sign of him at any of the tables near the counter. Did Isabella get the wrong restaurant? There are several cafes dotted around the zoo.

'Olivia?' says a voice behind me, and I spin around to find Will standing there, looking worried.

'Thank goodness!' I gasp. 'I was about to run around to all the cafes to find you.'

'With a sprained ankle?' he says.

'You're the one with the sprained ankle,' I say. 'Do you need to sit down?'

His face crumples into laughter. 'Did you by any chance receive a call from Mission Control?'

Did he hit his head when hurt his ankle? Is he convinced we're touring NASA rather than London Zoo?

'You should sit down,' I say again. 'I'll ask someone for help.'

'I'm referring to Isabella,' he says. 'Did she call you?'

'She did. She said you were hurt, and I should meet you here.'

'What a coincidence,' he says. 'She told me the same thing about you. I raced over here at top speed, only to find you standing here with both legs obviously in perfect working order.'

I drop into the nearest chair. 'I should have known she was up to something. Is she worried we won't have eaten, and this is her way of making sure we do?'

'I wouldn't put it past her,' he says. 'But I don't think it was that. I think –'

He breaks off and grasps my shoulder. 'Is that –?'

I look in the direction he's pointing. 'I don't believe it! What's Mrs Ogilvie doing here?'

I watch the woman as she moves along the counter. I've never seen Mrs Ogilvie wearing magenta. She usually sticks to browns and greys.

Will gives me an incredulous look. 'Do you think there's a chance that woman isn't actually Mrs Ogilvie?'

'You mean she has a doppelganger?'

'I don't mean anything of the sort.' He takes my arm and leads me over to the counter where the woman is selecting a slice of carrot cake.

'Excuse me,' he says very politely, tapping her on the shoulder. 'But would you by any chance …?'

She turns and surveys us, and her face breaks into a beaming smile.

'You must be Will and Olivia! How lovely to meet you both.'

Chapter Thirty-Two

Will and I look at each other in astonishment.

'You *are* Will and Olivia, aren't you?' says the woman.

It's bizarre. She looks exactly like Mrs Ogilvie. She even sounds like her.

'We are,' I say. 'But I don't understand. Are you really Mabel? This isn't some elaborate prank of Isabella's?'

She laughs. 'I'm Mabel. If you know Edie, you must have recognised me at once.'

'Edie?' I say. 'Oh, you mean Mrs Ogilvie. We do know her, and we knew she had a sister. What we didn't know was that she had a twin sister. An identical twin sister, at that!'

She looks surprised. 'She never mentioned we were twins? I can't think why not.'

The woman behind us in the queue clears her throat irritably. Mabel stares her down. 'You can go around me if you're so impatient.'

She sounds so like Mrs Ogilvie that I laugh.

'I need something to drink,' says Will.

'I could do with a coffee,' I admit.

He takes Mabel's tray from her. 'I'll get this. What would you like to drink?'

'I was going to get myself a nice pot of tea,' she says. 'The more British, the better.'

Mabel and I go upstairs and find ourselves a table on the terrace. I can't stop staring at her. Now that I observe her more closely, I can see her hair is styled differently to Mrs Ogilvie's. She's also wearing bright pink lipstick, which I can't imagine Mrs Ogilvie doing. But the resemblance is uncanny.

Mabel notices me examining her and laughs. 'Don't worry, dear. I'm quite used to it. People have been doing it since we were tiny. I always tell them I'm the good-looking one, but they never seem to believe me.'

'I wonder why Mrs Ogilvie didn't mention it,' I say. 'She's talked about you several times. You'd have thought it would have come up at some point.'

She stops laughing. 'Perhaps she doesn't like to remember how close we once were.'

'I'm sorry,' I apologise. 'I'd forgotten things were strained between you.'

'It's all so silly,' she says. 'Did she tell you that she and I and Edward planned to move to Australia?'

'She did. And then he had a heart attack.'

Her face clouds. 'That's right. Poor Edie. She and Edward were inseparable. I wanted her to come out to Melbourne after the funeral, but she wouldn't because of her dog.'

'She was worried about him,' I say. 'She still has him, you know. He's a gorgeous dog.'

Will arrives carrying a tray laden with plates of cakes, a teapot, and several mugs. 'What have I missed? Have you solved the mystery of Isabella's obsession with our ankles?'

'We were waiting for you,' I tell him.

'This Isabella sounds a bit of a live wire,' says Mabel. 'I spoke to her on the phone today. She wanted to ask me to come down for this party tomorrow. I told her I was already planning on coming down to Honeywell to surprise Edie. We had a good laugh about that. I mentioned I was coming to the zoo this afternoon, and she said that was a coincidence. Her two friends would be at the zoo, and they'd love to meet me and talk about the arrangements for the party. We agreed I'd meet you here at the cafe.'

'She didn't mention any of that to us,' I say, accepting the slice of coffee and walnut cake Will hands me. 'She told us you'd checked out of your hotel before she could talk to you and invite you down to Honeywell. But the receptionist told her you'd be at the zoo, so she said we should get over here as quickly as possible and look for a woman in a pink jacket.'

'All I know is that I got Edie's email recently,' says Mabel. 'I was so pleased to hear from her after all this time. It may sound silly, but I decided on the spur of the moment to come over and celebrate our birthday together.'

'I've just realised!' says Will. 'You two must share a birthday.'

I roll my eyes. 'Well done, Einstein.'

Mabel smiles. 'I booked myself a hotel in London for a week. Then I wrote and told Edie I was coming to England, and I'd come down to see her as soon as I'd recovered from the jetlag.'

'Will and I rushed over here as soon as we got Isabella's message,' I say. 'And we've spent the afternoon running around looking for you.'

Her mouth twitches. 'I wish I'd seen you at it. But I expect she had her reasons.'

She looks so unconcerned that I burst out laughing. 'You and Isabella will get along very well when you meet. When are you arriving in Honeywell?'

'She's booked me a train ticket for tomorrow morning,' she says. 'First class! She refused to allow me to pay. It was very generous of her.'

'Maybe Olivia and I should upgrade to first class on our way home,' says Will. 'We can charge it to the bank of Isabella.'

Mabel pours herself another cup of tea. 'Now we're all here, why don't we get to know each other?'

We spent the next hour chatting and laughing. Mabel tells us all about her life in Melbourne and entertains us with anecdotes of her and Mrs Ogilvie's childhood.

'Don't mention I've told you any of this,' she warns us at one point. 'She'd never forgive me. Particularly that story about the goat and her winter underwear.'

She's very interested in what Will does for a living. He goes into far more detail about his work than he's ever done with me. I listen with interest as he tells her about some of the trips he's taken in pursuit of once-in-a-lifetime shots.

'And then Olivia went and eclipsed me with a barely functioning mobile phone!' he says.

He tells her about the advertising campaign his firm is hoping to secure, and Mabel laughs. 'You have the wrong person in your photographs. You should have used me. Nothing says slow motion more than an eighty-year-old woman on a hot day.'

'Seventy-nine,' he corrects her. 'And you seem pretty active to me. You dropped everything on a whim and flew halfway across the world. Then, instead of putting your feet up and enjoying the hotel spa, you set off across London to visit a place knows for its tigers and wolves and snakes.'

'No worries, mate!' she says in a comical Australian accent. 'We're used to dangerous wildlife in Australia – and that's just the cities!'

She laughs heartily at her own joke, and Will and I join in. It's impossible not to like this woman. She's so friendly and genuine. I wonder if she was anything like Isabella when she was younger.

It isn't until past five o'clock that Will and I remember we have a train to catch.

'Will you be all right getting back to your hotel?' I ask Mabel.

'I'll be fine,' she assures me. 'It's been a long time since I've been in a London taxi. I'm rather enjoying the experience. I'll see you both on Saturday.'

We walk as quickly as possible to the exit and jump into a taxi.

'That was quite a day,' says Will.

'I still don't know what Isabella was playing at,' I say. 'I know she has a tortuous mind, but this seems unnecessarily complicated, even for her.'

'No doubt she'll have an explanation when we see her,' says Will. 'Not necessarily a good one, but an explanation.'

I yawn. 'I'm exhausted. It feels as though I left Honeywell weeks ago.'

'It's been a busy day,' he agrees. 'But I must say I've enjoyed it. And I got those pictures for the campaign, so I can't feel too annoyed with Isabella. How about you?'

I think back over the day. The first part is a blur. I barely remember meeting with Charlie, which is a good thing. He's a part of my past and growing more so by the minute. And this afternoon was fun. It was almost as good as our day at the mediaeval fair, which until now has been my favourite Honeywell memory.

Even better, the distance between me and Will has completely disappeared. It would be difficult to maintain an awkward coolness after racing around searching for an elusive, pink-clad Australian woman, conning teenagers into thinking I was famous, and both of us enduring imaginary sprained ankles. Maybe this is what Isabella had in mind when she sent us off on this ridiculous expedition.

Will is looking at me, a faint question in his eyes.

I smile back at him. 'Yes, it was fun. I'm glad I came today.'

His face relaxes. 'Me too. Here's the station. I hope your ankle has recovered from its fake sprain because we have exactly three and a half minutes to catch our train!'

Chapter Thirty-Three

We race across the concourse and jump onto the train, ignoring the disapproving look the guard gives us, before making our way to our carriage.

I collapse into my seat. 'I'm exhausted. We must have walked miles today. I'll have a lot to say to Isabella when I see her.'

He leans back in his seat and yawns. 'Like you said, it was a busy day.'

'It was more fun than I expected.'

'Which bit?' he says.

'All of it! Running around the zoo. Being mistaken for an influencer. The usual sort of thing.'

'How about the part before that?' he says.

'You mean Charlie?'

'He was the reason you came up to London,' he reminds me.

'I know. But it all seems so long ago now.'

'How do you feel about what happened?'

'Surprisingly good,' I say. 'I knew I was doing the right thing when I left London. I didn't know why, but I knew I couldn't stay with him any longer. I have no idea why I stayed as long as I did.'

'Why did you?' he says, and I'm surprised by the intent look on his face.

'I've asked myself that same question a hundred times, and the answer is I don't know. It felt as though it was my fault when things didn't go well. I thought if I could discover the one thing about myself I needed to change, everything would be perfect.'

'That's the definition of insanity,' he says. 'Doing the same thing over and over again and expecting a different result.'

'I thought the definition of insanity was leaving freshly baked doughnuts alone with Isabella.'

'I'm serious,' he says. 'Don't you see how useless it is to try to fix things by changing yourself? That's never the answer.'

'I must have known it subconsciously or I wouldn't have left the way I did. I'll always feel bad about that.'

'I don't see why,' he says. 'Do you think Charlie ever thought about your relationship and decided he needed to change something about himself?'

'Probably not. Anyway, it's finished now, so what does it matter?'

He sits up straighter. 'Are you serious? Of course, it matters.'

'Why? It happened, it's over, and that's that. There's no point in rehashing the past.'

'There's every point,' he says. 'How can you prevent yourself from making the same mistake next time if you don't know what went wrong?'

I'm starting to feel annoyed. This is none of Will's business. I don't want to argue with him. I'm too tired, for one thing. But neither do I want to delve into the details of my failed relationship.

I decide that the best form of defence is attack. 'Did you do that after you broke up with Melissa? Did you go back over every gory detail and ask yourself why it all went wrong and what you should have done differently?'

'I thought about what happened,' he says.

'And what conclusions did you draw?'

'That I had no chance unless I started bodybuilding and found myself a plastic surgeon who specialised in the Greek god package.'

'He was better looking than you?' I say.

'In the same way a Rembrandt is better than a finger painting. He was an underwear model, if that helps you to imagine?'

'You're right,' I say. 'How could a troll like you compete?'

He smiles. 'I can always rely on you to make me feel better about myself.'

'Are you telling me your relationship breakdown had nothing to do with you? It was sheer bad luck?'

'That's just what I told myself to soothe my injured pride,' he says. 'The truth was that Melissa and I had almost nothing in common. We met at a sports club, and we kept bumping into each other. I thought we were compatible because we had a shared interest, but that wasn't the case.'

'Isn't that the predictor of success in a relationship?' I say. 'All the magazines say you should enjoy doing the same things.'

'They also say you should drink hideous green smoothies in order to live an extra decade,' he says. 'I don't think we should base our life choices on what any magazine says. In our case, it didn't work out that way. In fact, it kept us together for far too long. We were so busy playing tennis and squash together that we never stopped to ask ourselves whether we wanted the same things for our lives.'

'You'll have to marry a photographer,' I say. 'It's the only way to ensure you're compatible with someone.'

'I could marry ten photographers without being compatible with any of them,' he says. 'That's my point. It doesn't matter what you do. It's all about how you see the world and what your goals are outside work.'

'There wouldn't be any outside work if you married ten photographers,' I say. 'You'd be in jail for bigamy.'

'Must you be so literal?' he says. 'But you get my point?'

'I'm not sure I do.'

He looks surprised. 'It's not about what you do in life. It's about what you want – what's important to you.'

'Like how many children you want?' I say.

'Maybe, for some people. For others, it might be about making a difference. Leaving the world in a better state than you found it or protecting the environment. It's different for everyone.'

'What do you want for yourself?' I ask.

'Lots of things. I want to travel as much as possible. It's a big world, and I'd like to see a lot more of it. I love the idea of using my photographic skills to bring places to people who can't visit them, and to show them in a new light to those who've visited them a thousand times.'

'I like that,' I say. 'But it isn't wholly unrelated to your work. What else?'

'You're embarrassing me,' he complains.

'I'm sorry, but I'm interested.'

'I want to become the best person I can be,' he says. 'I can't say what that entails, but I don't want to be static. I'd like to keep learning new skills and developing meaningful relationships. I'd like a family one day. I don't know what that looks like, but it doesn't matter. I'll know it when I see it. And I hope to be part of a community – not necessarily in a single place, but a group of connected people.'

This is a side of him I haven't seen before. It's somewhat unexpected.

'I hope it all happens for you,' I say.

'Thanks. What about you? What do you want out of life?'

I don't answer. Not because I don't want to, but because I can't. I have no idea what to say. I'm horrified to find my eyes filling with tears.

'Olivia?' he says.

I wipe my eyes on my sleeve. 'I'm sorry. I don't know what's wrong with me.'

'You're tired. It's been quite a day! It isn't the greatest time for these metaphysical discussions.'

I sniff. 'It isn't that. I'm upset because I can't answer your question. I've always thought of my life in terms of steps and plans. What am I going to do next? Where am I going to work? Where are we going to live? I've never thought about any of the rest of it, and now I'm wondering why.'

'I could make a suggestion why you haven't,' he says. 'But I'm not sure you'd like it.'

'Charlie?'

He nods. 'He seems to have done most of the thinking in your relationship. Whenever you talk about your life with him, you always say, "Charlie wants," or, "Charlie says." You don't seem to figure at all in your own life.'

'I can't put all the responsibility on him. I'm an adult. I should have seen that that myself and done something about it.'

He shrugs. 'Maybe. Anyway, that part of your life is over now. At least, I assume it is? Is there a chance you'll go back to him?'

'Not even the tiniest one. As soon as I saw him today, I knew it was no good. I kept telling myself I was being unreasonable, but I knew I wasn't.'

He looks uncomfortable. 'It wasn't because I arrived? I didn't mean to. I was trying to give that server a note for you, and unfortunately Charlie caught sight of me.'

'It wasn't you,' I say. 'It was all me. I may not know what I want, but I finally know what I don't want.'

He looks relieved. 'I'm glad. I didn't like the guy, but I'd hate to be the reason you two broke up.'

'You weren't.'

Surely, this would be the perfect opportunity for him to raise the subject of what he said to me in Mrs Carson's garden. But he doesn't. He picks up a magazine someone has left lying on a nearby table and starts to flick through it.

It's a good thing, really. I don't need any more complications in my life. Will has obviously forgotten about what he said that afternoon, or he's thankful it didn't come to anything. He was carried away by the excitement of the afternoon and almost created a very sticky situation for himself.

He and I can go back to being friends, with none of the awkwardness of the past few days. We won't be seeing each other for much longer anyway. Lily is returning to work next week, which means I'll be moving on. He and I will probably never see each other again.

I remember one of my high school teachers telling me that some friends are there for a reason and a season. That's the case with Will and Isabella. They both came into my life when I needed them, and I'm thankful for them. But it's time for me to move on and create my own future.

It looks very different from the one I planned with Charlie, but that isn't a bad thing. Now that I'm free again, there's almost nothing I can't do if I choose. I can create myself a whole new life. I just wish I knew where to start.

Chapter Thirty-Four

I arrive at the bakery early the following morning. As I expected, Abby is already there. As I also expected, Isabella isn't. She arrives twenty minutes later, looking cheerfully apologetic.

'My car wouldn't start this morning, so I had to wait for Georgia to give me a lift. She said she was almost ready, but I reckoned without her needing breakfast first.'

'She takes after you,' says Abby, emerging from the kitchen covered with flour to make herself a coffee.

'She's nothing like me!' says Isabella. 'I'm able to skip breakfast if it's in a good cause. I mentioned that to Georgia, but she said so could she if she worked in a bakery. There's no reasoning with that girl sometimes.'

'Perhaps you could help me in the kitchen,' says Abby. 'I'm on top of most things, but I still need to fill the sandwiches and ice the cake.'

'No problem,' says Isabella. 'But first, I want to hear all about your day in London, Olivia. Well done on locating Mabel, by the way.'

I give her an exasperated look. 'Well done? We wouldn't have needed to look for her at all if you'd told us the truth. Why did you send us on a wild goose chase?'

She gives me an unrepentant smile. 'I thought it would be fun for you.'

'Racing around London in the heat, trying to find an unknown woman, before discovering you knew where she was all along and there was no need for any of it?'

'That's one way of putting it,' she says. 'The other is that I was giving you and Will a chance to have some fun together and work through whatever's gone wrong between you.'

I grope for the appropriate words, but I can't find them.

She smiles again. 'Did it work? Are you two ok now?'

'I went to see Charlie,' I remind her.

Her face falls. 'Did you and he get back together?'

I'm tempted to tell her we did, just to see her expression change. She ought to realise that tampering in people's lives like this is a dangerous activity. But she looks so eager and friendly that I don't have the heart to. Besides, she's always been so kind to me. I can let this one slide.

'We didn't,' I say. 'But you couldn't have known that when you sent Will up to London on the same train as me. The whole thing could have been extremely awkward.'

'I know,' she says. 'But I couldn't think of any other way to get you two talking again. You are talking, aren't you?'

'We are.'

'And you're not angry with me?'

She looks so much like an excited pre-schooler that I laugh. 'I'm not angry with you. We had a fun afternoon. It's been a while since I've been to the zoo.'

'Good,' she says. 'Now we've got that out of the way, we have another crisis. I heard last night that Mrs Ogilvie won't be here for the party!'

'What?' I almost shriek. 'Do you mean she's managed to leave the village without anyone realising?'

Isabella gives me a pitying look. 'Do you think this is my first rodeo? I've been meddling in people's lives for years. I considered that possibility ages ago. Mrs Ogilvie has been under twenty-four-hour surveillance for the past three days.'

'She's been ...?' Words fail me, and I sit down at the nearest table.

'That's right,' she says. 'I didn't want to risk our quarry disappearing at the last moment. I mentioned it to Angela Carson, who suggested I talk to Mavis Sotherby. Say what you like about Mavis, but she takes her work seriously.'

'I'm almost afraid to ask,' I say. 'Have you had a group of women in disguise hanging around Mrs Ogilvie's house, pretending to read her water meter?'

'I thought about that,' she says. 'But Mavis said that kind of activity is strictly against the law. She was most emphatic about it. I wondered how she could be so sure, but she wouldn't say.'

'What a shame,' says Abby. 'What did you come up with instead?'

Isabella looks even more pleased with herself. 'Lots of things. Mrs Carson asked Mrs Ogilvie over for tea on Thursday afternoon. She kept her there until early evening. And Mavis took care of yesterday. She contacted the Silver Surfers and told them she was setting them homework, and she expected everyone to take part. They had to log on every two hours and complete assignments like downloading an image or sending her an email. She said there would be a prize for the competitors who completed all the assignments.'

'And Mrs Ogilvie fell for it?' I say, amused.

'Like a ton of bricks. It turns out she's very competitive. Mavis says she was the first one to log on and do each of her tasks. It helped that they were tailored to her interests. First, the class was told to download a picture of a cavoodle and add it to their photo album. Then they were asked to send Mavis an email describing the funniest thing their pet has ever done. After that, there was an online questionnaire about the history of Honeywell. Things like that.'

'I'm impressed Mrs Ogilvie managed all that by herself,' I say. 'She's only been to a couple of classes.'

'So am I,' says Isabella. 'But she's picking it up surprisingly quickly. Mavis says she's as sharp as a tack, and she doesn't like being told she can't do anything.'

'That figures,' says Abby. 'Remember when we closed the bakery for the first round of the competition last year? She was furious. She was standing on the doorstep with Bernie on the stroke of noon, glaring at the judges until they left.'

'So, what's the problem today?' I ask.

'She called Nigel Farrow last night,' says Isabella. 'He's retired, but he runs a sort of unofficial taxi service for the village. Mrs Ogilvie told him she was going up to London this afternoon, and would he please pick her up at one o'clock?'

'To London?' I say. 'To see Mabel?'

'That's right,' says Isabella. 'We should have thought of that possibility. But we didn't realise until yesterday it was Mabel's birthday too. Mrs Ogilvie told Nigel her sister had just arrived in the country, and she planned to surprise her at her hotel and take her out for dinner to celebrate their joint birthdays.'

'He didn't give the game away?' I say.

'Not at all. Luckily, he's one of the Silver Surfers, so he knew all about the party. He took the booking, then immediately called Mavis, who called me.'

'So, what's the plan?' says Abby. 'Will you tell Mrs Ogilvie about the party and stop her from leaving the village? You've done pretty well to keep everything under wraps so far. Maybe it's time to tell her what's going on.'

Isabella looks disgusted. 'I will not! We said this was a surprise party, and so it is. We only have to prevent her from finding out for a few more hours. If we can't manage that, we aren't worthy of the name of co-conspirators. We have a much better plan. Nigel will pick her up, as planned, and set off for

London. Halfway up the motorway, he'll develop engine trouble and have to turn back to Honeywell. He'll bring her back exactly in time for the party.'

'I don't think that's a good idea,' I say. 'You know it's all fake, but Mrs Ogilvie doesn't. She could be quite upset.'

'Oh, ye of little faith!' says Isabella. 'That thought crossed my mind too. Mrs Carson will be with her. She's told Mrs Ogilvie she's going up to London today and suggested they share the cost. When Nigel develops car trouble, Mrs Carson will tell him to take them both back to her house so that Martin can run them up to London.'

'You're wasted running a bakery,' I say. 'Why aren't you working for MI5? I'm sure they could use someone with your devious abilities.'

'Creative abilities,' she corrects me. 'Let's see how this plan works out first. I can send them the details later and offer myself on a consultancy basis.'

Abby finishes her drink. 'I have to get back to the kitchen. We don't want Mrs Ogilvie to arrive at the party and find there's no food.'

'Quite right!' says Isabella. 'I'll help you. Are you ok by yourself, Olivia?'

'I'm fine,' I assure her. 'We don't get many customers on a Saturday morning. And I have something of my own to work on.'

'That sounds exciting,' says Isabella, preparing to sit down again.

'Not now,' I say. 'Off you go and make yourself useful. I'll see you at lunchtime.'

I spend the next few hours serving customers and making coffees. I'm pretty good at this now. I've mastered the art of perfect foam. I haven't attempted any more complicated pattern than an acorn, but they're almost always recognisable. It should serve us in good stead if the bakery is ever attacked by a gang of rambunctious squirrels.

In my spare few minutes, I study the list I've been making and think about the conversation Will and I had on the train. It helped me to see more clearly what's wrong with my life. I don't know why I didn't see it before, but that's often the way things turn out. Something obvious stares us in the face for years without us realising. Then someone new comes along, and it's like a lightbulb going off in our head. That's what happened with Will yesterday. And whatever happens in the future, I'll always be grateful to him for that.

Chapter Thirty-Five

Abby and Isabella emerge from the kitchen at lunchtime, carrying Mrs Ogilvie's cake. They set it down on the nearest table, and we all step back to admire it.

'I can't believe you made that yourself,' I tell Abby. 'I knew you were a talented baker, but this is amazing!'

She looks pleased. 'It came out well, didn't it? I made the cake yesterday, but I didn't want to ice it until today. The buttercream needs to be fresh.'

Isabella checks her phone. 'Two hours to go. Mrs Ogilvie will be finishing packing her bags, and Mavis will have a couple of her best operatives lurking at the end of the street to let us know if she shows signs of making an early getaway.'

'What about Bernie?' I say. 'I'd forgotten him!'

'Tsk,' says Isabella. 'It's lucky you're surrounded by so many older and wiser heads. He's going to Will for the weekend.'

'To Will?' I say.

'That's right. As soon as Nigel told us what was happening last night, I dropped around to Mrs Ogilvie's house with some biscuits for Bernie. She told me about her plans for today and said she was about to call you and ask you to look after Bernie.

So, I told her you were going away this weekend. I suggested she ask Will instead and gave her his number. She called him last night, and he agreed.'

'Why did you say I couldn't do it?' I say.

'Because I need you here. Will isn't really looking after Bernie. It's all for show. He'll pick Bernie up from her house at one o'clock, take him for a long walk to shake the fidgets out of him, then bring him to the party. I can't spare you until then. Who knows what might go wrong here at the last minute? So, I dumped the job onto Will.'

I relax. It's true that Bernie will need a walk before he arrives at the Carsons' house. Even with a walk, he'll be bouncing off the walls. Without one, I don't like to think what havoc he might wreak.

Abby turns the shop sign to closed. 'We'd better transport this food to the party. Isabella is taking the savoury things in her car, and I'm taking the sweet.'

'Good plan,' I say. 'It's like the fox, the chicken, and the grain. We can't leave Isabella alone with the cakes, but we need to get all the food there in one piece. Who's taking the birthday cake?'

'That's going on your lap,' says Isabella. 'Unless there's any more rudeness from you. In which case, you can walk through the village with it.'

'Fine,' I say. 'But I'm sitting in the back seat.'

'Don't you trust my driving?'

'I don't trust you not to get hungry halfway there,' I say, and Abby laughs.

We pack the food into the two cars, and I climb into the back seat with the cake.

'Are you sure you wouldn't be better off sitting in the front?' says Isabella. 'It has air bags.'

'It's very nice of you to worry about my safety,' I say. 'But as long as you drive slowly, I should be fine.'

'I was thinking about the cake!' she says.

We drive to the Carsons' house by a circuitous route. Isabella explains she doesn't want to go near Mrs Ogilvie's house in case Nigel drives past and Mrs Ogilvie guesses what's going on. I'm unconvinced, but Isabella is having so much fun with her spy games that I don't want to burst her bubble.

We pass Will walking towards the high street with Bernie. He waves when he sees us but looks preoccupied. I'm not surprised. Bernie is running in alternate circles around a lamp post and Will's legs, creating a figure of eight. Will obviously doesn't know about keeping an excitable dog on a short leash.

'I hope they make it to the party,' says Isabella. 'The way Bernie's carrying on, he'll soon have Will tied to that lamppost, and Bernie will be able to make his escape. Maybe you should go back and help.'

'I have one job, and it isn't rescuing Will,' I say. 'I plan to deliver this cake in one piece or die trying.'

'That's mean,' she says. 'Will rescued you when you first arrived, and you're refusing to return the favour.'

'He'll figure it out,' I say. 'And from now on, I plan to rescue myself.'

She raises an eyebrow but doesn't say anything more as we pull up outside the Carsons' house.

Martin opens the car door and picks up the cake. 'Doesn't this look marvellous? Abby's outdone herself this time.'

We carry the plates of sandwiches and quiches to the back garden. I can't believe the change since I was last here. There's a large pink and white marquee in the centre of the lawn. There are about fifteen small tables dotted around the garden, each with its own umbrella. Each table is decorated with a floral centrepiece, and someone has arranged lanterns in all the trees. The Carsons must have spent days on this.

By the time, we've organised the food, people have started to arrive. I recognise a few of our regular customers, but Isabella seems to know them all. She greets them by name and ushers them into the marquee.

'Mrs Ogilvie mustn't see you too soon,' she explains.

'Were you planning for everyone to jump out and shout *Surprise!*' I say.

'I wanted to,' she says. 'But Abby talked me out of it. She said we don't need Mrs Ogilvie spending her birthday afternoon in the cardiac ward.'

'So, what's the plan?'

'Mrs Carson will take her into the house until I give the signal. Then she'll bring her into the garden to find Martin. I hope Mabel arrives in time.'

'I expect she'll be here,' I say. 'I've only met her once, but she struck me as a competent woman. Just like her sister.'

'It's in the lap of the gods,' says Isabella. 'We've done everything we can, and the rest is up to fate. In the meantime, I'll make sure everyone has something to drink.'

'Soft drinks, I hope. We don't want half the guests to be drunk before the guest of honour arrives.'

'Most of the elderly people I know can drink me under the table,' she says. 'But I'm way ahead of you. Mrs Carson has left several jugs of iced elderflower juice in the kitchen. I'll bring them out.'

I look around the garden at the people chatting and laughing in the sunshine. When I first suggested this party, I assumed we would just be offering tea and cake. I had no idea it would spiral into something like this. This must be what Will meant when he talked about community. An entire village coming together to support someone who needs it. I hope Mrs Ogilvie feels the same. It would be awful if she took one look at our arrangements and ran away.

A sharp yap rouses me from these musings, and I turn to see Will has arrived with Bernie. Will looks exhausted, but Bernie is as perky as ever. He gives an excited yelp when he sees me and tears across the lawn to greet me, with Will barely clinging to his lead.

'This is wonderful!' I say, bending to hug Bernie. 'Have you taken him on a nice long walk to tire him out?'

'About an hour,' says Will. 'I didn't want to be late for the party.'

'I was talking to Bernie,' I say. 'Remind me to show you how to shorten his lead. It will prevent you from being tied to stray lamp posts.'

He laughs. 'I hoped you wouldn't notice that.'

Lily comes out of the house, carrying Daisy. She waves when she sees me. 'Isn't this incredible?'

'It's amazing,' I say. 'Your parents must have worked so hard on all this.'

'They've had a lot of help,' she says. 'Mavis and the Silver Surfers have done most of the organising. They've loaned tables and chairs and plates. One of them knows someone who rents marquees, so they managed to get a huge discount. And they've talked all the local suppliers into donating things. Mr Peters told me it's one of the joys of getting older. You don't care what people think of you, and you have plenty of time to make them see your point of view.'

'Do you think Mrs Ogilvie will like it?' I say.

Will gives me a reassuring smile. 'You worry too much. She'll love it.'

Isabella appears around the side of the house. 'Mabel's here! Just in time. Angela has texted me to say they're almost back in Honeywell. Apparently, Mrs Ogilvie is most unimpressed with Nigel's car maintenance skills.'

'Whizzy!' shrieks Daisy, struggling out of Lily's arms and setting off at a determined crawl towards Isabella.

Isabella scoops her up and gestures to us all to join her in the marquee.

'We should all stay as quiet as possible,' she instructs us. 'Angela and Mrs Ogilvie will be out at any moment.'

'Whizzy!' shouts Daisy again.

Isabella lays a finger on her lips. 'Let's play a game to see who can be the quietest.'

Daisy gives a squawk of laughter and Isabella picks up an iced cookie. 'Don't talk until you've finished that.'

Daisy beams at her and crams the cookie into her mouth.

'You could have given her a piece of cheese,' murmurs Lily.

'Cheese!' says Isabella contemptuously. She lifts a finger. 'I can hear them.'

The marquee has fallen silent. Everyone is staring at the doorway. There's a murmur of voices, which grows louder.

'Let's see where Martin is, shall we?' says Mrs Carson's voice.

They appear a moment later. Mrs Ogilvie takes in the inside of the tent – the tables of food, the crowd of people, the bunches of balloons. She looks around without speaking.

Mabel has been standing at the back of the tent until now. She steps forward when she sees her sister. 'Happy birthday, Edith!'

Chapter Thirty-Six

For a moment, Mrs Ogilvie doesn't move. She looks at Mabel as though she's seen a ghost. Mabel looks back at her, an enquiring smile on her lips. It feels as though the entire crowd is holding its breath. Then Mrs Ogilvie throws her arms around Mabel and bursts into tears.

'Oh dear,' says Mrs Carson uncertainly.

Neither Mabel nor Edith takes any notice. They hug each other as though they never want to let each other go.

There's a chorus of happy birthdays, which seems to bring them back to reality.

Mrs Ogilvie lets go of her sister and looks around, dazed. 'I don't understand.'

'Of course, you do!' says Mabel, wiping her eyes. 'It's your birthday.'

'But you're in London,' says Mrs Ogilvie.

'I was in London,' says Mabel. 'You didn't think I'd miss your party, did you?'

'Both your parties,' says Isabella. 'Once I discovered you were identical twins, it didn't take me more than four or five hours to work out that you must share the same birthday. I'm quick like that.'

'Go on with you!' says Mabel. 'I don't need a party. I'm just happy to see Edith again.'

'Too late,' says Lily, reaching up and pulling a red ribbon hanging down from the top of the tent.

A rolled up banner unfurls itself and opens out. It reads *Happy Birthday, Edith and Mabel!*

'I made that,' says Isabella. 'You wouldn't believe how long it took me. I spelled the first one wrong.'

'Birthday is a tricky word for anyone to spell,' says Will, looking amused.

'I've known how to spell that one for ages,' says Isabella. 'But the first time I made the banner, I put two bs in Mabel. I didn't think anyone would notice, but Lily made me do it again. She's such a perfectionist.'

Mrs Carson has been handing out glasses of champagne to all the guests. She clinks her fork on a plate. 'We should drink a toast! I'd like to thank all of you who have so generously contributed to this party in various ways. We couldn't have done it without you. Also, many thanks to The Sugarloaf Bakery for providing this lovely food. Abby, you've surpassed yourself.'

'Don't forget Olivia,' interjects Isabella. 'This was all her idea in the first place.'

'I was getting to that,' says Mrs Carson. 'We're grateful to everyone who's contributed in whatever way. And last, but not least, the birthday girls! Thank goodness we managed to get you in the same place at the same time. I hope you enjoy your party!'

She raises her glass to Mrs Ogilvie and Mabel and drinks. We all follow suit.

'Help yourselves to this lovely food,' says Mrs Carson. 'We don't have room for it in the freezer, so it all has to go.'

People fill their plates and wander out into the garden. Mrs Ogilvie still looks dazed. 'I don't understand what's happened.'

Mabel takes her arm. 'I'll explain it to you later. In the meantime, you and I have a lot of catching up to do.' She leads Mrs Ogilvie out of the tent, and they disappear towards the house.

'Thank goodness for that,' I say. 'It was touch and go there for a while. There were so many things that could have gone wrong.'

'It was bound to turn out all right in the end,' says Mrs Carson. 'These things always do.'

'Where's Daisy?' says Lily suddenly.

I notice that Isabella is no longer holding her goddaughter. 'Have you lost her already?'

'She's over there.' Isabella points to where Daisy is sitting on the grass underneath a table, sharing a cookie with Bernie.

'Stop that!' exclaims Lily, making a dart for her daughter. Bernie takes advantage of the commotion to snatch the rest of the cookie, and Daisy gives a wail.

Isabella picks her up. 'Don't worry. We're cutting the cake soon, and you shall have the biggest slice!'

Lily groans. 'Don't say that. She'll understand you.'

'Of course, she understands me,' says Isabella. 'She's the cleverest girl in the whole, wide world. Come on, Daisy. We'd better get you something else to eat before we cut the cake. Your mother seems to have a cheese obsession. Let's start with that.'

Lily brushes the grass off her skirt. 'I sometimes wonder what was going through my mind when I made her Daisy's godmother.'

'It was an excellent decision,' I say. 'I wish I'd had a godmother like Isabella.'

It's late afternoon by the time Mrs Ogilvie and Mabel reappear. Their eyes are suspiciously red, but they're both smiling.

Bernie jumps up at Mabel, who pats his head. 'I see what you mean, Edith. He is precious.'

'He's all I have,' says Mrs Ogilvie, her eyes moist.

'That isn't true,' says Mabel.

Mrs Ogilvie gives one of her rare smiles. 'I suppose not.'

Mabel catches my eye. 'You and Will went to so much trouble to find me. You should be the first to know. I'm moving back to Honeywell!'

'Permanently?' I say, astonished.

'That's right. Australia is all very well and good, but I've found myself missing home more and more.'

'What a great idea!' says Will. 'Where will you live?'

'With Edith,' she says. 'I was planning to buy myself a small house in the village, but she won't hear of it.'

'I have two extra bedrooms,' says Mrs Ogilvie. 'There's plenty of room for us both. And Bernie will enjoy the company. He's quite taken to Mabel.'

Bernie has positioned himself under the nearest table in case anyone drops any food. He grins up at me and thumps his tail.

'He'll love it,' I say. 'Bernie is an extremely sociable dog, even for a cavoodle. He'll adore all the extra fuss.'

Mrs Carson bustles up, holding a bottle of champagne. 'Can I fill anyone's glass?'

'Good idea,' says Will. 'We have plenty to celebrate. Mabel is moving to Honeywell.'

Mrs Carson almost drops the bottle. 'That's lovely news! I'm so glad for you both. Will you be living in Honeysuckle Cottage together?'

'That's the plan,' says Mabel. 'But not immediately. Edie and I are going to London tomorrow for a few days. It's high time we spent some time together.'

She turns to me. 'We were hoping you might agree to look after Bernie? It's a lot to ask, but Edie tells me you're so good with him, and he loves you.'

'I'd be honoured,' I say. 'Bernie and I will have lots of fun together. If my landlady isn't keen on the idea, maybe I could stay at the cottage while you're gone?'

'Better still!' she says. 'Edie's always had a thing about burglars.'

Mrs Carson fills the rest of our glasses. 'This seems to be an afternoon for toasts. To the newest member of our village. Welcome home!'

'I'd better fetch another bottle of champagne,' she says when we've drunk the toast. 'In case anyone else has something to celebrate.'

'I'm happy to toast anything you like,' says Isabella, appearing in the doorway with Daisy in her arms. 'But I doubt anything will top that. I never dreamed this party would be such a success. That's all thanks to you, Olivia.'

'I hardly did anything,' I say.

'It was your idea,' she says. 'Without you, there wouldn't have been a party at all. And look what a great time everyone's having.'

Lily appears behind her. 'There you are! I couldn't find Daisy anywhere. She's supposed to be having a nap.'

'She can have a nap any time,' says Isabella. 'It would be a shame to miss this afternoon. She's been having so much fun. She's a party girl, just like her godmother.'

'What are you all talking about?' says Lily.

'The future,' says Will. 'Mabel is moving to Honeywell, and Bernie is getting himself a new servant.'

'I'm so pleased,' Lily tells Mabel. 'I hope you'll be very happy here. Honeywell has probably changed since you last visited. You'll have to get Bernie to show you our bakery. We have a cafe now, and he's one of our most regular customers. We're thinking of putting up a plaque.'

'Speaking of change,' says Isabella. 'Plenty of other things are happening. Lily is starting work back at the bakery on Monday.'

'Is that right?' says Will, shooting me a quick glance.

'It is,' I say. 'She and Isabella told me last week.'

Mrs Ogilvie looks concerned. 'Does that mean Honeywell will be losing you, my dear?'

'I'm afraid so. It's time I moved on. I've had the most amazing summer here, and I'll never forget it. But I don't think it's the place I'm supposed to be – at least not for now.'

She nods. 'You must do what's best for you. But Bernie and I will miss you.'

Will still hasn't spoken. I half expect him to ask me what I'm doing next, but he doesn't.

Isabella breaks the silence. 'Have you made any definite plans, Olivia?'

Everyone's eyes are on me. I hadn't expected to do this now, but why not? It's time I stopped caring what everyone thinks about me and the choices I make.

I reach into my pocket and pull out a crumpled piece of paper, which I clutch like a talisman. 'As a matter of fact, I have.'

Chapter Thirty-Seven

I turn to face the assembled group. Isabella looks amused, while Lily looks anxious. I can't quite read Will's expression.

I unfold the piece of paper. 'I realised something while I was racing around London yesterday. Somewhere along the line, I've lost the ability to say, "I want." I'm not sure when that happened, but it did. I spent a long time thinking about it last night, and I made this list. It isn't complete, but it's a start.'

I take a deep breath and start to read. 'I like mountains, but I'm not too keen on the beach. I love handwritten letters with real wax seals. I like rock music, but I hate jazz. I like thrillers, but I find romance films boring. I prefer plain apple pie and ice cream to Tiramisu. I hate flavoured coffees. I love rainy days and splashing through puddles. I like yellow, but I don't like red. I prefer the autumn to the spring. I hate the idea of going in a helicopter, but I've always wanted to take a trip in a hot air balloon. I love the idea of buying the first plane ticket to anywhere and seeing where I end up. I hate planning my life down to the last second. I'd rather chew my arm off than go to a nightclub. I want to swim with dolphins one day.'

'You can do that in Australia!' says Mabel. 'I'll send you a link.'

Mrs Ogilvie taps her sister's arm. 'This isn't the time.'

'Sorry,' says Mabel. 'I thought she wanted to know where she could find some dolphins.'

'No, she doesn't. Stop talking and listen!'

I resume my list. 'I don't want to be a general veterinary nurse forever. I want to take a post grad course and specialise. I want to travel and see the world. I want to go to California and see the sun rise over the Pacific Ocean. I want to sleep in a tree house in Kenya. I want to learn to cook Mexican food and make a proper margarita. I want to adopt a rescue dog and have my own garden.'

I'm so engrossed in my list that I've almost forgotten everyone is standing there, watching me. I look up and see Mrs Carson's encouraging smile. Isabella gives me a thumbs up, but no one else speaks.

Will breaks the silence at last. 'Is that all you want?'

I force myself to meet his eyes, aware of my heart beating uncomfortably fast. 'No, it isn't. I added one more thing to the list this morning. I want you.'

He doesn't move. 'Are you sure?'

'Yes. I want to do all the things I just said. But it won't be half as much fun doing them by myself. I'd far rather do them with you. It's fine if you don't want the same things I do. But I couldn't leave Honeywell without telling you.'

'I should point out the sun actually sets over the Pacific Ocean,' he says. 'Also, I prefer Italian food to Mexican. But if we're both willing to make a couple of compromises, I think we could make this work.'

'You do?' I say.

'The only thing on your list I care about is the last one,' he says. 'I want you too, Olivia. I've wanted you ever since the first day we met, when we argued about ping pong balls and giant omelettes. I even wanted you when you made fun of me at the quintain.'

'The what?' says Mabel, but Mrs Ogilvie shushes her again.

'So, the only question left unanswered,' says Will, his eyes fixed on mine, 'is whether I'm going to kiss you in front of this crowd of interested observers, or whether we're going to find somewhere more private.'

'Don't you dare!' says Isabella in such an indignant tone I can't help laughing.

Will smiles down at me, his eyes full of amusement. But there's something else there, something that makes my heart beat faster.

'The crowd has spoken,' he says, putting his hands on my shoulders and bending his head to mine.

It's nothing like our last kiss. This isn't a result of the adrenaline fuelled chase across the lawn and my successful picture of Bernie. It feels soft and sweet and familiar, as though I've been kissing him all my life. It's also unfamiliar and exciting, a promise of things to come – things I never knew I wanted, yet I now realise I can't live without.

Will suddenly staggers and slips, letting go of me just in time before he falls.

'Bernie, you naughty boy!' says Mrs Ogilvie. 'What are you doing?'

I look down to see Bernie's lead wrapped around my legs and Will lying in a heap at my feet. I drop to my knees next to him. 'Are you all right?'

He slips an arm around my shoulders and pulls me towards him. 'I've never been better!'

I sit back on my heels. 'Now isn't the time!'

'I disagree,' he says. 'I've been waiting for this for a long time.'

'Don't mind us!' says Isabella. 'Pretend we're not here.'

'You see?' says Will.

I untangle the lead from around his legs. 'I think the moment has passed.'

I help him to his feet, and he hands the lead back to Mrs Ogilvie. 'This is yours, I believe?'

'I'm so sorry,' she says. 'I can't imagine what came over him. He's usually such a well-behaved dog.'

'He's perfect,' I say, holding his paws as he jumps up to lick me. 'He's had an exciting day, that's all. Even the best-behaved dogs forget themselves at times.'

I turn to Will. 'Which reminds me. Where did you put that parcel?'

'In the hall.'

'I'll fetch it!' says Mrs Carson. 'Lily, can you pour some more champagne? It seems we have another toast to drink.'

She returns a minute later, carrying not one but two parcels. 'Are these both yours, Will?'

'That's right.' He hands the first one to Mrs Ogilvie. 'This one is from me. The other is from Olivia.'

She tears open the paper, and her eyes fill with tears. 'Oh, Bernie!'

Everyone crowds around to look at the picture she's holding. Will has framed it beautifully. I smile as I see Bernie sitting in the middle of the flowers, looking up at the butterfly and grinning. That was quite an afternoon.

Mrs Ogilvie wipes her eyes. 'It's so like him!'

'I should hope so,' says Will. 'It's what I do for a living. Open the other one.'

Mrs Ogilvie tears off the wrapping paper. 'However did you manage to take this?'

'I didn't,' says Will. 'Olivia did.'

'I'm impressed!' says Lily. 'I didn't know you were a photographer too, Olivia.'

'My girlfriend is multi-talented,' says Will proudly.

'Aren't you getting a bit ahead of yourself?' I say.

'I don't think so. If we were living in mediaeval times, you'd have to marry me after kissing me like that before all these witnesses.'

'If we were living in mediaeval times,' I retort, 'you'd have had to win me a lot more ribbons before I let you kiss me at all.'

His arm tightens around my shoulders. 'Isn't it lucky we're living in the twenty-first century?'

'They didn't have cameras back then,' says Lily. 'You'd have had to paint Bernie instead.'

'He wouldn't have sat still for long enough,' I say. 'All you'd have seen was a blur of oil paint.'

Mrs Ogilvie lays the pictures on the table next to her. 'I shall hang these over the fireplace as soon as I get home. Bernie will enjoy seeing them each evening as he lies in front of the fire.'

'Good idea,' says Mabel. 'And I'll put up some pictures of Melbourne. It will remind me of all the fun I've had over the past few years.'

'You'll have lots more fun over the next few years,' says Isabella. 'Both of you together.'

'I hope so,' says Mrs Ogilvie.

'Of course, we will,' says Mabel. 'The three of us will make a great team.'

Lily fills everyone's glasses. 'That's the last of the champagne. There's enough for one final toast. We'd better make it a good one.'

Mrs Ogilvie surprises me by speaking first. 'I'd like to propose this one, if no one minds. First of all, Mabel and I would like to say thank you to everyone who has worked so hard to make this wonderful party happen. I haven't enjoyed myself so much since our fifth birthday, which we also celebrated in a garden in Honeywell.'

'That was a corker!' says Mabel. 'You made yourself sick on blancmange, and I fell into the stream at the bottom of the garden.'

Mrs Ogilvie ignores this. 'I'd like to say a special thank you to Olivia. She may not be staying in Honeywell forever, but I'm so pleased she came to visit. I'm even more delighted she found what she was looking for.'

'Hear, hear!' says Will.

'There's something very special about Honeywell,' she goes on. 'I knew that when I was younger, but I've rather lost sight of it. I'm glad both your paths converged in this place so we could all be here to see you start off on your journey together.'

She lifts her glass. 'To Will and Olivia – may your lives be filled with adventure and love.'

Bernie gives an excited yap and tries to knock Mabel's glass out of her hand.

'Steady on, old fellow,' she says, moving it out of his reach. 'You and I will be setting some guidelines before we move in together. The first rule will be that you never, ever touch my drink.'

'He's excited,' says Mrs Ogilvie. 'You'll find he's as good as gold once you come to know him better.'

'He's lovely,' says Isabella. 'But he doesn't enjoy being left out. We've drunk to everything else this afternoon, but we shouldn't forget it's his birthday too. There's enough champagne left in everyone's glasses for one more toast. And I know the very one. To Bernie – may your paws always remain free from thorns, and may you keep The Sugarloaf Bakery in profit for many years to come!'

I hope you enjoyed this book. If you did, please consider leaving a review on Amazon. It helps new readers find my books, and I really appreciate it.

Join my mailing list to receive a free story about a reluctant bridesmaid and be the first to be notified about my upcoming books.

rosemarywhittaker.com/signup

A Sugarloaf Valentine

When the ingredients for love turn into a recipe for disaster...

Lily's world is turned upside down when her ex-boyfriend Stephen walks into her bakery, hoping to buy Valentine's cookies for his new girlfriend. To make matters worse, he wants Lily to decorate them with a message of love.

Determined not to let him see her heartbroken, Lily tells him she has met someone else too and has never been happier. It's a risky deception, but luckily, she knows just the man to help her out.

She doesn't count on ending up on a double date with Stephen and his new girlfriend. Nor does she expect her fake boyfriend to have a secret of his own.

As Valentine's Day approaches, and Lily struggles to create the perfect cookies, she wonders whether the recipe for happiness has been in front of her all along.

With a cast of charming characters, and a dash of sweet romance, A Sugarloaf Valentine is a delightful read that will have you falling in love with love all over again.

Available now in paperback and Kindle ebook

A Sugarloaf Mix-Up

Welcome to the latest romance at the Sugarloaf Bakery, where love and baking are always in the air.

Abby has returned to Honeywell to care for her father and is delighted to land her dream job at the bakery. Her career is starting to flourish, but her efforts at online dating have been a total disaster – at least until Chris, a fellow baker, literally knocks her off her feet.

As their romance heats up faster than a batch of fresh scones, Abby finds that someone is sabotaging their entries in the local baking competition. To make matters worse, she begins to suspect Chris might be involved.

Can she save her bakery and her heart before it's too late? Or will she discover the recipe for love may be a little more complicated than she thought?

Join the delightful cast of characters from the Sugarloaf Bakery for another deliciously funny and heart-warming story...

Available now in paperback and Kindle ebook

A Tale of Two Christmases

Annie never comes home for Christmas. There's too much chance of running into Alex. He broke her heart, and she never wants to speak to him again.

Alex always comes home for Christmas. He's desperate to talk to Annie about what went wrong between them.

Faced with a family crisis, Annie reluctantly agrees to spend the holidays with her parents. It shouldn't be too difficult to avoid Alex for just one week.

But she didn't expect to arrive in the middle of the wedding of the year. The entire village will be there, and no one will be able to avoid anyone else.

It's a battle of two Christmases, and only one can win.

Snuggle up in front of a roaring fire with a mug of hot chocolate and enjoy this sparkling Christmas romance.

Available now in paperback and Kindle ebook

The Cinnamon Snail

She's found the love of her life. He just hasn't realised it …

When Christian moves from Copenhagen to London, Kate quickly tumbles into love. He's the most handsome and charismatic man she's ever met, and she's all set for her Happily Ever After.

Until he announces that he's returning to Copenhagen, and he doesn't want her to go with him. Nothing Kate can say will change his mind. All she can do is plan a new future without him. And if that future happens to be in Denmark, that's entirely her own business.

She gets a job at The Cinnamon Snail Cafe and sets out to win Christian back. His new girlfriend is a slight problem – but when true love is on the line, anything goes.

Kate has a year to prove she can settle into a new country and persuade the love of her life she means business. A piece of cake!

A delightful new story of Danish pastries, romance, and lots and lots of hygge.

Available now in paperback and Kindle ebook

About the author

Rosemary Whittaker wanted to be an author as soon as she was old enough to hold a book the right way up. From that moment on, she was the despair of her teachers, who attempted to impart the basics of an education while she stared out of the window, making up characters and situations.

Having accidentally absorbed enough to graduate and become a teacher, she spent the next few decades moving around the world with her husband, children, and menagerie of unexpected pets.

She accidentally found herself in Australia some years back and intends to stay there for a very long time. She currently spends her time writing, sourcing English marmite and salad cream and wrangling her two determinedly destructive house bunnies – Pumpkin and Midway.

Rosemary has written several light-hearted romance novels set in the different countries in which she has lived. She also writes children's books as R J Whittaker – in particular a series of books about a recalcitrant monkey named Pom Pom, who is not in any way, shape or form based on her experience of raising her own four boys.

Printed in Great Britain
by Amazon

25431922R10156